A BREATH AWAY FROM SLEEP . . .

By

Edward Nubian James

ISBN: 0-7596-9400-1 (e-book)
ISBN: 0-7596-9401-X (Paperback)
ISBN: 0-7596-9402-8 (Hardcover)

This book is printed on acid free paper.

1stBooks - rev. 08/08/02

CHAPTER 1

Paris

It was seven years ago when I took off all my clothes, stood in front of the mirror, and looked at myself completely naked as though for the first time, almost gagging at the sight of my reflection therein. It appeared that I was growing larger and larger with each passing moment. No, let's face facts and be for real here. *I was fat*; a size eighteen with visible ripples even! That was when I dropped the bag of Cheetos I held in my trembling hands to walk, waddle, and then run over to the telephone. I called Jenny Craig and joined right on the very spot that I stood. I lasted about two weeks. Directly after that fiasco, I went out and bought a Richard Simmons's Deal-A-Meal fitness package with daily recipe cards and a workout tape. Now, there is nothing I hate more than a man trying to tell me what and what not to do, so after two hours a day, three times a week of hearing his high-pitched voice squeaking out commands for me to lift my legs higher and burn off excess cellulite by doing power jumping jacks, my ass landed in the bed with a quart of Ben & Jerry's ice cream. They kept me company until I'd gained five additional pounds and was completely nursed back to hefty. I won't even try to front or perpetrate; there are occasions when a box of chocolate has satisfied the yearning between my thighs, taken boredom along with its friend, Lonesomeness, and sent them both scurrying to offer me a brief reprieve from living in my own world of isolation.

No matter what the exercise or diet regimen I just couldn't seem to lose any weight, that is, until the night of a Sadie Hawkins dance. The celebration fell on the evening of my fifteenth birthday. Earlier in the week I had worked up enough gumption to ask this fine, chocolate brother out to the dance and after-party, thanks to the constant badgering and coercion of my best friend, Butter. Butter was fine herself with a twenty-nine inch waistline, cocoa cream complexion and a perfectly shaped apple-round behind screaming out for attention from all of the boys in class. At this point in our lives, she was fighting off everything that was wearing pants and metamorphosing through puberty.

Anyway, getting back to what I was saying, Barry Maloney and I were in the same fourth period science class together. They say love is blind, but in this case, it was also deaf, dumb, and stupid, which was the exact way I acted whenever I was around Barry. Since we both held the highest grade point averages in our class, sometimes the instructor would couple us together to work on experiments or call upon Barry and me to decipher equations on the blackboard, the worst and best times of my life in junior high school. Unless I was speaking to him about something related to the rate at which a chemical burned beneath a Bunsen burner, my voice came out in an interminable stammer. Without Barry ever knowing this, of course, he was my entire life. There was nothing he could ever want that would be too much, not anything he could say, at least in my eyes, that would be in any way wrong. For a time we had what some would consider to have been *the ideal relationship*. On occasion at bedtime, after I had taken my shower and climbed underneath the sheets, I would slip out of my nightgown then lie flat on my back completely naked. As my nipples became hard and a throbbing sensation began to envelope both my perky breasts, I would cup them in my hands and start to

3

massage their mounds. However, in my mind, the hands I felt would not be my own at all, but Barry's large dark fingers. His hands would slide to my belly button and linger for a trice, then glide down between my legs where they would commence stroking, gently probing in and then out until my entire body became electrified from his contact, causing my juices to maturate almost to their boiling point. And when his fingertips found their way to my spot, I opened both legs to allow him a deeper penetration, jerking in an orgasmic rhythm until my body became aflutter. Afterward, I would pick up a pillow and squeeze until it felt just like a man, feeling a single teardrop slide from the corner of an eyelid to roll down my cheek. I'd grit my teeth and close both eyes even tighter, wanting to forever be inside his arms while they kept me warm, safe and secure from the outside world.

It was Monday during class when I asked Barry to go with me to the Sadie Hawkins dance. It took all the courage I could muster not to stutter.

"Barry, are you going to the dance with anyone?"

"No," he said, not bothering to look up from the worksheet he was completing.

Anxiety was causing my throat to constrict and I almost couldn't continue. But, at the same time, hearing the answer "No" from him would be better than never knowing what he might have said, so I composed myself again and spoke with only a smidgen of hesitancy inner my voice, trying even harder to keep my words from becoming repetitious.

"The reason why I'm asking, well…uh…how would you like to go with me, to be my date for the evening?"

And to my total surprise, no, let's make that shock, Barry immediately said "Yes" and told me that he would come pick me up from my house on Wednesday evening at around six-thirty. This is when I *really* started to freak out. I mean here I am, larger than life, and this gorgeous man is willing to embarrass himself by being seen in public while his friends, classmates and onlookers see *me* hanging onto his arm all night long? *Something smells like shit!*

"We can go out to dinner beforehand then continue on to the Sadie Hawkins," Barry added, his utterance trailing off just a bit as

5

though he were in the middle of a thought, "maybe hit the after-party once we finish on the dance floor. How does that sound?"

"You and me…do all of that together?"

"Yes," he laughed, then finally looked up from his paper, turned in my direction and smiled at me, "you and me together."

"Where could we go to eat?"

"There are lots of places to go. Like, for instance, the Angus Barn on Glenwood Avenue. By the way, what types of food do you enjoy eating?"

A more accurate question for him to have asked me is what, *don't,* I enjoy eating. I was suddenly very sorry that I'd ever brought up the subject of food.

"Barry, are you certain about all of this, about the two of us going out I mean? If you've changed your mind or have completely lost it for the moment, I really would understand."

"Yes, I'm certain, unless you're planning on attending the function with someone else. But then again, if you were going to do that, then why would you have asked me in the first place? Right?"

"Well, there were quite a few gentlemen who expressed interest in being my date for the evening," I lied, half joking while I spoke with a surprisingly casual ease. "But by me being such a stunningly beautiful woman and having to think about my social standing in this school, I decided to settle for you."

After I arrived home that afternoon and told my grandmother I'd actually been invited out on a bona fide date, my first one ever, she was so excited that we went out that very day and bought a dress for me to wear to the dance.

On the night of the Sadie Hawkins, Big Mama (a.k.a. my grandmother), warned me to keep my legs closed and not to even think about engaging in any kind of sexual activity. However, she gave me a twelve pack of Trojans to carry with me inside my purse anyway. I was dressed in a size eighteen, double breasted black chiffon evening gown embroidered with rhinestones that shimmered like melting silver against a backdrop of midnight. The dress cost several hundred dollars and was the most beautiful frock I had ever owned. When I emerged from my bedroom to show my older brother and Big Mama how I looked inside of the gown, there were teardrops within her eyes. Both she and Derick gave me a big bear hug at the same time. Then, I went into the living room and sat down on the sofa, waiting for Barry to drive up in his parent's 1995 Volvo station wagon.

Six-thirty came and went. No Barry. I figured he must be running late, probably stuck in traffic or spilled something on his clothing and had to change into another shirt. Seven-fifteen came then went, and still, Barry hadn't arrived yet. Most likely he rented a tuxedo and had to go back to the formal wear shop to be refitted at the last minute, I told myself. A quarter of eight crept into being. I hope he wasn't in some kind of automobile accident, maybe lying in a hospital bed beside my father. While I remained seated on the couch, silently twiddling my thumbs, Big Mama never said a word to me. She only gave me an occasional glance every now and then, acknowledging me whenever I caught her peering in my direction. That was probably the worst part of it all, not the prospect of me having been stood up by my date, but by the overwhelming pity I could see within the etched lines upon her face.

Then, in a last desperate attempt to cling onto hope, I decided that I'd misunderstood our arrangements and that Barry had meant for me to meet him over at the Angus Barn. I borrowed some money from my brother, Derick, who offered to come along with me and I quote, "Give the Negro a beat-down!" I forthwith declined then caught a taxi over to the eatery alone. For a long time I just stood outside the establishment looking very much out of place, feeling a chill since I'd forgotten to bring a jacket along with me. Fearing that I may miss Barry if he were tarrying outside in his parent's car, I walked around the entire parking lot, making sure he wasn't waiting for me in another area that could not be seen from the entrance. At nine-thirty I decided to step out of the cold and go inside the restaurant to wait for him in the foyer.

The scent of something delicious wafted through the air, *and yes, by this time I was hungrier than hell!* I gazed further into the dining hall to find out which entrée it was. When I saw what I saw, I could not believe my eyes. There, sitting down at an intimate table set for two where Barry and I should have been seated, was my best friend Butter dining with my date, a basket of steaming hot French bread between them. Although they were staring into each other's eyes, seated interior a setting that was in every way romantic, Butter seemed to be upset about something. However disturbed she might have been, believe you me, Butter couldn't have been as angry or upset as I myself was! Seemingly emerging from out of nowhere, a maitre d' appeared from around a corner and asked me for the name of the party my reservation was in. When I didn't answer the question and pushed past him, he tried to prevent me from entering the dining room by placing a hand in front of me. I outweighed his frail body easily by about forty pounds. Without a police escort to help him, the poor boy didn't stand a chance at stopping me or my attitude from doing what we were about to do next. I was determined to confront Barry and my so-called best friend amidst the act of their betrayal.

Have you ever seen a man caught out with another woman? He is so proud to be seen with her until you catch them together. That's when they start looking around for shit that isn't there, acting like they've misplaced their wallets or integrity.

"Hello, Barry. Fancy meeting you here with Butter, seated between a hot buttered roll."

They could see my hands were balled into two fists, and that I was mad enough to punch someone, but hadn't decided which one of them to hit first.

"Now don't go getting your panties all into a wad, Sister-friend," Butter said, wearing what I thought was a guilt-ridden mug. For some reason she was dressed down in casual attire, decked out in a pair of blue jeans with this black cotton top and duo of brown loafers. To be perfectly honest, since she was in this bourgeois, overpriced restaurant, I was surprised that the management had even allowed her to cross the threshold wearing that outfit.

"Don't even talk to me, bitch!" I yelled, almost shouting at the top of my lungs. Fury dwelled within every fiber of my being.

"Bitch? There ain't no reason for you to come up in here and disrespect me like that. I am your closest friend, Paris, or at least I'm *trying* to be."

"Okay, you're right," I agreed in a much calmer voice. "I shouldn't be calling you outside your name like that."

11

"Thank you, that's much better," Butter replied.

"Excuse me, Miss Bitch, but do you realize how long I've been waiting for this bastard to come to my house and pick me up?"

Butter seemed taken aback by what I was saying to her. This annoyed me to no end and pissed me off even more, especially when the look of shock came across her visage.

"Barry, you told me that she called you and had canceled your date for tonight!" Butter accused as she turned to glare across the table at him. "You told me that Paris didn't feel well, that she was going to stay home and lie down for the rest of the night. You said she insisted that you and I go to grab a bite together, rather than for us both to stay at home while everybody else was out having fun. Why you dirty, little dick, sorry excuse for a man! You're nothing but a lying dog."

"Don't even try to act holier than thou with me, Butter, cause this is all your fault!" Barry shouted as he rose out of his chair and backed away from the table, a cloth napkin sliding from his lap onto the plush burgundy carpet. He was clad in the tuxedo I had imagined him to be wearing, albeit the actual color was an unusual gray and blue mesh.

"Shut up, Barry, and stop talking so much," Butter protested as she too rose from her chair and stood up.

We now all formed a semicircle around the table. I'm certain by this point people were staring in our direction, but I was so mad and confused that I couldn't see any of their faces. I could only focus upon the three of us, on our confrontation and conversation.

"Let me make one thing crystal clear to you, Paris. The only reason I accepted your invitation to the Sadie Hawkins dance in the first damn place is because your friend Butter here begged me to. I told her that *she* was the one I truly wanted to go out with, but Butter won't trying to hear me unless I took your fat ass out to the dance. But now, to tell you the truth, I don't need or ever want to see either one of you two whores again!"

"Oh, no, you didn't," I yelled as I moved around the table to stand by Butter's side, "*no you did not just call me and my girl here a couple of hoes!*"

"Oh, yes, he did girl, so now let's jump on his ass!"

And that's precisely what we did, too. I sat on the bastard while Butter scratched his face up. During the scuffle a few chairs were knocked over on to their sides, and the laced tablecloth was pulled free from its wooden slab and landed on the floor. From a distance away, I heard an elderly woman yelling for someone to dial 911 on their cell phone. By the time the police arrived on the premises, Butter and I were long gone. Beyond that night, neither Butter nor I were ever contacted by the authorities or anyone else concerning the incident that took place in the restaurant. I guess Barry didn't want word to get out around school that he'd been attacked and beaten up by two women. If the information had been leaked, all of the guys on the basketball team upon which he played would have thought Barry to be some kind of punk or sucker. And don't think for one moment that he tried to retaliate against me or Butter, not with my big brother Derick around. In school Derick had acquired a reputation of fighting at the sound of a heartbeat, so no one ever dared to mess with me, his little sister, no matter what size they were. Derick never met a man he couldn't defeat in under two minutes flat. He lifts weights four days out of the week and although he's only five feet, seven inches in height, Derick boxes like Evander Holyfield and eats like Mike Tyson as if they were all rolled together into one person, only with an appetite more voracious than the two of them combined.

Neither Butter nor I ever spoke anything more about what happened on the night of the Sadie Hawkins dance. I understood why she had manipulated Barry into asking me out. After that particular incident, no one else ever invited me to any functions or even out to our high school prom, so my date with Barry was the one and only social engagement with a man that I'd ever have during my high school years.

◊   ◊   ◊

But that was then; this is now. Seven years later at the age of twenty-two, through a sensible diet and regular exercise, I've trimmed down to a slender build of one hundred and forty-two pounds. On my smaller frame of five-feet, nine inches, my breasts now poke out like huge horizontal mountains. Whenever I get depressed and simply *have* to have me a piece of chocolate, I've learned to break off only a small portion then place the rest inside my freezer for another day. Since I'm still a virgin and oftentimes become lonely, I wind up doing that quite a bit throughout the month.

Currently, I'm in my sophomore year at the University of North Carolina in Chapel Hill, majoring in Psychology and Sociology between ethnic groups as they relate to the European influence of past times up-to-date. In other words, I'm studying White people and how the influence of slavery has transposed from being a physical bondage into an economical suppression among the haves and have-nots, namely persons in political power and economic control. Not all Caucasians have this mentality of yesteryear, merely the majority that I've encountered. One exception would be President Clinton and his lovely wife. I voted twice for them.

Today I'm moving off campus into an apartment located in West Raleigh, near Cameron Village. It's a secure building that costs an arm and a leg to live in, with a guard booth that requires all visitors to log in ahead of their admittance. There is even a doorman who announces every non-tenant before anyone is allowed to go upstairs. My brother took the day off from work and borrowed a truck from one of his friends to help me move a few items, so he should be driving up any minute now with the rest of my things. He's supposed to help me take these boxes I have scattered down here on the sidewalk up to my unit on the third floor. When I heard music booming from several blocks away as it traveled in my direction, I knew Derick had arrived. He was driving a brand new four-by-four that I'd never seen previous to today, and I wondered why one of his homies' would allow him to help me move in such an expensive vehicle. Because it was early spring and the sun shone brightly from above, Derick removed the top from off the cherry red Trooper and placed it inside the trunk.

"Hop in, Paris. We got to go make a withdrawal from my bank so I can fill this truck up with some gas."

Just the other day I had given him an advance of money to assist me with moving, so I couldn't figure out where all of his cash had gone to so quickly. Since the doorman was standing outside anyway, I asked him to watch my cartons for a few minutes until we came back. I climbed into the passenger side of the sports utility and caught a glimpse at the pair of two hundred dollar sneakers Derick was wearing. Without an ounce of doubt, my question about where all of his dough had gone to so quickly was answered in that single, silent glance. *We* spend mad money on dresses; *men* blow theirs on sneakers.

"Derick, why are you dressed like that, clad in a sports shirt, Silver Tab jeans, and a brand new pair of Air Jordan's when the only thing we're going to be doing is lifting a bunch of crates?"

"I be clocking mad honeys everywhere I go. You feel me on that, Sis? Can't be seen by whatever ladies living inside of that expensive ass apartment building you moving into without my props."

"Whatever…Where is your bank located? I didn't know you'd opened up an account anywhere."

"It's near Moore Square, you know, close to where the city park is downtown."

"The only banks I know of nigh the park are several blocks away. What's the name of your institution?"

"You ask too many questions. We'll be there in a few."

And so I remained quiet, quiet at least until we pulled into a parking space at the city park instead of the lot at a bank.

"Derick, what is this? Why are we here, sitting in front of this cement fountain as opposed to being at a drive-thru window or teller machine?"

"Paris, stop mouthing off and grab that pot from the backseat."

"Am I missing something here?" I asked as I reached backward to seize my grandmother's good Tefal.

We got out of the truck and I followed him as he stepped closer to a cascade of falling water. There was no way in the world that I could have foreseen or expected what was about to happen next. Derick took off both shoes, removed his socks, and rolled up each pant leg to then hop inside the pool. He stooped down to wade around in the water using both his hands as scoops, sifting all the way down to the bottom of the fountain as though panning for gold in a stream. He repeated the procedure several times, coming back up to dump fistfuls of change into the utensil before returning to the bottom for more.

No he didn't just jump into a public water fountain and wishing well...having me standing here holding a pot for him to throw loot into while the police station is located only two blocks away! As the reality of what was happening left my subconscious to reach my conscious mind, I threw the pot into some bushes and started cursing Derick out. When I threatened to call the cops on him my damn self, he leapt from the water and walked with me back over to the Trooper. While we were riding back to my new apartment, I swore under my breath then told him that I would move everything by myself. Yes, I know this was a stupid thing for me to say, but what the hell. I was angry, damn-it!

So here I am in all of my glory, standing outside this apartment building with all of these boxes to lug upstairs by myself. I peered up into the sky and followed the exposed brick until it led to the three tall windows of my unit. 'This really is a beautiful brownstone,' I thought to myself.

"This really is a beautiful brownstone. You moving in here today?"

I spun around on the heels of my navy blue clogs to see who'd made the inquiry or was reading my mind. When I did, I had to look up...and up...and up. Once my eyes settled on those muscular arms, I was almost *too* through. This man had shoulders like a quarterback, long legs like a tree trunk, and there was no visible body fat on him anywhere to be seen. He easily weighed every bit of two hundred pounds, all of it nothing but lean masses of sinew. Closely cropped hair, faded and tapered along the sides, let me know that he must have recently gotten a haircut. And his eyes…oh, what eyes…they were brown with flecks of gray and green, set behind a countenance that exuded an intense scrutiny. His thick ebony lashes complimented a clean-shaven complexion that reminded me of black grapes. His nose, an aquiline work of art resting prominently above a pair of ruddy, succulent lips, appeared to be chiseled away from a solid piece of bittersweet chocolate. I suppose if I had to use only a couple of words to describe him with, they would be "strikingly handsome."

"Are you all right, Miss?" he asked.

I just stood there without responding, frozen as I stared up at him with a silly glaze covering my eyes. My throat immediately became parched, and my mouth watered as if it were literally washing away the power of speech. I tried to say something, to say anything at all, but instead I just glanced down at my two paralyzed feet. Yes, I'm embarrassed to admit that he did have this affect on me. Since he

21

stood in front of me wearing a jogging outfit and I'd read within a brochure that there was a gym located somewhere on the premises, I surmised that the guy lived in the building and must've been returning from there.

After a long while had passed and I still hadn't answered his question, he flashed me a sexy grin and posed his query again, "Miss, are you all right?"

Finally, I found a voice to speak back with.

"Yes, thank you. I'm fine."

"You certainly didn't tell a lie when you made that statement. I can see that for myself," he complimented, then smiled, *that smile,* again.

Due to my lingering chagrin, I wasn't in the least bit amused. I merely averted eye contact with him then gazed down and around at all of my things resting on the grass and sidewalk. I was feeling very disgusted by the amount of work I had ahead of me. Something told me that the guy was staring and when I looked up again, he certainly was.

"Why do you have that smirk on your face?" I asked him with a frown upon my own.

My workouts during the morning time, before having that first cup of coffee must've been paying off, because twice his eyes left my visage and fell further southward. Though I really didn't mind the attention and was somewhat flattered that he felt compelled enough to look, it made me realize that I was dealing with a player or possibly even worse, maybe just a plain dog. Trust me; I can spot them from a quarter mile away, swooping in like vultures down to a sushi buffet. And this one standing before me, being at home during the daytime and on his way back from a gym, obviously has no job to keep him occupied in the mornings. I don't know about any of the other women who reside in this complex, but I'm not looking for a man who needs me to support him. Case closed!

"You about to move into one of these apartments?" he continued as though I hadn't asked him anything at all, nodding toward the ground to indicate one of the boxes that rested directly in front of me.

"I saw you attempting to check me out on the sly. Is this the way you view all women? Do you look at your mother or sister in that same way, too?"

"Of course, not."

"Okay then, don't be disrespecting me that way," I said tartly.

My words didn't seem to bother him at all. He merely beamed at me as if he was thinking about something secret, and then continued on without ever missing a beat.

"Well, do you mind if a brother admires your hairdo, or is that off limits too?"

"That depends on the brother who's giving me the admiration."

I turned my back to him, picked up one of my cartons, and began to ascend a stairwell that led into the main lobby of the building. A plastic cup fell from my box onto the pavement, and when I bent over to grab the vessel, I caught the handsome stranger sneaking another peek, observing my posterior from the rear with an unabashed enjoyment. Ignoring him and his actions, I stood back up then continued on into the building, boarding an elevator whose doors were about to close to allow it to move upward.

CHAPTER 2

Tyree

When I picked up one of her boxes and followed her into the building, footing with her onto an awaiting elevator, she turned around and gave me a hard glare. There were two other people inside the car who were watching our exchange, a white man and his Hispanic girlfriend or wife.

"What are you doing with my things?" she interrogated with a sour bore, looking at me as though I were a total stranger. Come to think of it, to her, I guess I was.

"I'm performing my neighborly duty by helping you to move into your apartment. Since I don't have anything else to do at the moment, I might as well be doing something productive and assist you. Don't you guys think so?" I turned and asked of the man and woman couple.

They both smiled politely although neither of the two responded, not that I wanted them to.

"I don't know you from Adam. You could be some sort of pervert."

"No, you don't know me, but it will take you forever and a day to do all of this work by yourself. Besides, if I was some kind of cretin, I wouldn't be flaunting it in front of these two witnesses, now would I?" I reasoned.

She just looked at me, glanced over to the people riding with us on the car then visually acquiesced, shrugging both her shoulders in a defeat of reason.

"I guess not, but keep your distance outside of an arm's length," she said sarcastically.

Her tone didn't bother me none, cause playing hard to get gets me hard in the first place.

"And I will pay you for your efforts," she continued.

"That's good, cause I don't do anything for free. I expect due payment for my time and services rendered."

"Now why doesn't that surprise me?" she remarked in an inflection that required no response.

She looked up toward the ceiling and remained quiet until the elevator stopped on the third floor, the same floor where I also lived. We walked out into the corridor, and I followed until we reached her apartment, a tenement that also just happened to be located directly across the hallway from my own. May wonders never cease! As I took inventory from the rear, I could see that Mother Nature rules in one of her greatest creations known to man, cause this is one woman who's got it going on from her backside clear round to the front. I won't lie, it took everything within me not to drop the box I was holding to run over and squeeze that juicy, curvaceous ass of hers until I could feel some meat through those formfitting khaki shorts she was wearing. I swear; this woman has got the legs of Tina Turner and a face resembling that of Whitney Houston when she played in that movie, *The Preacher's Wife*. Yeah, that's who she looks like in the face, hairstyle and all, exactly like Whitney in that film. And talk about nipples! The titties were shaking every which way, poking through the front of that cacao colored T-shirt she was wearing.

Once we reached her door, she unlocked the entry and pushed it open with her shoulder. She stepped across the threshold, placed the carton she was holding down on the floor and put both hands on her hips. For a minute she just stood there, scanning the interior from left to right as though she were trying to figure out where to position the rest of her boxes.

By request of the renter, these apartments already come pre-furnished with several different styles from which the tenants can choose, so the larger items were already inside the living area. A brand new sectional sofa and mahogany dining set, with its matching china cabinet situated inner an adjacent room, made the apartment already seem occupied. Except for the furnishings and color scheme of the walls, I could see that the floor plan of our apartments were identical. They were both "T" shaped with the couch positioned in front of three tall windows that spanned from the ceiling almost down to the floor. Sunlight filtered through them to illuminate most of the interior without the need for any artificial lighting until well into the late afternoon or evening hours. Further down the hallway was positioned the kitchen, lavatory, and a rather spacious master bedroom.

"Well, let's get started," she sighed.

And for the next hour or so we trod up and down the stairwell or we used the service elevator, hauling box after box while working up a serious sweat. I insisted on carrying all of the larger cartons myself, sliding them against the living and dining room walls before going back downstairs for more. On occasion, we would simultaneously enter the doorway leading into her apartment and brush up against one another by accident. All I could hear myself thinking was that I bet some man loves to roll over at night to find her inside his bed, a bedroom that, quite frankly, I myself wished and wanted to be my own.

Once we finished moving everything, I approached her from behind, standing beside her in the living quarters with my chest pressed ever so slightly against her back. She inched away and then turned around to face me. For some reason the look she gave me, made me feel a little bit nervous. I don't know why this was the case, because women throw themselves at me all the time. I don't normally have to deal with all of the rejection crap that other guys usually do, not unless the woman is married or otherwise engaged; and sometimes, I can even get the draws under those circumstances.

There are a lot of hoes out there prowling the streets, married or not. But, there's something different about this girl, something mysterious that I can't quite place my finger on. Whatever it is about her, its peaked my curiosity to a point that I can't let go. I know she finds me attractive by the way she was staring at my body when we first met; however, that's where her interest seems to have come to an end.

"Thanks," she said, then turned away from me to walk down the hall and enter her bedroom.

If this was her way of flirting it sure as hell worked, cause I could feel my dick rising as I watched her from the rear. Umm, umm, umm, that is my kind of woman, one who's as tough as nails and can offer me some form of a challenge. She didn't seem to care one way or another whether I liked her or not. And let me tell ya, this attitude was turning me on like a dog in heat on a hot summertime day during mid-July!

Then I heard her yelling something to me from the back room. She didn't need to call me twice. I was back there before she could draw another breath to repeat herself with. Forgetting that I needed to duck underneath an archway leading into the bedroom like I usually do when I'm at home inside my own apartment, I bumped my head with an audible thud as I went into the room. That shit hurt like hell, but I drew in a deep breath and pretended not to be going through any major changes, hoping that a lump wouldn't develop before I could get home to place an ice pack across my forehead.

"How much do I owe you?" she bade in a serious, businesslike tone.

She was standing near a canopied bed, holding an oval beaded purse in her left hand while rummaging inside of it using the other. An oak vanity rested in the space between two windows, both panes allowing light to shine down on bronze skin that looked flawless in a glow of late noon light. I couldn't tell if she was wearing any makeup or not.

"You don't need to pay with money. Why don't you cook me dinner one night next week? A rain check will be sufficient enough payment for now."

"How much do I owe you?"

Her expression went stone sober. When I winked at her instead of answering the question, she merely withdrew forty dollars from her pocketbook then tossed it onto the bed.

"That's all I have on me at the moment, but if there is a teller machine somewhere in the neighborhood, I can go and get you more money."

"Keep your cash. Just answer one simple question for me."

"Take the money. I don't answer personal questions for strangers, at least not in what will soon become my bedroom. Let's go back out into the living area."

She dropped her purse on the bed, walked past me, then headed down the hallway while I trailed closely from behind.

"After moving all of those boxes, I would hardly consider you and me strangers anymore."

"I don't even know what your name is. By *my* definition, that would make you fall under the category of being a strange man."

"My name is Tyree, Tyree Dick."

"You're joking!"

"I've had a lot of jokes made about it, but no, Dick is really my surname."

"What is it that you'd like to ask me, Mr. Dick?"

Since I knew she intended for me to leave soon, I sat down on a box nearest the exit and folded both arms, my back pressed firmly against the wall. She peered over to a box labeled 'BOOKS' that was sitting directly across from me, then carefully alighted herself down upon it.

"What is your name?"

"Paris Hightower," she answered and then stood back up, like that was my one question and now it was time for me to go.

Damn, talk about being direct. I knew she wanted me to go home, but I wasn't ready to part-company with her just yet.

"Paris, can I ask you another question?"

"You just did."

"Then may I ask you two more questions beyond this one?"

She sat back down, crossed her legs and then just looked at me like I was starting to get on her nerves.

"Am I getting on your nerves?"

"Tyree, do I look like you're getting on my nerves?"

"Yes."

"Well then, you've just answered your own question, now didn't you? Look, I'm not trying to be rude because you really were of great help, but I'm not in the market for a man. I just want to be up-front with you about that."

"Does that mean women turn you on instead?"

She stood up and immediately marched over to the front door, holding it wide open for my departure.

"No Tyree, what it means is it's time for your nosy ass to leave my apartment and go home. Can you not read the signals? All of mine are saying 'STOP!'"

"Since I assume the only person who'll be living here is you, why would you want to pay extra rent to have a unit with this much square footage? You could have gotten a price break if you'd have chosen something a little smaller in size," I asked.

I was really trying to find out if there was going to be a man moving in here with her, right now or later on down the line.

"You *would* have to make it sound like I'm some old maid or damn spinster."

"Now, don't get so touchy. If you play your cards right, I might even want to ask you out on a date myself," I suggested, half joking while at the same time being serious. Without delay she looked at me as if to say, 'Does this guy *ever* quit or give up?'

"Okay, Mr. Dick."

"Paris, please call me Tyree."

"Okay, Tyree, when I get settled you can ask me out on a date but not right now."

"Cool. Do you have any idea as to when that will be?"

"Sure," Paris said as she glanced up in the air as though she were deep in thought. "Ask me out when there are no more men, or batteries, left upon the surface of the planet."

"Would that be Duracell or Energizer?"

For the first time in the two-and-a-half hours of our knowing each other, Paris laughed with me. It kind of surprised me because one thing is for sure, something smells damn funky up in here and I do believe it to be me. Sweat and perspiration was pouring off of my

35

body like I was a racehorse sprinting around a track. No wonder she wanted me to leave.

"You know something, Tyree, you certainly ask a lot of questions for them to only be a couple. Can you count?" Paris observed while opening the door even wider.

I rose and met her at the threshold.

"You want me to help you unpack some of these cartons?"

"Are you on drugs or some form of medication, Tyree?"

"After moving all those boxes, you're looking a bit rough around the edges yourself, Paris. What kind are *you* using?"

Her expression went completely bland, not even cracking so much as a simper.

"Thank you again for all your help, Tyree. I have some things I need to get done around here. A friend of mine will be dropping by to see my new apartment, and then we have plans to go out for the evening, so if you won't mind leaving now I'll chat with you some other time, neighbor."

Why do women have to be so damn sneaky about their shit?! All Paris had to say was that she was going out on a date tonight, was having some dude come by to take her out on the town for an early dinner and some late night dancing. As I walked toward the sill, I purposely allowed my forearm to brush up against her chest before she could step back and avoid the contact. When I spoke, I tried hard to keep the jealousy from piercing through my words.

"He must be a good friend for you to start getting ready for a date this early in the afternoon."

"The very best," Paris confirmed, running her fingers through a flowing mane of jet-black hair. The curls on her head appeared to be natural, not some frizzy-assed perm or one of those played-out Jheri-Kurls. Damn, this girl is fine!

CHAPTER 3

Paris

"Girl, we're going to be late arriving at the club. All the straight men will be taken by the time we get there. When I spoke to you on the telephone three hours ago, I told you that I'd be right over. What took you so long to answer the door?" Butter inquired with a slight impatience, never stopping to take a breath between words.

After stepping across the threshold of my apartment, Butter hoofed past me and went straight into the living room, plopping herself down on the couch. After I closed the door I stood inside the foyer for a moment longer, pushing a pin through my earlobe to finish attaching a pair of topaz earrings I'd bought from a jewelry shop in the Crabtree Valley Mall. As usual, I knew Butter would be tardy as hell and then act all innocent and dramatic, as though we were in need of a heart transplant and were going to miss the surgeon who'd be performing the operation if we didn't leave out for the club immediately after she arrived at my apartment.

Once I came around the corner Butter stood up, placed both hands on her hips, and smiled as she scrutinized my new outfit from head to toe. I wore a cranberry, crushed velvet evening gown that hugged every curve of my body. A silk sheath concealed its seductively plunging bust line, while my hair was pulled around to hang over one shoulder, fastened by a diamond studded clip with the ponytail dangling above my cleavage. Butter resumed speaking without waiting for me to respond to her first question.

"Paris, girl, you look gorgeous! No harm intended, but since we both graduated from high school years ago, you've transformed into some kind of Cinderella. I don't know whether you're wearing that dress or if the dress is wearing you, but damn if somebody ain't in charge!"

"Thanks, Butter. These days I've been feeling gorgeous."

"Now come on and let's hit the road. I'll drive while you just keep looking cute."

"Butter, we go though this every single time you drag me out to some club. I am not showing up at anyone's bar on a Friday night

39

before eight o'clock just so we can seem like two spinster sisters who're out on the prowl, searching for a husband before we leave."

"Okay then, then tell me more of this guy you started telling me about on the telephone, the fine chocolate neighbor who helped you move into your apartment."

"There really isn't anymore to say, other than he probably has no job."

"Yeah girl, but he's got to at least have a dick. And judging by your description of the man, he sounds like my type."

"Butter, if a man doesn't have a car or a pot to piss in, then he won't be having me."

"*She-it*, the guy wouldn't be having your virgin ass if he were welded to it. Back when we were in high school and you weighed a lot more than you do now, you couldn't find a date with a flashlight during the daytime. Now you have men throwing themselves at you all day long and you don't seem to want to catch. I know you ain't no bull dyke, so what's the problem here?"

"I'll tell you what the problem is, Butter. Back when we were in high school, when I weighed so much more than I do now, I was still the very same person on the inside that I am today. The only things that have changed are my figure and maybe my self-esteem, but nothing else. I don't need a man to use me for my body, and then toss me away when he's through. Before you met me, when I was just a little girl, I watched my mother allow my father use her until there was almost nothing left. Even though she had me and my brother Derick around her, she still seemed to be so extremely lonely. Oftentimes I would cry myself to sleep at night, not because I was sad for my mother, but because I didn't want to end up as unhappy as she was when I grew up. I guess mother was afraid that if our father ever decided to leave her, then she would truly *feel* alone. Some women believe that possessing half a man is better than having no man at all, and I guess maybe she was one of them. But as for myself, my virginity is my refuge, the one part of me that I know is truly my own. Since my grandmother ended up raising Derick and me from the time we were children into our adulthood, I had to give up my mind so that it could be molded by her, and subsequently on to teachers for training in school. Every day I get up and go to work in order to pay taxes, extending the use of my body to the government and for

41

everyday livelihood. However I refuse to do that with my maidenhood, a gift that cannot be retrieved once it has been bestowed."

"Honey, I've given that gift away to several men on many an occasion. Most of them can't even figure out when you're faking an orgasm," Butter chortled, glancing about the room as though she were looking for something she'd misplaced.

Upon spotting an antique mirror that I'd hung on the wall near a window, she removed a pick from her purse and went over to it, teasing out bronze curls that were black at their roots. She smoothed out her leopard print spandex suit, dropped the comb back into her pocketbook, then took out a small compact to apply some more makeup, not that she needed to be wearing anymore. Butter is a size seven and has perfectly even toned skin, although she's forever applying a layer of foundation or cover-up. The girl reads nothing but fashion magazines, and then follows every clothing or cosmetic trend known to man. No matter what the time of day it is, Butter always looks as though she's going to a party.

"That is precisely my point, Butter. Why would I want to have sex with a man who doesn't satisfy me intimately, only to fake an orgasm so he never knows or learns *how* to make me come? I say, instead of trying to convince him that you're a virgin, just communicate with him or leave his ass. Chances are he isn't one himself, nor does a man care about making you believe that he is, so what is the point in lying about it?"

"Well, I say having a man or two in your life never hurts anybody and can definitely help to pay bills at the end of the month. If I'm lying I'm flying, and you sure enough don't see a pair of wings strapped on my back, now do you?"

"No, I don't see any wings, but maybe a mattress and some dirty sheets. Besides, I can't tell if you're lying to me or not. You've got too much makeup on top of that foundation for me to distinguish your facial features."

"Bitch! Girl, I love those red pumps you're wearing. Are they new?"

Butter was still peering into the glass, looking at the reflection within it to see me standing behind her.

"That's Miss Bitch to you, and yes, these shoes are new. Furthermore, I called you at home today on three separate occasions to see if you wanted to go shopping with me, only to get your answering machine."

"Yeah, so what?"

"Butter, I hope you know that I know you by now. The only reason you don't pick up your telephone these days is because you've been juggling too many men around at the same time. You probably gave all of them your digits and now you're scared that two or more might want to show up at your apartment on the same night. You may not have answered the phone, but I know you were at home. Now, weren't you?"

"You think you know everything, Paris. However you're speaking from a standpoint that lacks any hands-on experience. My phone might be ringing off the hook at night, but I've dated some fine men who were sexy as hell and could screw their ass off."

"Oh yeah, well where or what has all of that gotten you?"

"Well for one, it's gotten me off; and for two, it's gotten me a gourmet dinner whenever I get hungry and my rent paid on a days when I'm broke. But all of that is beside the point. We're supposed to be talking about you and this new neighbor of yours, not the men in my life. You're the one with the frigid ass, not me."

Butter left the mirror then went back over to the couch and sat down.

"From the way he was acting when he was here, the man's probably on crack. I almost couldn't get him to go home."

"Paris, trust me Sister-friend, if he was using that stuff you'd know about it without having to guess. From the way you described him to me, I doubt very seriously that it could be drugs anyway, not with his physique. The man obviously cares about his body. He probably likes you and became nervous once he spent some quality time around you and that smart-ass mouth of yours. You might have intimidated him by your attitude. How old is he?"

"He looks to be in his late twenties."

"Where is he from?"

"He has a slight Southern accent, so I assume he's from somewhere in the Carolinas, or at least, the Southeast."

"What's his name again?"

"Tyree."

"Tell me his last name. Maybe I know some of his family if they live here in this area."

"Dick."

"What did you say?" Butter guffawed.

"I said his appellation was Dick, Dick is his surname."

For some reason I didn't appreciate Butter laughing at him. Don't ask me why, because I scarcely know the guy.

"If he's got one, then I'd like to get with his older brother myself, Mr. Big Dick! Does he have any other family living in the area?"

"How should I be aware of information like that, Butter? I only met the guy for the first time earlier today. For all I know, the man just got out of prison and is some kind of ex-con. Come on now, girl, the brother helped me to move into my place at eleven o'clock in the morning. He can't be employed anywhere."

"Paris, you is a straight-up trip. Do you know how rare it is to find a man with a car?"

"A car? Butter, what are you talking about?"

"Do you know how many guys there are in the streets who don't own or drive a vehicle? Me myself, I get tired of going over to some dude's mama's house to pick up the dick. Then, after we're finished knocking boots, I got to drop him and the dick back off where I picked them up in the first place!"

Butter gazed at me like *I* was the one who was crazy.

"Please, Sister-friend, this man must be working somewhere if he lives in one of these expensive ass apartments. Maybe if you told me that Tyree wanted to hang out at your place all the time and never allowed you to come visit him, I could believe that he was married and hiding a wife and three kids from you. But this isn't the case. If you ask me, he already has a couple of things going for him. It's obvious that he doesn't still live at home with his mama, and for two, you wouldn't have to travel anywhere if you ever wanted to get some dick. No pun intended. Sounds to me like this Tyree has potential."

"Do you know what potential means, Butter?"

"No, Paris, what does potential mean?" she quizzed with an obvious disinterest, rolling her eyes at me.

"Potential means that he doesn't do jack now. You're the one who's looking to get your rent paid by a man, so how about me and my needs?"

"Let me put it this way, sister. When money, some good lovin', and a man comes knocking at my door all rolled into one handsome package, I don't allow happiness or a free meal to slip through my fingertips."

Butter picked up a glass jar of jellybeans that was resting on an oak coffee table between the sofa and a cedar television cabinet, and popped a handful into her mouth at one time. How she manages to do that without smearing her lipstick or ever gaining any weight, God only knows. She chewed, swallowed with several hearty smacks of her lips, and then continued on like she'd never stopped talking.

"I remember when I was dating Dan, a corporate lawyer who handled multi-million dollar deals for *Fortune 500* companies. *Girl*, when he and I met at the art museum, it was like meeting my soul mate. Something magical happened between us. Dan stood across from me on one side of a dinosaur exhibit, staring into my eyes until he walked around it to introduce himself and say hello. Over the days and weeks that we dated, taking time to get to know each other better, there was an unspoken bond that allowed me to know that our love would last forever. And if he hadn't left me nine months later because he found out that his wife was pregnant, then I just know he would have gotten out of the situation and then proposed to me."

"But he already had a wife, and that meant he couldn't ask you to marry him, Butter. And what did you do after learning that fact? I'll tell you what you did. You blackmailed Dan into buying you that condominium and a Porsche, a car you can't even afford to pay the maintenance or upkeep on. Is that story supposed to encourage me to jump into a relationship with Tyree, a man about whom I know absolutely nothing? Plus, you're darn lucky that Dan didn't call the police on you during all of that extortion business, because I know you knew that was illegal."

"*Damn skippy,* I blackmailed his ass! I won't about to walk away from the situation with nothing to show for all my efforts, not after I'd given that man the best nine months out of my life. Got me a nice chest of jewelry out of the deal too, but that ain't the point I'm trying to make here. Do you know what your problem is, Paris?"

49

"No, Butter, what *is* my problem? Please tell me."

"You're a damn fool! You need to let your hair down and get your freak on. Live a little for a change instead of keeping your head buried inside some textbook like a damn ostrich. You know what I mean? Now can I borrow five dollars, girl? I don't get paid until tomorrow."

"Kiss my natural brown ass, Butter."

I reached into my purse and handed her a crisp green bill. She began to gaze around my apartment and study its interior, taking in the floor plan like she was planning on renting a unit herself. Upon stuffing the five down between the cheeks of her bosom, Butter rose to stroll throughout the room. She went over to a box labeled *Kitchen/Fragile Bottles and Glassware,* and then started to rummage through it.

"You got anything to drink up in here, some cognac or a forty-ounce? We can christen your new apartment before we leave out for the club. God, this place makes mine look like a pigsty."

"You won't be drinking and driving with *me* in the passenger's seat. You already know I don't consume hard liquor anyhow, only an occasional wine cooler every now and then. If you decide you want something other than alcohol to swallow down that scratchy throat of yours, then there's some pineapple juice in the refrigerator."

Butter raised an eyebrow and glowered back at me, then withdrew a silver frame from one of my cartons. For several long moments she peered down at it, focusing on the photograph of a woman, a small girl with braids, and a little boy. The photo showed the three of them standing near an artificial Christmas tree during wintertime.

"Paris, this is a photograph of you and your brother Derick when you were children. Is the woman whose hand you're both holding in the picture your mother?"

Damn, Butter would have to find the one photo I don't want to discuss. I could've sworn that I'd put that inside my bedroom already. Should I lie and avoid a lot of probing questions, pretend that the woman in the picture is not my mother? No, Butter is my best friend and knows me all too well. I can't be dishonest with her, she'd see right through my deception before I could finish the sentence.

"Yes, Butter, that is my mother."

"But you've got to be at least seven or eight years old in this shot. When I first met you back in high school, you and your brother Derick were each living with your grandmother then, so I just assumed that your parents had died while you both were still at a very tender age; I thought that maybe they'd been killed in an automobile accident or some other form of tragedy. Where are your mother and father at now? Are they both still alive?"

"I thought I told you about what happened," I fibbed with a flutter of my eyelids, trying my best to feign an innocent expression.

"Yeah, right," Butter said skeptically. "You thought you told me about what?"

"That my mother is wanted by the police. She fled from the authorities when I was seven, soon after my brother Derick had turned ten years old himself. We haven't seen nor heard anything else from her since then."

"Wow, no freaking way could that be true! You're pulling my leg, aren't you sister-friend?"

"No, Butter, I'm not. To God's ears I wish I were, but I am not."

"What has she been charged with doing?"

"The warrant out for her arrest is for the shooting and attempted murder of my father, Joseph Morgan. Fifteen years ago she was charged with plugging him in the back during a domestic dispute."

"Attempted murder! Where is your father at now? Is he dead?"

"No, but he might as well be. He's still in the hospital. When he was shot in the spinal column years ago, his mind and body fell into a coma from which he has never awakened. His condition has remained unchanged for the past fifteen years up to this present day."

"Paris, girl, what took you so long to tell me about all of this? Damn, I'm supposed to be your friend!"

"Outside of God, my grandmother, and my brother, you are now the only other living soul that I've ever discussed this situation with. You are and always will be my friend, Butter, but reliving my past through talking about it can be so darn painful. It's most especially true for my brother. I was in elementary school at the time, but Derick was there when my father got wounded. He was waiting outside in the car while my mother went into our house and caught my dad with another woman. For several years now, Derick has been in and out of therapy, trying to deal with and work through his emotions surrounding that event. Before leaving town, our mother dropped us off at my grandmother's house. I think the reason why Derick never moved away from living with our granny is because when Mama left us there years ago, she promised that she'd come back for us, that he and I would never be apart from her for very long. It's like he's still waiting for our mother to come back and get him. *Thank God* he doesn't recall anything about what happened on the afternoon that our dad was shot and injured. He already has enough anguishing memories to last him a lifetime,"

"Why can't Derick remember what happened that day?"

"The medical term is called *selective recall*. His brain blocked out an event that was too painful or stress ridden for his conscious mind to deal with."

"Damn, girl, just when I thought I knew all there was to know about you and your family, you turn around and pull some shit like this out of your hat."

"Suffice it to say, that now you know me much better than you ever did before. We all have skeletons in our closets that can cause us great pain if they're ever unearthed. Some are buried deeper than others. This one just happens to be mine."

"But still, Paris, with as much stuff as you and I have gone through together over the years, I can't believe that you waited until now to reveal all of this to me. You know that you can confide in me, girl. At anytime during the day or night, you always have my ear. You're my sister-friend and I love you no matter what; come rain or come shine, till death do us part."

"I know that, Butter, and I love you all the more for it."

We hugged, and for the first time I noticed that tears were falling freely from my eyes. Butter soon followed, releasing a flood of waters from her own.

"Now, no more talking about such serious subjects," I insisted. "This is supposed to be a celebration, so let's embark for the club A.S.A.P., and go get our groove on."

"You know, I had a cousin once who cut off two balls when she caught her man sleeping with the babysitter. She went to jail for a few years, but is out now. Maybe I can ask her if she knows your mom. What do you think?"

"No thank you, Butter. I would prefer you not do that. This has always been a private matter between me, the rest of my family members, and now you. I want it to remain that way. Do you understand what I'm saying?"

"Yes, I do know what you're saying. Okay, girl, but you never know when your mother might decide to pop back up from out of nowhere, straight out of the blue. There may yet be hope, so don't be sad or ever give up on the possibility."

"That would never happen, Butter. Since we haven't heard a word from her all these years, most likely she's dead. And, to be perfectly honest, it's just as well. My mother is still wanted by the police to be held accountable for the crime of attempted murder. It has taken me years to realize that our mother is gone forever and will never be coming back. Hopefully, my brother has reached this conclusion, too, or someday soon will."

Butter dropped the frame back into the box with a clatter of metal against glass, then started jogging in place. Initially, I thought her mind had snapped. Maybe she and Tyree had been brother and sister in a past life.

"Butter, what is wrong with you?"

"Shit, I got to go pee like a racehorse. Point me in direction of your bathroom, girl."

Before I could finish indicating the way Butter was gone, dashing down the hallway as her clothing became unzipped or pulled off during mid sprint. She raced into the bathroom and slammed the door behind her. A few minutes later I heard the toilet flush and Butter came back out, entering the living area to grab her purse and car keys from off the coffee table.

"Let's roll on out of here, sister-friend. I'll drive."

When Butter turned on her high beams, honked the horn, and made a third motorist careen out of our way, I could have spit nails at Dan for giving her this car. The more I pleaded with her to slow down before a cop pulled us over, the faster she drove in the hope that the one who stopped us would be young, African American, and single. For Christ's sake, Butter drives like she's flying an airplane! I was grateful she had left her convertible top closed. If she hadn't, by now my hair would have been blown all to hell and back again.

Butter herself wore a style that appeared as if it had been created inside of a wind tunnel anyway, so even the stiffest gale couldn't have destroyed her hairdo.

For the third time since I'd climbed into the car with her, Butter drove over a speed bump that tossed me from my seat up into the air. Thank goodness I was wearing my seatbelt. Otherwise, I'd have flown right through the roof like Dino does on the *Flintstones*. I glared at her real hard, and then erupted at the mouth.

"Butter, I'm telling you this for the last time. Slow down before we get into a wreck and never make it over to the club alive! You're making me anxious, damn-it."

CHAPTER 4

Butter

"*I said*, slow this automobile down before we get into a wreck and you kill us both!" I heard Paris yell to me, shouting to be heard above this phat' rap playing on the car radio.

I had the stereo blasting with one of Tupac's slow jams from off his last release before he was assassinated by a ghost. At least it might as well have been one for all the effort the police put into finding his murderer. Time was pushing eight-thirty faster than my period can dispense out cramps, so the lead in my foot had taken control over my better judgment. Speeding doesn't bother me one bit, and I have the traffic tickets to prove it. Besides, I would love to be pulled over by one of them fine ass cops. A black man in uniform can slap a pair of handcuffs on me any day.

The moon was full and illuminated the heavens above with glow, while the stars overhead twinkled amidst a dark gray sky. I would have lowered the top of my convertible to feel the breeze blowing through my hair, but Paris was sitting next to me with her face all torn up, like her eyes were about to pop outside of her head at any moment. When she gets attitude, *she really gets an attitude,* so I decided not to push my luck with her since this was a celebration in honor of her finding a new apartment. I simply wanted us both to have fun tonight.

We were approaching a yellow stoplight at the intersection of Capital Boulevard and Millbrook road, when once again the impulse to depress the accelerator clamped onto my ass. Quickly, I fought off the urge and slammed on my brakes, bringing the car to a screeching halt. Not wanting to look over at the passenger seat to see the hard glare I could feel Paris was giving me, I glanced into my rearview mirror and pretended like someone else had caused me to almost have an accident. I swore at the person driving a Toyota Celica who was directly behind us, like it was his fault instead of mine. The vehicle had to switch lanes and pull up alongside us to keep from ramming me in the bumper. Though I knew the blame was all my own, I still had to play it off and roll down the passenger window so I could cuss the driver out.

"What's the matter with you, brother, can't drive and listen to music at the same damn time?"

The guy shook his head back and forth and then just laughed, as though I'd told him a dirty joke. Paris started groping around in her purse like she was Wonder Woman and could see in the dark, searching for shit that won't there in the first place because she was embarrassed to be seated between our exchange of words. I, on the other hand, ignored the both of them. I turned down the radio and swallowed so that my voice wouldn't crack, preparing to shout out what a jackass I thought this brother to be. When I started fussing, working my neck to and fro as only Black women can do whenever we become upset, I realized that the volume of music never went down and the jackass couldn't hear a word I was yelling at him. Damn, he's listening to the same radio station we are. The guy chortled even harder when he saw me becoming agitated. At the changing of the traffic light, I raised the window back up and sped off through the intersection, driving the last two blocks to reach the club that Paris and I were going to. I circled into the lot, parked, and then turned off the ignition. We climbed out of my car as I complained.

"I get so sick and tired of people playing music so damn loud, thinking everybody wants to hear what they're listening to."

"Butter, quit complaining and let's go on inside. We're here now, so just forget about it, okay."

"Well, I can't help it, girl. My day is going every which way but right. When I got home from work this afternoon, I discovered that my pussy was gone. First, I looked under the couch because it sometimes likes to play games and hide from me there. Then I went into my bedroom to search for her under my bureau, thinking maybe she decided to get the two balls of yarn that I keep stored beneath it for her to play with. That's when I saw that I'd forgotten to close my window before I left out for the job this morning. My belief is that the pussy climbed onto the pane and leapt outside."

"Butter, why don't you go ahead and give that feline of yours a real name? Whenever you start talking about that cat, I always have to remind myself that you're speaking of the one living in your condominium and not the stuff resting between your legs."

"Cause since I never gave her a name when she was a kitten, that darn cat thinks her name *is Pussy*. She won't come to me if I call her by anything else. Besides, Paul gave her to me and I always promised him that I wouldn't name her until our first wedding anniversary."

"Since you slept with his brother on the same day you two were going to announce your engagement, I'm sure that after three years beyond your breakup with Paul, he won't mind it one bit if you finally give that cat of yours a name."

"*Damn Skippy,* I freaked his brother and then told him all about it! Let's not forget that Paul made a pass at you once he'd already proposed to me. If you hadn't been my friend or woman enough to tell me about the advance he made towards you, then I might not have ever found out what a creep he really was, at least not before we were married and then it would have been too late."

Paris and I began to move toward the entrance of the club. Just as I was trying to decide whether to find a payphone to call Paul at home and cuss him out about some things he'd done to me that I'd forgotten to mention back then, or not, we heard a reggae beat so loud that the tone caused me to forget what I was bitching about in the first place. An emerald green Celica swerved into the driveway of the lot then pulled into the space next to my Porsche and parked.

"Paris, look over there girl!"

"Look at what, Butter? We don't know him."

"Yeah, we do too. It's that rude ass from back at the traffic light."

Paris cringed then turned in the opposite direction, once again peering inside her purse to search for something nonexistent. I love the girl, but damn if that ain't the silliest habit. Even if she had found whatever it was she was pretending to look for inside that pocketbook of hers, she wouldn't have been able to see it in the dark anyway. There's less light here than there was on the road a few minutes ago, when we were back inside my car.

The guy switched off the music, turned off his headlights, and alighted from the vehicle, approaching us with a strut that was sheer poetry in motion.

There ain't nothing like the swagger of a brother, the utter glide at which they perform with the dignity and grace of a strutting peacock in motion. And this brother...all I can say is, umph, umph, ummm. He's all that and a large bag of chips! Broad shoulders under a brown leather jacket, copper slacks tethered at the waist by an ebony belt, with a pair of matching Timberland boots. Thin sideburns complimented a faded haircut and goatee. We appear to be about the same age and height, so he's not the tallest thing in the world. But I am wearing a pair of high heels, which means that he's not too short. I wanted to get a quick glance at the print between his legs; however, my concentration was broken when Paris started calling my name.

"Butter...Butter."

"What, damn-it!"

I was frustrated that Paris had interrupted my train of thought just when I was about to check out one of his best attributes.

"Don't you see me here deep in thought, thinking about how much I owe on my next electric bill?"

"Please, girl, instead of lusting after that guy, undressing him with your eyes and then trying to lie to me about it, you'd better hope the man isn't crazy as hell since you almost ran him off the road back there. If you ask me, him playing that gangster rap is *not* a good sign."

"He was listening to the same radio station we were, Paris. And what are you trying to find inside of that pocketbook of yours? You can't see anything in this dark ass parking lot, anyway."

"I was searching for this," she said, and then withdrew a can of Pink Moisture Oil hairspray from a side compartment of her purse.

I knew Paris must have meant to take out her key chain with the container of mace attached to it. We both carried some inside of our purses.

"Moonlight can bring out some of the strangest people, folks who'll do some very weird things," Paris continued. "You yourself proved that theory true tonight when you were acting so foolish while maneuvering that car of yours. Here he comes, girl. Stand close to me in case I have to use this stuff. Two screams will be louder and easier to hear than just one."

"Paris, unless you're planning on deep conditioning his hair right here in the parking lot, I'd suggest you put that stuff away."

The embarrassment on her face was so funny it almost made my toes curl up inside my pumps. I wanted to laugh out loud so badly that I felt like I was going to pee in my panties. I did neither. Instead, I just watched while Paris stuck the can of aerosol back inside her bag. She then readjusted her ponytail even though it didn't need readjusting.

"Calm down and don't worry about nothing, cause I got this situation under control. Watch, listen, and learn, while I do what I do best," I said. "I'll expose the man to my delicate side and win him over with some good, old-fashioned, feminine wiles and sweet southern charm."

"Just remember, Butter, lunar madness can be a trip, and road rage isn't much better than."

When my eyes went to find him again, he was already standing by our side, positioned closest to me. His gaze darted to Paris, and he nodded an unspoken hello, then his eyes fell back upon mine. Since I couldn't be for certain of what his attitude was going to be toward us, I resolved within my mind to let him know that I held no fear inner my heart.

"Don't even try to clown on us about what happened back there at that intersection, because we ain't in the mood. Today hasn't been the greatest of days for me, and my pussy is already missing, so I would hate to have to open up a can of scratch-ass and serve it to you!"

Judging by the confusion I could read in his face, I realized that my statement hadn't come out exactly the way I meant for it to sound. Damn, I guess maybe it is about time for me to name that cat of mine. Otherwise, I might find that I've picked up a very strange reputation in the streets.

"Well, that's too bad, my Nubian sister. Hope you find her in the same condition she was in when you lost her. I love animals myself, grew up with two pedigree dogs that I still take care of. They give me mad love, so it would hurt me to the core if anything ever happened to either one of them," he explained as we moved forward along with the rest of the line, stepping closer to the club entrance.

That's when I looked up to see that he, Paris, and I were now all standing underneath a streetlamp. Above our heads were flying gnats, each swooping and swirling to form a cloud of living haze. I said a silent prayer to myself, asking that the bugs wouldn't be attracted to and then electrocuted by the light, to then fall down atop my head, their little corpses stuck in my hair like deceased Christmas tree ornaments. PLEASE, STAY AWAY FROM THE LIGHT! DO NOT WALK INTO THE LIGHT! That's all I need to happen to me tonight, for some of those flying ants to adhere to my styling moose, having me running up into this club for the very first time wearing live creatures that are buzzing inside my ears all night long. If that happens, Lord only knows which rhythm I'll end up dancing to.

"By the way my name is Angel, Angel Spirit."

"The name accurately describes the face," I flirted.

He blushed at my compliment and then spoke in that articulate, smooth voice of his.

"I've never seen you here before. Do you ladies drop by this club often, or are you both newcomers?"

"Not until tonight we haven't. My friend here just moved on this side of town and so here we are, checking out the scene. How much will it cost for us to get into this joint?"

"Twelve dollars for the guys, six a piece for both of you girls. Tonight is Ladies Night, so you two will get into the club for half their regular admittance."

"Oh, I see..." I said, and then paused like I was thinking over something, even though I wasn't. "Now, can I borrow five dollars?"

He pulled out his wallet and handed me the bill without giving it a second thought. One thing's for sure, this man is definitely not one of those cheap brothers whom I've had the misfortune of dating lately. .

Since I knew that Angel and I were going to be talking for awhile, at least if I had anything to say about it we were, I turned around to ask Paris if she had a stick of gum. If his or her breath ain't smelling right, a brother will leave a girl real quick and vice versa, as far as I'm concerned.

That's when I noticed that there was some old man in front of her, attempting to make a pass of some sort. He had to be at least fifty years old if he was ever a day, and he wore a set of false teeth with several of them trimmed in gold. Every time Paris told him that she wasn't interested and didn't even know what a telephone was, the man continued to ask her for a number where she could be reached. Angel was just about to intervene and send pops on his merry way, when I told him to just chill and allow Paris to handle the situation herself.

"Come on, now, why don't you just give me your digits? If you don't want to do that, then we could leave right now and head back to my place. All I want to do is to get better acquainted with you," said the old fart. "Sweet thing, don't let some years and a few gray hairs fool you now. You don't know what you're missing. I'm a real man and could eat you out like no one has before."

"What? You want *me* to go back with *you* over to your sitting parlor? Then allow you to use those false, big-ass gold teeth to chew and gnaw between my legs all night long?" Paris countered with a glower of indignation. "You'll never give me a hysterectomy!"

"If I were you, I'd leave the girl alone before she starts hurling some roots or berries over your way," I interjected for good measure.

I traded places with Paris so that I could stand next to the old fart and look him straight in his one good eye. I hadn't noticed it before now, but his other eye was orbital and spinning around like hell. I resumed speaking even though I was becoming dizzy and wasn't sure if he could see me or not.

"My friend over there is a voodoo princess who just moved here from New Orleans. She can, and will, cast a spell on your ass in a heartbeat, have you waking up in the mornings sucking your own dick! So be afraid. Be very, very afraid."

71

Old pops must have already had some previous experience with one of those Louisiana women, because after I said that, he clutched at his heart as though my words were causing him some sort of an attack, then got out of line and ran off in direction of the parking lot.

CHAPTER 5

Tyree

Because the club was running a promotion for women to be charged at half the regular admission price, the barroom was busier than it ordinarily is on a Friday night. Due to several radio ads that had been running for over a week now, and the generous cut in price to promote the attendance of more female patrons, several new male customers were drawn into the club who were all spending freely at the bar, buying beers for themselves and any attractive woman who'd join them for a drink. Many of the usual patrons are here tonight; some dancing while others nursed drinks in their hands, cruising as they moved from one booth or table on to another. Several chic ladies were leaning against large marble columns that supported the ceiling. Others milled around from place to place, holding onto an arm of their potential mate. Loitering near the entranceway, smoking cigarettes or cigars while being boisterous with an animation that suggested each one of them may have already been intoxicated, stood three men who were asking every woman that walked by them for a dance.

As I tended bar and fetched a beer for this teenager whom I knew had just showed me a fake identification card, I could overhear a conversation between an extremely beautiful lady and her very attractive friend, down at the opposite end of the counter. They were sitting on barstools next to some dark-skinned brother who had a goatee and wore a high-grade leather jacket. Though I knew these women were not regulars and didn't frequent the establishment often, one of them seemed so familiar to me that I had to glance at her two or three times. I was staring at her intently when I suddenly recognized the face.

Paris! Oh my God, this girl becomes more stunning each time I see her. Damn, look at that cleavage trying to escape from that dress!

Paris glanced away from the conversation with her friends to see that I was staring at her. I walked over to where she and her group were seated, reading the cast of shock and utter surprise that she wore upon her face.

"What are you doing here?" Paris asked.

Down at the end of the bar nearest to Paris was a second cash register that wasn't in use, so I leaned up against it, peering out over the crowd. I scanned from left to right and made certain that none of the waitresses needed me to fix them a drink before I focused my full attention back on Paris, answering the question she'd asked me with yet another question.

"What does it look like to you that I'm doing?"

"Being a smart ass," Paris mumbled.

I pretended that I couldn't hear her above the din surrounding us.

"What's that? I can't hear you above all this noise?"

"I said that you must be racking up some mad cash, especially tonight, with all of these people who decided to come out and take advantage of the half-price special."

"Maybe I am, but right now *you're* my main concern. I will be at your beck and call all evening long, checking in with you from time to time to make sure that your every need or whim is taken care of, that your every desire of thirst is quenched before you can ask twice."

Paris laughed out loud. And not one of those fake, dainty chortles either, but rather, a genuine chuckle from way down from within her gut. Her two friends stopped conversing and stared at us, both looking somewhat perplexed by what I'm sure they assumed to be our first encounter with each other.

"Tyree, it sounds to me like *you're* the one who either needs a drink or has already had too many."

"Tyree!" exclaimed the woman seated next to Paris.

The woman swiveled away from the man to whom she was chatting with to spin her chair completely around, look from me on to Paris and then did it all over again, watching us both as though we were in the middle of a tennis match.

"Paris, girl, is this your next door neighbor, the guy without no job who sits at home all day long, farting and eating corn flakes while clicking the television remote between *Oprah* and The *Young and the Restless?*"

"I didn't say all that, Butter," Paris replied in a defensive tone, appearing somewhat embarrassed that I now knew she and her friend had been discussing how we met.

To keep from just standing there and being idle as I listened to the girls talk, I grabbed a wet towel from off the bar then began to wipe down the countertop.

"I know you didn't, girl. I just threw in the rest of those comments because I thought that this Tyree fellow might have been some sort of bum," Butter explained, then gaped over at me as though I were a selection on a menu. "But damn, girl, this guy looks like that super model, Tyson Beckford, only with some hair on his head and a couple of shades lighter in complexion."

"Butter, quit talking about the man as if he weren't standing right here in front of us and order something."

"I'll have a cognac, and Mary Poppins over here will have a decaffeinated coffee with some sugar and cream. What do you want, Angel?"

"Bring me a Miller draft, my man. Shaken and not stirred. Tonight, I want my buzz to be on like double-o-seven."

Even though I hoped they were finished speaking about me for the moment, there was a faint grin in my expression when I served them their beverages. I now realize that because I'd been home earlier today to help Paris move into her apartment, she and her friend, Butter, thought that I was some kind of unemployed vagabond. No wonder Paris won't trying to give me the time of day. I was deep in thought when a couple, perched on the opposite end of the counter, waved a hand in the air to flag me down. After I went over to them, took both orders and rang them up, I meandered my way back to where Paris and her loud mouth associate were seated.

"This all must seem very strange to you, Paris."

"Strange?" she parroted wearing a perplexed expression. "What are you talking about, Tyree?"

I turned away to prepare an order for one of the waitresses before I could respond to her question.

"Meeting me here like this. Our running into each other is starting to become repetitious. If you and your friend Butter are following me around for some reason, the man waiting for you back at your apartment isn't going to appreciate the habit. What happened? Did your man cancel out on a double date tonight, so you decided that contrary to popular belief, three *is* company and not a crowd after all?"

"What man are you talking about, Tyree?"

"The one you said you had a date with tonight."

"The *friend* I said I was going out with is Butter. And as you can clearly see, she's already here."

"Well, that didn't take long," Butter piped into our exchange.

At that moment I heard another customer calling to me from behind, so I turned and moved away from their discussion, walking round to the other side of the bar to see what drink the guy wanted me to fix him.

"See, girl, I knew you would enjoy yourself if only you'd get out and meet some new people. Now aren't you glad that you stayed here tonight, instead of slipping away and disappearing from the club like you normally do?"

"I don't have a choice either way, Butter. You drove us here tonight, so my car is at home. I couldn't have left if I wanted to."

"And that's just the way I planned it, too. Besides, girl, that Tyree wants you something fierce. I've been watching him whenever he thinks no one is looking and I can see it written all over his face. He's trying not to seem too anxious about it, though. I'm glad you and he are talking, because that can lead to something more substantial. But what you need to do if you really want to trap the man is this: find someone to groove with out on the floor. Get somebody to dirty dance with you and make sure that Tyree is watching. Make him jealous and wish it was his ass you were rubbing up against."

"Let me get this straight, Butter. You want me to grind my behind into some stranger so that his wife or girlfriend can wait for me outside of this club and kick my ass? I don't think so! That must be the cognac talking."

"Cognac my ass, that Tyree has got the deepest dimples I've ever seen on a human."

"On a human? Butter, I'm not even going to bother asking you what *that* statement is supposed to mean. Besides, with him working in this place, I wouldn't be surprised one iota if Tyree has women throwing themselves at him all the time."

"What do any of those hoochies have to do with you, Paris? In case you haven't noticed it yet, the man has been ignoring everything wearing a skirt in here tonight, including me for that matter, to make his way back over here and hover around your ass. And although I'm certain that Tyree has slept with some of these girls, because honey, they always do, you're a woman of intelligence and sophistication, not some schoolgirl wearing a pair of hot pants. Why don't you invite him to take a short break and have a drink with us?"

"One reason would be because Tyree is the only bartender. Who else would serve the customers if he took a break?"

"Here he comes, Paris. To give you two a semblance of privacy, Angel and I are going to locate an empty booth somewhere and move over there. When he gets back over here, order yourself another coffee and find out what sort of movies he likes to watch. Even if you've already seen the flick Tyree says that he'd like to go see, tell him you haven't heard of it before and would like to go with him some night to catch it. In other words, work him like a baby does a bottle of milk and suck him dry by whatever means necessary. And if you don't know what that means, then just use your imagination."

"Butter?"

"What?"

"You're just plan nasty! You know that?"

"Yeah, I know. That's way I'm driving a Porsche and you own a Honda. Need I say more?"

No sooner than I reached the cash register to come to a stance near Paris, did her two friends hop up and vanish like a pair of ghosts into the crowd. One minute Butter and Angel were there; the next, they were on the far end of the barroom, sitting across from each other in a tiny booth. I saw Paris glancing round, trying to locate them within the darkened room by peering between the gyrating motions of hoofers atop the dance floor. When I came to stand in front of her again, I leaned on the counter, then pointed out their table before I spoke.

"I guess the third wheel caught a flat, huh? It's a good thing that I have a flat, too, because now we can keep each other company."

"You must be an out of work comedian, moonlighting here part-time as a bartender in this club," Paris suggested in a slightly playful tone, rather than the wall of sarcasm to which I'd first become accustom. "You should drink less of your work."

"I don't consume alcohol during working hours, but I *will* join you in a cup of java."

She watched me closely as I pour myself a cup of coffee.

"Have you gotten everything unpacked from all of those boxes yet? After I left this afternoon, it must have taken you years to do all the work by yourself."

"Home is where I should be right now. I have so much unpacking ahead of me that my joints are aching just thinking about it."

"I could see you had good taste when we carried everything upstairs. You actually own real China instead of that tacky plastic stuff you find in most people's cupboards. What do you do for a living?"

"You know, to me that sounds a bit snobbish, Tyree. But, to answer your question, I attend school in Chapel Hill. Between my classes there, I work on campus as an assistant to the administrator in the infirmary for students and faculty."

I decided to mess with her some and see how far I could cast out the line before Paris would reel me back in.

"That's a good thing, because I sure could use some medical advice about now. I haven't been feeling too well lately and need an expert opinion."

"Unless you want advice on how to run an office more efficiently, then I'm not sure that I can be of any real help to you, but shoot. What seems to be your problem, Tyree?"

"Women are the problem, especially a woman like you."

"Excuse me?"

"Normally, I'm an extremely confident man; however, you have really thrown me for a loop. I know you want to see me again but you keep avoiding me, pushing me away just when I'm about to ask you out on a date. ·You act like you're afraid that if you said yes to me this one time, your head would fall off and roll away, or you'd lose your drawers or something. So now you leave me no choice but to resort to the caveman approach. Look, woman, I like you and you might like me if you gave me half a chance, so I'm going to pick you up from your apartment tomorrow at five o'clock sharp for some dinner!"

Paris rolled both of those pretty brown eyes at me, shaking her head in what seemed to be disbelief. When she opened her mouth to speak, what I heard shocked the hell out of me.

"No, make it six o'clock, and don't be late."

"That sounds cool to me. You better believe I'll be there on time," I said in an even tone, even though I could feel my heart skip a couple of beats.

Since I seemed to be on a roll, I decided to push the envelope even further.

"Now that we have all of that settled, what are you and I going to be doing later on tonight?"

"How would you like to come back with me to my apartment? All of the shades are drawn there, so it'll be pitch black when we arrive. Would you like that, Tyree?"

"Oh, yes, baby. Please, go on."

"I could light a few scented candles, put on some soft music…maybe by Luther or D'Angelo. How would that be?"

"Oh, yeah, that sounds like the bomb to me, Paris!"

"Then I would go into my bedroom and slip on something a little more comfortable. Would that turn you on?"

"You already know it would."

"Then, after I was certain that I'd gotten you all hot and wet, ready to become the tender lover I know you must be, do you have any idea of what I would turn on next, Tyree?"

"No, but I'm dying to find out. What would that be?"

"All of the lights, so you could see how to get the hell out of my apartment!"

"That's cold, Paris…real cold."

CHAPTER 6

Tyree

The day dragged on as though I were working down at the bar. The clock ticked so slowly that it seemed like it would take forever for six o'clock to arrive. I'd been looking forward to my date with Paris all day long. Earlier in the afternoon I spent a few hours at the gym, played a little racquetball, and then headed for the steam room to lie back, relax, and give my muscles some time to get rejuvenated. From there I went back upstairs to my apartment and plopped down on the couch, just staring at the four walls with nothing else to do but kill time. No matter how much I tried to push thoughts of Paris from my mind, I could still sense the image of her smooth skin and flawless complexion writhing their way back into my concentration.

The living room was feeling kind of stuffy, so I hopped up and went into the kitchen to go peek inside the fridge. Obviously, I need to go to the grocery store, because the only things in there were an apple and a six-pack of Budweiser. I grabbed a bottle and, using my teeth, twisted off its cap. I downed the brew so fast that I didn't know whether it was regular or Lite, causing me to wonder if there might not be some recessed alcoholic genes that run in our family, starting with my own.

Once I returned to the living room, the first thing I did was to go over to a window and raise the pane, opening it up as wide as possible to allow plenty of fresh air to circulate inside the room. Then, without a moment of hesitation, I stripped out of my sweaty workout clothes and let them drop to the floor right where I stood, standing there completely naked while allowing a cool breeze to blow over me until my entire body became cool.

Back to the sofa I went. I picked up a day old newspaper from the coffee table and turned to the sports section only to see that my team had lost again. Damn! Just then, I could feel a drip of sweat from my armpit fall down to seep into the fabric of a throw pillow I was using to support my upper back and neck. Tossing the periodical aside, off to the bathroom I went. For a few minutes I used a pair of clippers to groom myself in the mirror above the sink, using them to shapeup my sideburns and snip away any stray whiskers. I turned on the shower and, upon taking a long, hot bath, dried myself off then slapped on a generous amount of aftershave lotion...probably too much. I threw on a cream colored shirt and black tuxedo, cinched an ebony tie about my neck, and slipped into a pair of size twelve Versaci designer shoes.

Don't ask me why I did this because I don't even know, but I left the lavatory to go all the way into the living room to glance at the grandfather clock in there. I had on a wristwatch so I could have easily looked down at my arm, but it was almost time for me to go pick up Paris and I guess, as silly as this might sound, I just wanted to be as close to the front door as possible.

Shortly thereafter I found myself in the hallway, walking up to her unit wearing this ridiculous grin on my face. I rang the chime and immediately started pounding on the door, knocking like the building was on fire and there were some kind of an emergency. When Paris yanked the door open with a look of alarm on her face, I merely laughed and walked past her into the apartment.

"You were taking too long to answer the door," I playfully complained.

I watched as her eyes glazed over into something resembling vex, and I could tell that she wasn't the least bit amused. Man, this girl was looking some kind of cute! The dress she wore was tight, black, and supported on both shoulders by thin chainlike straps. From the rear her back was completely exposed, with slits on either sides of the frock showing nothing but legs from her waist down to the floor.

"So how do I look?" she asked.

"Like the bomb, baby! Toni Braxton better look out, cause she ain't got nothing on you wearing *that* dress."

"Tryee, this is only our first date and we don't yet know if there will ever be another one, so please call me Paris. No offense intended. I'm just trying to keep it real and be up front with you about that."

"Since we're being so up front about things, I have a personal confession to make to you about myself," I explained.

Her expression transformed into a serious bore. Even though Paris was apparently ready to leave for our date, I walked over to the couch and sat down without her ever inviting me to do so. I continued.

"I need to be straight with you about an event concerning my recent past."

Since she didn't know how long my confession was going to take, Paris walked over to the sectional, sat down beside me and crossed her legs. Once she got settled and looked comfortable, I commenced speech.

"Before you go out with me tonight, I should be honest and warn you about a couple of things."

"I'm listening. You want to warn me about what, Tyree?"

"Well, I'm not always the mentally competent person you believe me to be right now."

"Okay. I appreciate your sharing that information. And appreciate the fact that you feel comfortable enough to speak with me about such a personal matter," Paris countered with the professionalism of a trained psychiatrist, never once batting an eyelash while she spoke, "but what exactly does that mean, Tyree?"

"It means that I murdered my last girlfriend."

I watched as a large lump formed in her throat. Paris swallowed hard before she continued.

"Really?"

"Yeah," I said with a demeanor and tone that...excuse the pun...was deadly serious. "In the state of mind I was in that night, she never stood a chance."

"What happened to her?" Paris asked in a really low voice, like she was afraid of sounding too judgmental and ticking me off. "Why would you do such a thing to someone you loved? Or maybe she didn't love you back. I mean...ahh..., of course she loved you. We all do!"

"I've been to prison and have paid for my crime. But what happened was really quite simple, just a ridiculous misunderstanding really, even though a judge and twelve-panel jury didn't think so."

"What did you do to her?"

"I strangled her to death using my bare hands."

"Why in the world would you do something like that?"

"Well, when I went to her apartment on an evening much like this one, she refused to go out with me even though we already had plans for dinner and a movie. On that particular day, I had gone overboard and tried to look especially good for her, had spent a lot of money to buy myself a new tux and everything. Actually, now that I think about it, I wore the very same suit that I have on here tonight. How do you like it?"

"It looks absolutely fabulous!" Paris complimented, even though she never once took her eyes off of mine.

As we sat next to each other on the sofa, she was watching my every move very closely, leaning far away from me as though I had really bad breath and she might have to sprint away from it and me at any moment.

"Now please go on with what you were saying, Tyree."

"After I had gone through the trouble of making all of those preparations for our date, the girl just dissed me for no reason and said that she wasn't going anywhere with me, told me that I was acting all strange and shit! I *do* have to give her credit for something because she did have one thing right. I usually take medication to control episodes of dementia, but on that particular night, I'd forgotten to bring my pills along with me and had left the bottle somewhere at home. So when I got there and she refused to go out with me, I just kind of snapped; I actually heard something pop within my brain that sounded like a rubber band breaking into two separate pieces. Ain't that funny?"

"Absolutely hilarious," Paris said as she stood up, glancing over at the front door as if she were considering whether she could make it outside of the apartment and into the hallway before I could catch her.

She looked back at me wearing a polite smile.

"Don't play games with me, Tyree." Paris demanded. "Is any of this true?"

"I'm not playing games with you, Paris. In fact, I've been forgetting to take my pills for the last couple of days as it is. I think I can feel one of my anxiety attacks coming on right now, so I really should take some of this medication. Could I trouble you for a glass of water?"

"Sure, thing. Stay right here while I run into the kitchen and grab you a bottle of Evian from the refrigerator."

When she left the room and was out of sight, I started laughing uncontrollably. I didn't think that she would fall for it so completely, but Paris actually believes that I'm some sort of psychopath in desperate need of his medicament. All I could hear for the next

94

couple of minutes was her opening and closing each of the cupboards one by one, frantically searching through all of them in a frenzied pace. Since she just moved into this apartment all of her glassware is probably in unfamiliar places, I thought to myself. I decided that when she returned from the kitchen, I'd tell Paris the truth and let her know that I'd been pulling her leg.

When I heard a floorboard squeaking from behind me, I turned around just in time to see that Paris had crept back into the living room and was swinging an iron skillet at my skull. It was too late for me to duck out of the way; and the next thing I felt was this heavy ass frying pan smashing hard against the back of my head. There was a loud metallic ringing that reverberated all around me like an echo, but I couldn't tell whether it was coming from inside or outside of my mind. It sounded just like the bong you hear in those Bugs Bunny cartoons. Seriously, it did!

Through blurred vision, I could see that Paris had dropped the skillet and was running toward the front door. She attempted to pull it open several times; however, the portal must have been stuck because it never budged. I was so dizzy that when I climbed up from the couch to follow her, I literally had to stagger over to where she stood. Once Paris saw that I was moving in her direction, she darted back into the foyer, pulled open the coat closet, and leapt inside of it, slamming the door behind her entrance.

"Paris, I was only playing around with you," I shouted.

Since I didn't know whether she could hear me or not, I waited until I'd reached the closet before saying anything more. My head was hurting like hell, but I didn't want to scare her any further so the next time I spoke, I tried hard to keep the strain of pain free from my voice.

"I'm not on any kind of medication so you can come out of that closet."

"Yeah, right," she screamed skeptically through the closed door. "I leave you all alone in my living room with the television turned off, and then you start laughing like you're a one-man audience at some kind of comedy show. And now you want me to come outside of this closet to find out what was so damn funny! What do you think I am...some kind of fool? Tyree, get the hell out of my house before I call the police."

"Sister, if you keep a telephone in the closet, you just might be a fool after all!"

God, why did I say that? The thought just slid through my teeth before I could catch it. At that precise moment I started to feel faint and my head began to throb, like someone was in-between my ears pounding down hard on a bongo drum. The beating was keeping in the exact rhythm of my heart, which was already accelerated and sounded as though it were threatening to leap from my chest at any second. I took several deep breaths, placed both hands against the closet and leaned into it, bracing myself against the door until the spell had passed. I heard Paris trying to move further to the back of the walk-in, as though she expected me to yank open the door and come inside to get her. She must have fallen and then gotten back up from the carpet, because I heard several hangers clanging together, followed by loud thuds against the wall and floorboards.

"Paris, even if I were some kind of nut, why would you stay with me here in your apartment, trapped and locked up inside a closet with nowhere else to run? Now, maybe the things I said to you were in poor taste, but I was merely having some fun and just kidding around

97

with you. I am not crazy, nor was it my intention to be cracked upside the head with a freaking frying pan. Look, I can understand why you hit me, and if I were you, I probably would have done the same thing too. So please come out here and talk to me about this situation, then allow me to apologize to you face to face. I'm sorry to have frightened you that much, really I am."

"No Tyree, *you* look; I don't believe you, and I'm not about to come out of this closet until you leave my apartment. So if you plan on staying *in this house with me inside it*, you'd better pull up a chair because, buster, we're going to be here for a while."

"I have a better idea. I'll go and get your telephone, and place it down on the floor by the closet door. Once you get it, you're more than welcome to call the police or anyone else you'd like to come to your aid, but I can promise you none of that will be necessary. I don't have a criminal record, and none of what I told you about my murdering a previous girlfriend is true. This was all just a very bad prank gone awry."

"Okay, then, I can go for that. My cordless is on the coffee table near the recliner in the living room. Go get the phone, put it down by the door, knock three times, and then back the hell away from the closet. After that, I want you to say or yell something so I can hear where you are in my apartment. Then, *and only then,* will I come out of this closet."

Following her instructions, I placed the telephone on the floor in front of the closet, rapped three times on the door, then left the vestibule and backed far away into the living room. Paris cracked the door open just wide enough to poke her head outside the closet, peered over to where I stood with a suspicious glare on her face, then grabbed the cordless from the floor. She was just about to dart back inside and start dialing numbers, when she saw that her actions were causing me to grin even harder. Without uttering a single word, she bounded from the closet and walked right past me, went down the hallway, then headed straight into the bathroom. I heard some running water and once she came back out into the living area, a wet towel was pressed firmly against her forehead.

"What a lowdown, dirty trick for you to play on somebody, Tyree. Don't you ever pull a stunt like that on me again, do you hear me? Not if you want to live to tell anybody about it! Are you all right?"

"Yeah, I guess so. I hope you can cook with that thing as well as you can kill with it."

"You deserved everything you got, and much more. I'm not like those silly women in the movies, the ones who become lightheaded and fall down on their knees from being too frightened to put up a fight. Consider yourself lucky, Mr. Dick, if that's even your real name...that I didn't jump outside of the closet brandishing a coat hanger for a weapon."

Wearing a broad smile, I reached out and pulled Paris close to me. To my surprise, there was no hesitation on her part as I pressed her body firmly against my chest, embracing her in a strong, bear-like hug. After all the drama I'd just put the poor woman through, I think she needed to be held as much as I myself did. Don't ask me why I was feeling this way since I'd just been knocked senseless by the girl, struck upside the head with a utensil intended for cooking, but for some strange reason, I believe I'm the one who felt the safest in our embrace. Inner my mind, the last thing I can recall thinking to myself was *'to be continued...'*

CHAPTER 7

Paris

Just as my telephone began to ring off the hook at work, an older lady walked into the reception area and stood directly in front of my desk. As I picked up the receiver to place several of the calls on hold, she began to stare at me with this blank expression on her face. The woman was Asian and looked to be in her late fifties, her hair styled in a rebirth of the cut made famous by Jacqueline Kennedy Onassis in the early sixties. She wore a business tailored bolero jacket with a matching cashmere blouse, clothes that screamed expensive and were probably original pieces by whoever had designed them. The cream-colored set went well with the eggshell shoes she was wearing. Her outfit, which looked like something straight off from one of those Academy Awards presentations, made the simple burgundy dress that I had on appear antiquated and behind the times.

I knew…without a doubt…this woman could not be on staff anywhere here at the university, not since she was wearing such an

101

extravagant suit. If money could don on a pair of high heels and then walk into an office, this was one female who could play the part, looking every bit of a million dollars and then some. Even though she hasn't spoken a single word to me yet, the authority in which she carries herself is self-evident.

I finished transferring calls, answering quick questions, and placing people on hold before I was able to look up and offer her some assistance. When I did, I saw that she was still watching me with a hard glare and looked sort of pissed-off.

"I apologize for keeping you waiting, Ms. Now that I have those callers on hold, how may I help you today?"

"No, my dear, you can't possibly be of any assistance to me," the Asian woman said in a calm, but stern voice. "I merely wanted to drop by and see for myself what you were like."

"You came into the infirmary because you wanted to see what I looked like?"

"Yes, that is precisely why I came here, to take a look at you and learn what you're all about. And now that I have, it's painfully clear to me that you must have been reared in some low-income tenement, raised by a person or persons who were anyone else but your biological parents. Oh yes, you *do* speak the Queen's English and you *are* clad in some halfway decent clothing; however, class and breeding cannot be taught in a school or rented from a domestic boutique. In other words, my dear, however you may dress yourself up to feign a modicum of decorum, you're still nothing more than an unsophisticated sister from the projects."

That's when I stood up to leap across my desk and slap her, but somehow God gave me the strength and will to restrain myself. Even so, just in case I had to fight this venom-spewing witch, I kicked off my shoes and watched them land underneath the chair in which I'd been sitting before I replied.

"Do I know you, Madam?" I asked.

"Know me? As much as I'm sure that you would like to know me, as of now you don't."

"I'm assuming that somewhere in your mind, you believe I was supposed to comprehend that statement," I said in an overtly sarcastic tone, then placed both hands on my hips. "Are you here to see the doctor about a head injury of some sort? Because I'm about two seconds away from calling security. In fact, never mind my calling them. If you don't leave this office immediately, I'm going to come from around this desk and personally escort your ass outside *my damn self!*"

"I would expect no less of a reaction from a girl such as you, a hussy playing secretary as it were."

"Look, lady, I don't know you from Adam. You have some nerve coming into my office, my place of employment and going off on me like this. Who are you, and what do you hope to accomplish by barging in here to toss around insults?"

"Who am I? Oh, you will know that in due time, my dear. But as far as you yourself are concerned, I've learned all there is to know about you and your sordid little affairs."

"Affairs! Me, having an affair with someone? Lady, you don't know what the hell you're talking about. If you have a husband who's going through a midlife crisis or something, sleeping around on you because you're not using enough moisturizer at night on those crow's feet around your eyes, then I would suggest you take the issue up with him and leave us innocent folks out of it."

"Remember this face and all of its lines, study it well before I take leave of the building, because it will be the last thing you see before you yourself depart. Just you remember that, Miss Hightower! And remember it well," the woman warned dryly, seethe enveloping her every word.

Without further exchange or even looking back in my direction, she turned around, walked to the door, and left the office, vacating the room as quietly as she'd come inside of it.

"God, there certainly *are* some strange people in this world."

While I drove down the highway to meet Butter at the city park, I pulled the cell phone from my purse to call home and check for messages. She had given me a ring earlier in the day, wanting to know about how my date went with Tyree over the weekend. The forecast for today was for clear and sunny skies, so I suggested that we meet for a bag lunch around noon, and, told her that I'd fill her in on all of the details then.

Since our engagement began with me cracking Tyree over the skull with a kitchen utensil, I'd been altogether reluctant in speaking with Butter about the entire incident. I know how her mind works and already knew she would say that I'd overreacted to nothing more than a bad joke, that I'd ruined any chance of him wanting to see me again because our misunderstanding was entirely my fault rather than his. Though it's true that I haven't heard anything more from Tyree since that night, I still think I did the right thing in hitting him upside the head with that frying pan. These days you never know about people, and I for one, wasn't about to take the chance that he could've been the least bit dangerous. Maybe this incident will teach him a lesson. Although, now that I think about it, judging by my not hearing anything else from the man since the night of our date, maybe Tyree is trying to teach me one too. Could that be why I'm calling to check my voicemail during midday, something that I usually never do, all because Tyree purposely hasn't phoned and wanted me to be thinking about him? Well, if that was his game plan and part of his little bag of tricks then it sure worked, because for the third time today, I found myself clicking off my Motorola after having checked my voicemail for messages.

"Nope, not a single call yet," I said aloud to myself.

◊   ◊   ◊

I reached the park and saw that a bright red Porsche was turned sideways in the parking lot taking up not one, but two spaces, and realized that Butter had beaten me there. Since the campus where I work and attend classes is only a few blocks away, she must've sped big time to have arrived here before me. I parked, climbed from my car and locked both doors, then headed down a cobblestone walkway leading through the entrance of the gardens. Butter was already perched on a bench, eating from a box of KFC that rested on her lap atop an outdated fashion magazine and some napkins. Using a drumstick she held in her right hand, Butter waved me over and slid sideways on the bench to make room for me to join her. I have to go back to work this afternoon, so utilizing a paper lining or not, I wasn't about to use myself as a makeshift table and take the chance of spilling anything on my clothes. So, I sat down, placed my sandwich and Mountain Dew down on the bench between us, said my grace, and began to eat.

Butter was wearing a gray pantsuit that I hadn't seen before. It looked good on her, and showed off her cleavage in a tasteful way

107

without being too sexy or overstated. I'll have to remember to ask her where she bought it from, I thought to myself, took another bite of my BLT and then spoke.

"I hope you know that if you keep on parking like that, taking up multiple spaces just so nobody can park next to you and accidentally scratch up your car, the police are going to eventually give you a ticket."

"We ain't here to talk about my automobile, Paris. Today is already Wednesday and neither of us is growing any younger, so stop wasting my time and yours and tell me all about how your date went with Tyree last Saturday night. Was it as long as you thought it would be?"

"How am I supposed to know about the size of the man's penis after one date, nasty? You must have meant to meet a hoe here for lunch instead of me."

"Paris, *you're* the one with your mind in a gutter. I was just trying to find out how long your date lasted. I tried calling you late Saturday night and all day Sunday afternoon, but got no answer. Where were you all day long?"

"I don't even know where to start, girl. The first part of our evening didn't exactly turn out the way that I would have liked, but Saturday night and all day Sunday ended up being one of the longest, best dates I've ever had."

I took another bite of my sandwich and then began to lick my lips very seductively, chewing slowly with an exaggerated sensuality. Butter and I laughed before she started quizzing me for more information.

"Saturday and Sunday? You guys were together for two whole days? Well, don't keep me in suspense, girlfriend. Tell me what happened so I can dream about it later on tonight."

"At the risk of sounding like an infatuated schoolgirl developing a crush on someone, all I can say is that *magical* is the only word I could use to describe our time together. Tyree picked me up at my apartment and, after the dizziness left and he no longer felt faint, we went downstairs to where a black limousine was idling in front of the building. A uniformed chauffeur was standing outside the car, holding open the door for us to climb inside."

"After the dizziness left," Butter repeated wearing a frown.

Confusion and a lack of oxygen distorted her features as Butter began to choke from having eaten a piece of chicken too quickly. Each time she attempted to speak, a coughing sound instead of any words came from her mouth. Without asking for my permission, Butter grabbed *my* soda, took several long swallows that left the can completely empty, and continued speaking as though she'd never stopped.

"You're kidding? The man sprang for a limousine and chauffeur! No wonder his ass became dizzy. Now *that* must have cost him some real bucks."

"Once we climbed inside the limo, I asked Tyree where we were going for dinner. He merely smiled, asked that I trust him, and pulled out a silk handkerchief from an inner pocket of his tux. He wrapped it around my head and covered both eyes so that I couldn't see anything, then instructed me not to remove it until we'd reached our first destination."

"You weren't afraid that his hands might wander during the ride to wherever it was you were going?"

"Tyree was a perfect gentleman during the entire trip."

"I'm sorry to hear that," Butter lamented, then thought for a moment and realized what I'd just said to her.

Butter's eyes opened widely before she continued.

"Trip! What you mean by trip?"

"If you would stop interrupting and listen for a change so I can finish telling you what happened, you just might learn something. When the limo stopped I could hear the roar of a loud engine, and since I knew we probably weren't about to eat at a truck stop, I became even more intrigued. Tyree helped me from the vehicle and led me up a small ramp. I smelled perfume and felt soft fingers, obviously those of a woman, take hold of my shoulder to assist him in directing me into what I assumed was some sort of establishment."

"So, where were you?"

"We were at the Raleigh/Durham International Airport, and I was boarding a private jet," I explained, then heard Butter make an audible gasp.

I continued speaking, still not quite believing my own self what I was saying to her. Even to me, my date with Tyree felt like a scene from out of a movie.

"An hour or so later we landed in New York City, then thirty minutes after that, we were being whisked via a limousine and second driver to a restaurant on the east side of Manhattan. Upon entering the establishment, the host seated us at a table near this enormous fireplace, separated by a single burning candle resting atop the intimate dinette.

"I don't know what to say, Tyree. I never expected you to go through the trouble of doing all of this for me," I grinned.

The waiter brought a basket of piping hot garlic bread to the table, then Tyree selected a hundred-year-old bottle of wine for us to enjoy. We both ordered the steak aujus, asking that each entrée be cooked well done.

"Paris, do you know how long I've wanted to ask you out on a date?"

"Stop trying to be funny, silly, or all of the above. You couldn't have been waiting for very long, because you've only known me for just a few days now. That's why I don't understand any of this treatment, not that I'm not complaining about it. Tyree, how often do

you do treat a woman like she's a princess and then spoil her rotten? Am I among a long line of descendants?"

"How's this for being serious? You're enjoying my company and you know it, Paris. And as for how I usually treat other women, normally I don't have to do much at all to capture the interest of a female. But you, you're different somehow. Let's face it. You act like you don't give a damn one way or another about what a man can or would do for you. So, for you, our date had to be as special as I perceived you yourself to be. That way you would remember it and me, above all the other men that you've gone out with in the past. Trust me, you're one woman who's worth all the time, energy, and effort that I've placed into our date."

"I know I am. I was just making sure that somebody had told you," I joked.

Tyree had just taken a bite of bread and was so caught off guard by my jest, that he started laughing and almost spit the entire thing out. A piece of dough flew from between his teeth, and if I hadn't ducked, it would have struck me directly in the eye.

With a look of skepticism plastered clearly on her visage, Butter chimed in and interrupted my recollection.

"I assume that checking yourself into a hospital and then suing your date for the bill was something that never occurred, but Paris girl, how can a guy who works in a bar afford to reserve a private plane? You know it must have cost him an arm and a leg to pay for. This is all sounding just a tad too strange for my tastes. He must be a numbers runner or even worse...perhaps involved with drugs in some way."

"Butter, forgive me if I'm mistaken, but aren't you the person who's been pushing me toward the guy all along? Now you want me to think that Tyree is some sort of criminal because he took me on an expensive date? For all you or I know, the pilot who flew us there could be a friend of his and was doing Tyree a favor by not charging him regular fair."

"But all the way to New York, Paris? Flying you there on a private plane merely to have dinner and impress your ass? Things like that just don't happen every day."

"Well, that's precisely what *did* happen, Butter. Now, getting back to my recount of the events, there was a live jazz band playing in the restaurant and, in between our slow dancing out on the floor, we ended up closing the place down, not leaving until well after two in the morning. Tyree had reserved two connecting suites for us at the Radisson, and we both stayed there overnight."

"Like I couldn't guess that you each stayed in separate rooms. There ain't nothing new about that where *you're* concerned, sweetheart. What I'd like to know is how Tyree figured it out. So what happened next? Was there any hugging or kissing going on between those adjoining doors? You know he planned for there to be whether he told you about it or not, right?"

"I don't know any such thing, Butter, but I'll tell you what *did* happen. When I walked into the bedroom of my suite, a terrycloth bathrobe and single red rose lay atop the pillows on the bed. I still haven't been able to figure out whether it was Tyree or housekeeping that left it there for me. Early the next morning he came over to my suite and we both ordered breakfast from room service, then ate out on the terrace. Since I hadn't brought any other clothing with me besides what I'd worn the previous night, we left the hotel and did some shopping at a couple of boutiques lining Fifth Avenue. Tyree tried to insist on paying for this stunning taupe dress and a matching pair of shoes that I liked, but instead, I used my Visa and purchased the items myself."

"Damn if I would have! Woman, are you crazy? I'll tell you this much. You won't find *me* turning down free fashion any day of the week."

"He'd already been overly generous and had done so much, so I wasn't about to take advantage of the man, Butter. What do you take me for, some kind of gold digger?"

"No, but I myself am a professional, card holding, World Federation Class Gold Digger. Now, would you like to borrow one of my shovels?" Butter asked as she reached for her purse as though she were about to pull one from it.

"I don't know why you didn't leave that pocketbook of yours inside the car anyway," I teased. "What, you couldn't stand to be away from your compact for that long?"

"Cunt!"

"Whatever. As I was saying before being so rudely interrupted by a woman sitting at this very bench who shall go unnamed because she already knows exactly who she is, Butter; once we returned to the hotel, Tyree went to his own suite and we both showered and changed into what we'd just bought. From there we headed over to a riverside bistro and had some lunch. Late Sunday afternoon we went back to the airport, flew home, and then attended an evening service together at my church. The end. So, tell me, is that not one of the best first dates you've ever heard of?"

"Yes, it sure is."

"And is that not one of the sweetest things you've ever heard of a man doing for a woman?"

"Oh, please, girl, get off it. That man wants a piece of ass just like they all do. If you expect any more treatment like that, you'd better not let him find out he won't be getting any of the poo-nanny before marriage. During the conversation you and he had at dinner, did it come out at all that you're still a virgin? You know men like that kind of thing, don't you? And in your case, it's for real."

"No, it didn't come out, and I'm not ready for him to learn that information about me just yet, not this soon into our getting to know each other. I don't want Tyree to see my body as a prize to be won, or me as a quest to be conquered. The man is so good looking and in such great shape that he could have most women at the drop of a hat. In time he will come to figure out that I'm not 'most women,' but I want Tyree to reach that conclusion on his own. Besides, since I haven't heard anything back from the man since our date last week, who's to say that he isn't already seeing someone, and that's the reason."

"Well, it's your life, and you can do whatever you want to, Paris; however, as far as I'm concerned, I don't see your point in dragging out the sex part of getting to know a man. Everybody knows that Black men make better love when they're involved with other women."

Just then my cell began to ring, so I finished the last bite of my sandwich, told Butter to hold 'that thought' as if I really wanted to hear what she was about to say next, and then answered the phone.

"Hello, Paris speaking."

"Hey, Paris, are you guys finished with lunch yet?"

"Who is this?"

"Oh, how soon they forget. It's me, Tyree."

"How did you get the number to my cell? I only gave you the one to my line at home."

"I looked up your job in the white pages, and then telephoned the department you work in. The woman who took your place when you left to go on break told me that you'd stepped out for lunch and were going to meet a friend, so she wasn't certain as to when you'd be coming back into the office. It took me forever to convince her to give me your mobile number, but once I asked if it was your friend, Butter, with whom you'd gone out to eat, she realized me for the close and personal friend that I am and finally relinquished the digits."

"How cleaver of you, Inspector Gadget. Miss Thompson would usually never hand out that sort of information, most especially, not over the telephone to someone she has never met face to face. Are you always so convincing with women?"

"You tell me. Listen, I know that I haven't called you since last week, but I had to leave town on an unexpected business trip. I'd forgotten to take your number with me, and upon calling information to find out what it was, I learned that you weren't listed in the book. I'm due back in Raleigh later today, sometime in the early evening. I was wondering if you wanted to do dinner and go see a movie."

"Sure, just as long as you're on your medication and our date takes place in state this time," I playfully insisted.

At this point Butter must have realized that it was Tyree with whom I was speaking because she brushed my paper bag, Mountain Dew can, our dirty napkins, her journal, and empty chicken box all on the ground. She quickly slid over to my side of the bench and leaned inward so that she could listen in on our conversation, pressing her ear next to mine between the battery pack and antenna.

"I think I can handle that," Tyree chuckled. "Once I arrive home, take a shower, and become settled, I'll give you a call back and we can go from there. In the meantime, you be thinking about which flick you'd like for us to go see."

"Okay, but what if I pick something that you've already seen?"

"Then I'll fake it and pretend like I haven't. It's an old trick, but it usually works when you just want to spend time with someone in whom you have an interest."

"See, girl, I told you!" Butter blurted out, and then realized that I was still on the phone with the man.

With a tangible chagrin, I pulled my ear away from the unit long enough to give Butter a hard stare before I found the words with which to continue.

"Ahhh…, okay, Tyree, I should be home after five-thirty this afternoon. I'll speak with you then."

"Sounds good to me. Goodbye for now."

"Bye, Tyree."

"I was talking to Butter, Paris."

"Aloha, Tyree," Butter yelled back into the mouthpiece.

Without uttering another word, I clicked off the phone and glowered.

"Thanks a lot, Butter."

"You're very welcome, girlfriend," Butter laughed, but then abruptly stopped and looked at me wearing a frown. "Now what's this about Tyree being on some kind of medication?"

CHAPTER 8

Paris

Tyree and I have been dating for well over eight weeks now, seven more than I had expected for us to be. On the day we first met, when I was moving into this apartment complex, he was the last person on earth I would've guessed that I'd become romantically involved with. Pretty boys just aren't my usual cup of tea. Most of them can be as vain as some women, only without the layer of foundation and a matte finish. Today of all Fridays, Tyree has invited me to come and have cocktails with his parents before we go out to dinner at a new comedy club located somewhere in Durham. He says they're interested in meeting me, although I can hardly see why that would be the case. It isn't like Tyree and I have been seeing each other long enough or, seriously enough, to warrant any of their attention. Our relationship, if you can even call it that at this point, is in its infancy stage.

As I remained seated upon the sofa, becoming more deeply enveloped in my thoughts, I glanced over to a photograph I'd hung on a wall in the corner of my living room. It was of me as a little girl, with my mother and brother Derick standing nigh a Christmas tree during wintertime. If the situation were reverse and it was Tyree wanting to meet my parents, what in the world could I say to him? *Well you see, Tyree, I can't introduce you to my folks because my father is in the hospital, lying in a coma from a bullet wound inflicted on him by the hand of my mother. I'd introduce you to her, but we haven't seen nor heard anything from Ebony Hightower since she disappeared when I was seven years old. The authorities are more interested in meeting up with her than you yourself could ever be; however, that isn't likely to happen because she's probably dead and buried somewhere.*

Throughout the years of my childhood, I often watched my father beat our mother until there was nothing left but a lump of raw flesh. I believe that she stayed with him because there was no emotion left inside her, no strength remaining to try and love another man, only to have him hurt her in the same ways that my father did. There was no more hope, no more sorrow, just a void that she filled by taking care of my brother, Derick, and me the best she could. Even though our father did not, or perhaps even could not, show us any genuine affection, I know without a doubt that my mother loved Derick and I more than she did her own life. If there were any way she could've come back home to us, facing the threat of life in prison or not, then she would have done just that. Ergo, my mother is dead. Big Mama, Derick, and I were all she had left in this world, everyone that she knew would never cause her pain in the ways that a lover could.

The ringing of the doorbell suddenly pulled my mind back to the reality of present day. My vision was blurry, and I realized that salty tears were causing my mascara to run. I hopped up, yelled to Tyree that the door was unlocked, and instructed for him to come on inside and take a seat on the sofa. Without waiting for him to enter, I made a mad dash for the bathroom to compose myself and fix my makeup before he could see me.

As I stood before the mirror and glanced at my reflection, I realized that my dress, an olive caftan that complimented my figure with a subdued femininity, looked even better on me now than it did on the mannequin in the store window. The cleavage was tastefully cut and didn't dive too low, wholly appropriate for the occasion at hand.

With my makeup repaired and emotions again intact, I headed back to the living room only to find that there was no one in sight. The front door remained wide open, so someone must've come inside my apartment. Apparently though, whomever it was decided to leave in a big rush, because they didn't take the time to close the entrance upon their exit.

Could this be Tyree playing one of his jokes again? No, he wouldn't do that to me anymore, not after what happened to him the last time. My heart began to beat faster at the prospect of someone, a complete stranger, entering my abode and catching me off guard. Instantly, the entire house felt colder, as though the breeze blowing through the open door and windows had changed the current sixty degree temperatures outside, into just seven degrees on the inside.

With rapid footsteps I moved towards the foyer to close and lock the entrance; however, before I could do so, the silhouette of a man appeared inside the doorframe. I took several steps backward before the racing of my heart slowed long enough to allow my eyes to come back into focus. Standing outside in the hallway, there stood Tyree. He seemed puzzled by my startled reaction to his appearance.

"Is anything wrong, Paris?"

"Tyree, were you just inside my apartment?"

"When?" he asked, stepping across the threshold into the foyer.

Tyree looked so sophomoric wearing a blue sweater, pair of khaki slacks, and a duo of ash-brown loafers.

"Just, now. Someone rang the doorbell and I assumed it was you. I told you to come inside and have a seat, and without waiting for you to enter, I went on into the lavatory to...to check myself in the mirror. When I returned to the living room, my door was left ajar and there was nobody here."

"Naw, that wasn't me, Paris. But if you want me to have a look around your place for you, then I will."

"No, that won't be necessary. Since the door was left open when I came back in here, whoever it was must have left. All the floors and hallways of this building look identical when you first get off the elevator, so perhaps someone just came into the wrong apartment and then realized their mistake. I'm sure it was nothing."

"But still, I'll tell my parents about what happened here tonight. This is supposed to be a secure building, so if there's a problem with the security around here, somebody needs to know about it ASAP."

"Tell your parents? What do you expect for them to do about it, write the management here a scolding letter? Don't worry about it, Tyree. There's no need for us to overreact about the situation. Let's just leave now so we can arrive at their cocktail party on time tonight. Where do your mother and father live, anyway? I hope they're not way on the other side of town," I said as we moved toward the door and walked out into the corridor.

After making certain my apartment was indeed locked, I took hold of the arm Tyree was extending to me. With my hands draped around his muscular limbs, we footed over to the elevator and boarded an empty car. Before I could stop him, Tyree depressed a button for the top floor rather than down.

"Baby, you hit the wrong key. We're going upstairs when we should be going down to the parking deck."

"Say that again, please," he requested, wearing a silly grin.

Tyree pulled me closer and kissed me passionately upon the lips, neck, and somewhere else that I don't care to mention.

"I said, we're going upstairs when we should be heading down," I repeated and then pushed him off me.

I couldn't deny the fact that his mouth felt good pressed against my own, but I wasn't about to let him smudge my lipstick and have his parents thinking that their son was dating some kind of clown who'd escaped free from a circus.

"No, not that. Call me 'Baby' again. This is the first time you've ever referred to me by a pet name, and I kind of like it."

I was just about to press a button for the parking deck downstairs, when Tyree brushed my hand away from the panel.

"What's wrong with you, Tyree? Stop playing these games, because we need to get a move on. I know how women think, and if we're late in meeting with your parents for cocktails, your mother will assume I took way too long to get dressed and that our tardiness was my fault. That's not the sort of first impression I'd like to make."

"I'm not playing games with you, Paris. My parents live upstairs on the top floor, on the penthouse floor of this building."

"No, they don't, either, because I know for a fact that that's where the owners of this building live," I said and then felt my mouth grow completely dry.

The words reverberated inside my head several times before my brain ever processed their meaning or significance. Tyree wasn't smiling at me in the least bit, and at this point, neither was I toward him.

"What did you just say to me, Tyree?"

"My last name isn't Dick. It's Dickerson."

"As in the owners of this apartment complex, Dickerson? As in my landlords and the people to whom I pay my rent, Dickerson?" I inquired as I backed far away from him into a corner of the elevator.

Tyree reached out to take my arm again but I pulled away from him.

"Why haven't you told me about any of this before now, Tyree? Who do you believe me to be, some sort of gold digger who couldn't be trusted with the truth, someone who should never find out your family owns this property?"

"No, that's not it at all, Paris. Whenever I meet anyone who moves into this building, I always introduce myself as Mr. Dick instead of using my surname of Dickerson. In the past, once new tenants found out I was the son of the owners, they were forever knocking on my door for this or that. My folks travel a lot and are always out of town checking on other properties they own, so whenever renters couldn't get hold of them, they would seek me out. If there was a problem with the plumbing or someone's heating wasn't up to par, they came looking for me. I'm not the owner of this property, Paris, my parents are. You just don't know; whenever people have a problem they don't care what time of the day or night it is, they'll come and get your ass out of bed! I just got sick and tired of that sort of thing happening day in and day out. You understand what I'm saying to you?"

"Yes," I begrudgingly responded, realizing that he'd made several valid points that I could not refute.

Just then the elevator doors opened to reveal the top floor, one that was dedicated solely for the entrance and exit of the penthouse suite. All I could think at that moment was, 'Gosh, their apartment must be huge. I should've worn a more expensive dress.'

"Oh, and since I'm coming clean about everything, we own the bar in which I work, too," Tyree confessed as he ushered me toward the double doors of the penthouse.

Mounted on the portal were the faces of two lions whose noses were touching, both their bodies cast from what appeared to be solid, twenty-four karat gold. He pressed one of their noses to ring the chimes.

A maid wearing a black and white uniform opened the egress and stepped aside to allow our entry. She motioned for us to walk into the suite before she herself disappeared quietly through a side service exit. As we trod down a narrow passageway leading to an enormous living area, I took notice of several figurines placed upon a beautiful antique table made of marble and pewter. The sound of classical music emanated from a baby grand player piano situated in the rear of the room, as hidden speakers softly amplified its tunes and produced melodies from multiple directions. A skylight placed directly overhead caused the piano and a porcelain vase resting atop its lacquered surface to glow brilliantly by a refraction of moonlight. Two modern glass end tables, a white leather sofa, and matching Queen Anne loveseat occupied the center of the room. Hanging directly above the couch was some projection equipment suspended from a housing embedded in the ceiling. It was casting an image of a sports program upon a screen built directly into an east wall. This was a home television setup that would rival most professional theaters, with digital Surround Sound and a crystal clear fifty-six inch, high definition picture. As I observed the formal, extravagant lifestyle his parents seemed to live, I wondered how Tyree himself could have such a very low-key, down-to-earth personality.

While waiting for his parents to make their entrance, Tyree and I took a seat on the sofa, feeling leather that was as supple as silk against our skin. I took a long glance around the room before I decided what I wanted to ask, and then turned to face him.

"Tyree, is this where you grew up?"

"No, we actually lived at another property my parents used to own in the Cary city limits before my mom shipped me off to a military academy in Vancouver. They bought this place and then sold the other one shortly before my sixteenth birthday when I came back to live here in North Carolina."

"Military school? Although at the moment you certainly do look the part, you hardly seem the boarding school type. At least not personality-wise, you don't."

"Believe you me, I'm not. You just can't imagine how it feels to be separated from your parents at such a tender age, to feel like your mother is sending you away because she's too busy with her friends at the country club to make time for her own son."

"But what about your father? Surely he had an influence in wherever you were to be educated. Did you discuss with him your misgivings about traveling so far away from the two of them? Maybe that could've made a difference."

"When I was growing up, Pops was so busy acquiring realty holdings or securing contracts with builders that he probably never realized I was gone. I really can't blame him, though, since my mother enjoys shopping like it was an extreme sport and makes the habit her pastime. He was merely trying to be a good provider for our family. Beyond that, well, let's just say that my father does whatever my mother wants him to do, only she makes him feel like the ideas are all his own. The bitch!"

At that precise moment, two large mahogany doors opened from behind us to reveal a library with hundreds of books lining each shelf. A distinguished looking man who appeared to be in his late fifties walked out holding the hand of a woman who followed him closely from behind. They were each dawned in exquisite attire, he in a gray pinstriped suit and she in an emerald and gold evening gown. As I gazed into the face of an attractive African American man, right away I could see from whom Tyree had inherited his rugged good looks. Then, as I looked onward into the face of his mother, I saw a bitch.

"You," I called out with an audible gasp as I gaped at Ms. Dickerson, then glanced at her husband, on to Tyree and then back again at his mother. "I don't believe this, you...you're..."

"I'm an Asian American, my dear," his mother interjected before I could finish my sentence describing where she and I had first met.

She was the same woman who'd visited me on campus while I was working in the infirmary, the very same venom-spewing witch who'd hurled several nasty insults toward me, before turning around and taking leave of my office without any explanation.

At the time I merely thought she was some kind of nutcase or, at the very least, a misguided socialite who was accusing me of having an affair with her husband. Now, I realize that she wasn't speaking of Mr. Dickerson *at all*. She was upset because of my involvement with her son, Tyree.

Oh, my God, what kind of setup have I just stumbled into? I don't know if her husband knows anything about what happened between us, but by the way Ms. Dickerson cut me off mid-sentence, it's obvious to me that she doesn't want Tyree to find out that we've already met. She's probably afraid that I'll tell him, or them, of how she came into my office to wish me her distasteful greetings. I never dreamed of seeing this woman again, and here she is, the mother of the man with whom I'm falling in love. Love? Did I actually just admit to myself that I've fallen in love with Tyree? Yeah, I guess I did at that. Go figure.

"Hi Pops," Tyree said as he rose, went over to his parents and gave his father a hug.

Without uttering a single word, Ms. Dickerson turned her cheek upward for Tyree to kiss and he followed suit, an obvious ritual of greeting between mother and son. The three of them sat down, Tyree reclaiming his seat next to mine as his mother and father alighted themselves upon the loveseat positioned nearest the couch.

Mr. Dickerson had beautiful eyes with highlights of brown and gray inner each iris, while his wife held golden flecks of hazel within her own. That would explain why Tyree himself has green eyes. I should have realized long before now that his heritage was multiracial, but never in a million years would I have guessed that his mother would pay me the kind of visit that she did.

What did Ms. Dickerson mean by saying her face would be the last thing I'd see before my departure?

"You look like your mind is a million miles away from here, my dear," Ms. Dickerson observed, her face and expression cast in the same bland smile of a painting on display directly above the fireplace.

It was an extremely handsome reproduction of the Mona Lisa.

"So tell us, Pairs, my dear, do your mother and father live in this area also?"

"Umm…yes, Ms. Dickerson, my father still does live here," I admitted in a stammer of my words, not quite knowing what else to say.

Her question had caught me completely off guard.

"Our son tells us you take classes at Carolina State, and that you also work on the campus there," Mr. Dickerson commented with enthusiasm. "I think it's wonderful that you young people value a good education. Never stop learning, young lady. It's what the experience of life is all about."

"Thank you, Mr. Dickerson, I've always been taught the very same thing."

"I suspect this will be one of many occasions that my wife and I will have the pleasure of seeing you, so let's keep it as informal as we can. Call me, Mitchell, and I shall refer to you as Paris if that's okay with you."

"That would be more than fine, Mr. Dickerson," I agreed, hearing the sincerity and warmth in the tone of his voice. "I mean, Mitchell."

"Very well, then. So, you're the mysterious woman who has stolen the heart of our son here," Mitchell commented as he looked from Tyree onward to his wife.

Ms. Dickerson remained silent, wearing a face that reminded me of cold, hard stone, until her husband glanced over in her direction. At that precise moment her expression changed into the ones that politicians use whenever they speak to their constituents during an election campaign.

"*Dad*," Tyree called out in an elongated whine, utilizing a voice that made him sound more boyish, rather than manly.

Embarrassment was causing Tyree's cheeks to flush with a rosy hue.

"I have to give you props whenever they're due, son. You have as much of an eye for beauty and grace as does your old man. Paris is absolutely lovely," he declared, reached out for my hand and then kissed it.

Mitchell made eye contact with me and spoke several phrases in French that I didn't comprehend.

"Though I don't speak the language those were certainly beautiful words, Mitchell," I complimented. "What do they mean?"

"He said," Ms. Dickerson interjected in a course, annoying pitch that spoiled the entire mood and atmosphere of the moment, "that 'God has embellished the earth of much adorn; however, true elegance is a treasure possessed only by a select few.' Obviously, my husband has forgotten about me, the woman who went through twelve hours of labor to bring his only child into this world."

Since I didn't know how to respond to her comment, I merely looked away from Ms. Dickerson and then back to Mitchell.

"Thank you very much, sir. I really appreciate all of your kind words."

"My husband is absolutely correct about one thing. You certainly have managed to capture the interest of our son here."

"You give me way too much credit, Ms. Dickerson. Tyree and I are merely dating, but the level of our interest is something that's completely mutual."

"Of that, my dear, I'm most certain is true. But getting back to what we were speaking about earlier, by whom were you taught the value of a good education?" Ms. Dickerson prodded. "By your mother, perhaps?"

"Ahh…no, Ms. Dickerson, that was actually something instilled in us by my grandmother. I have one younger brother."

"Your grandmother? Please, do explain."

"Good luck, ma. I can't get the woman to talk very much about herself at all. To tell you the truth, though, modesty is one of the qualities that I love most about Paris."

"Ashley Abbot, the woman you dated for three years and almost married, may not have had a modest bone in her entire body, but she was well bred and as pretty as they come," Ms. Dickerson countered in an even tone, looking at me just in time to see the startled expression on my face.

Mr. Dickerson glanced at his wife sternly while Tyree turned to engage her, his voice raised and expression irritable at the revelation.

"Mother, Ashley is also as artificial as they come, like a fragile doll that is easily broken if it doesn't get its own way."

"Please don't take my fondness of Ashley the wrong way, dear. I meant no disrespect at all toward your friend, Paris. I'm sure she hails from a wonderful family about which I'll take an interest in learning everything that I can, most especially for your sake. Your father and I are wholly interested in your happiness, and if Paris is the person who can help you achieve this, then we have no choice but to support you in that decision."

"Excuse me for interrupting you folks, but Tyree and I are merely dating, not engaged."

"Ashley is a wonderful person who will make some man a terrific wife," Tyree readily admitted, his tone much calmer and disposition notably appeased. "But she is my past while Paris is my future, and the only person I'm interested in dating for the time being."

"Then enough said. I'm looking forward to showing Paris just how welcome she is in my household," Ms. Dickerson offered wearing a smile that, to me, looked forced and contrived. "And I guess I'll start by inviting you both to stay for dinner. Miguel prepared enough brisket for an entire army tonight, so you're more than welcome to dine here with Mitchell and me. Some hors d'oeuvres and cocktails should be on their way out momentarily."

"Oh, no. No thank you, Ms. Dickerson. We already have reservations elsewhere, and I wouldn't want to put you or your staff through any additional preparations," I declared before Tyree could accept her offer.

Chatting with Tyree and interacting with his father has been a real pleasure; however, as far as his mother is concerned, the woman just won't quit with her thinly veiled digs or probing personal questions. She might be able to fool her husband and son, but as I look around this place at all of their expensive trappings, including a live-in maid and cook, this woman sees me as a threat. Not a threat to Tyree or his emotions, but one to their money. Lord, why couldn't I have seen or realized all of this before now? If she only knew the truth about my family and our background, about the poverty and violence that has tainted every day of my childhood; I can only imagine what her attitude towards me would be like then. *I have to get out of here!*

Just then, the maid who'd answered the door when Tyree and I first arrived entered the room carrying a tray full of drinks. *Never*, was I so glad to be interrupted in my entire life. Two goblets of champagne, a martini, and some sparking water sat atop a gold serving dish etched with silver filigree. I myself reached for the water, Tyree for the martini, and his parents each took what remained. Since Ms. Dickerson had the beverages prepared without first asking me what I wanted to drink, the last thing I was about to do was to grab anything alcoholic from off that tray. There isn't a doubt in my mind that she was attempting to test me in some way, probably trying to find out just how much alcohol I'd consume in an evening to see if I might be some kind of lush.

With his drink in hand, Tyree got up and strolled over to where his father sat, coming to a stance by Mitchell's side.

"Dad, why don't we give these two ladies some privacy for a little while? I have some business questions concerning stuff at the bar, about how you want me to handle the new promotion coming up next month. Those executives from the advertising company you hired contacted me today, wanting to know if I would okay an alteration of their campaign strategy. I explained that I'd talk to you over the weekend about the changes they suggested and then get back to them by sometime late Monday afternoon. Mom, Paris, this will only take dad and I just a few minutes to iron out, then we'll come right back and join you guys. You don't mind if we step away for that long, do you, baby?"

"Well, I…"

"No, she doesn't mind at all, son," Ms. Dickerson answered in my place, never giving me an opportunity to come up with a valid reason to voice any protest.

Nursing a drink in one hand, she used the free one to wave them both away, pointing to indicate that her husband and son should use the library.

"You two get along while Paris and I have a little chat," Ms. Dickerson insisted. "I'll try and convince her to allow you both to stay for dinner."

"Okay, dear, work your magic on her," Mitchell told his wife as he rose to follow Tyree into the library.

"Take care of her until we get back, Mother."

"Don't worry yourself any about that, son. Taking care of Paris is exactly what I intend to do."

CHAPTER 9

Paris

I've always wondered, at what precise moment does the dark of night transform into the dawn of day. If people and personalities were capable of such a feat, then Ms. Dickerson would be a prime example. No sooner than after Tyree and his father had stepped outside the room, walked into the library, and closed the door behind them, did Ms. Dickerson place her glass of champagne down on the coffee table. She rose from the loveseat in which she'd been perched and walked over to me. Right before my very eyes, I saw the woman change and allow her true nature to come out of hiding. Bracing both hands on the sides of her hips, Ms. Dickerson began to stare down at me where I remained seated upon their couch. When she opened her mouth to speak, her demeanor was as unadulterated and mean spirited as it had been on that first day we'd met.

"Are you pregnant? Is that why it's so important to my son that his father and I accept you into this family?"

"No, I haven't known Tyree long enough for me to even consider making love with him, much less having his baby," I explained with a nervous tremor in my words, observing that her entire posture was rigid and arched for defense, like an animal poised for battle and ready to pounce in order to protect its offspring. "I have too many goals in life yet to accomplish than to be thinking about bringing a child or children into this world."

"Like what? Finding a rich husband so that you won't have to work for a living?"

"Ms. Dickerson, I've known your son for less than two months now, and I haven't gone to be fitted for a ring or wedding gown yet. I don't live inside a cave nor do I own a club, so Tyree should be fairly safe from me dragging him off by the hair to be married by a justice of the peace."

"Your jokes are amusing, dear, but *you yourself* are transparent, nothing more than an educated slut devoid of any social standing."

"I'm a what?"

"You heard me correctly. You're nothing more than a stray, like all the other whores Tyree brings home every few months for his father and me to meet in an attempt to get our approval of."

"Okay, lady, that's it! I've completely had enough of you and your nasty, arrogant attitude."

I leapt off the couch so abruptly that Ms. Dickerson quickly backed far away from me, not quite knowing what to expect from me next.

"You have some nerve, inviting me up to this suite to listen to you hurl malicious insults from that foul mouth of yours. I'm leaving. So why don't you stop playing games and try being honest with people other than just me for a change? Explain to your son and husband that you can't stand to be in the same room with me, near you or your precious pocketbook."

I turned my back to her and began to walk toward the exit, heading into the foyer. Suddenly, Ms. Dickerson grabbed my arm and jerked me back around using such force, that my entire body spun counterclockwise until we again stood face to face. She was using a vice-like grip to hold onto my wrist, exerting strength that I hardly expected to be contained within her petit, middle-aged body.

"Yes, you *are* leaving here, Paris. However you will not merely be leaving my penthouse, but will take leave of this building as well. You shall stay away from me and my husband, but most especially our son. In other words, my dear, get the hell out of my house and stay the hell away from this family! Do I make myself perfectly clear?"

"Woman, are you crazy? You'd better release me this very instant!"

I yanked my arm free from her hold and started to massage where she'd gasped me, concentrating on a dull pain I could feel throbbing at its joint.

"What on earth makes you believe that I'll do either of those things, jackass?" I asked incredulously. "I have a lease with an option to renew for the next two years."

"You know, I saw you on the day when you first moved into your apartment. Tyree was on his way back from the gym when some thug, driving a jeep with its music blasting, dropped you off in front of our building. A mother knows her son, sometimes better than he even knows himself. And as I watched and listened to the both of you on the closed circuit equipment in our security room, I knew that with every carton he lugged upstairs for you, you'd be just the kind of girl my Tyree would fall for. Not long after that is when I made up my mind, and decided to have you and your family investigated by a private detective."

"You did what?"

"You heard me. I know all about the sordid details of your past, about how your unwed mother shot your father in the back fifteen years ago to leave the man in a coma from which he'd never awaken. Before fleeing the authorities, she did have the good sense to leave you and your brother in the loving care of your grandmother with whom you both grew up. I understand that the poor woman is disabled, though she proved to be an outstanding surrogate parent in the aftermath of her daughter's disappearance. The police never have been able to locate your mother these many years, have they Paris?

I must admit, though, I made a serious error in judgment with respect to you and my son. I figured that you were using sex to hold onto Tyree when, in fact, you've been withholding it, securing him by exploiting one of the oldest tricks in the book. You're much smarter than I ever gave you credit for being. I observed the way my son lusted after you on the day you moved into our building, and if you'd only given him what he wanted back then, Tyree would've used and been done with you long ago. Instead, you posed to be a challenge for him, something most men can't bear to resist. Brava, my dear, Brava. Well done, though not well enough."

"Well, so what? You've learned about my past? Like I said before, my lease in this building is good for the next couple of years, so you'd best become accustom to seeing my face around here until then, because lady, I won't be going anywhere anytime soon."

"On the contrary, Paris, you will be moving from your apartment by the end of this month. You will tell my son that you've had a change of heart, that the thug who dropped you off when you first moved in here means more to you than you ever realized."

"The person you keep referring to as a thug is my brother, not some lover or ex-boyfriend."

"Look, bitch, I don't care what you tell my son as long as it doesn't involve me! Just make up something and then step far away from all of our lives. You're the daughter of a felonious fugitive. Do you honestly believe that I'm going to sanction or allow you to embark on building a relationship with my son, risking the chance of him falling in love with you to propose marriage so that you can make the troubles of your past part of our future? You're the one who's crazy if you think that I'd ever permit that to happen."

"I don't see what choice you have, since I don't intend to comply with any of your wishes. If you have so much of a problem with me living here in your building, then *you* move the hell out!"

"You brazen, little, harlot! How dare you even suggest such a thing? I don't give a damn about how much rent you people pay to us, this is *my* complex and when you go to sleep at night, you're doing it under *my* roof. You will depart my home by the end of this month because if you don't, your mother and grandmother will be sharing the same cell."

In direct contrast to how the atmosphere had been only moments earlier, the entire room suddenly felt still and seemed unoccupied, as if there wasn't a single sound or melody floating in the air. I'm sure the baby grand was still playing somewhere in the background, that the movie showing on their television continued to surround us with its lesser tones; however, I simply couldn't hear them. When sound finally returned to my ears and mind, it came back in the form of sequences, starting first with the beating of my heart, followed by a tune of music wafting in the air, and lastly with me recognizing the tone of my own words.

"Wha…, what are you talking about?"

"I'm talking about your mother, dear. I've found her for you. And if you don't want the authorities to learn where she's been hiding out all these years, then you'd best leave my house, my son, and this building, and never return here again."

As I listened to the threat and demands spewing from Ms. Dickerson's mouth, I could actually feel my heart lurch at the sound of her words, as though the organ itself were having an epileptic seizure.

"That's impossible! My mother vanished without a trace years ago and is thought to be dead. So how could you, of all people, find her when an entire police department could not?"

"Quite simply, because they don't have the resources at their disposal that I do, dear. After a period of time the state simply gives up its manhunt to leave the case file open or pending. Without someone to offer them a substantial lead, or heaven forbid, if there isn't an election to be won, police officials can't make an aggressive search due to their lack of money or manpower. Too many crimes occur at any given time for them to concentrate on every domestic dispute that crosses the law enforcement desk.

The detective I hired to investigate you and your family came up with some very intriguing information. Imagine my surprise when he told me that, after having run a background check on all your social security numbers, you had a grandmother working somewhere in the city of New York. I distinctly remember Tyree telling me that your only living grandmother was disabled and resided somewhere here in Raleigh. So which is it, Paris? Where *does* your grandmother live? I'll tell you what I think. I think that someone who can't use her own social security number for fear it could give away her identity and location, is using the only one she has access to, one she knows won't be used during the same period that she herself is seeking employment. I believe your mother, Ebony Hightower, *is* that person. I also believe that she is as alive, *as surely*, as you and I are standing here today."

"Why would you say such a thing? You're nothing but a damn liar!"

I was yelling at Ms. Dickerson, but didn't realize it until I'd finished my sentence. She looked over to the library to see if Tyree or her husband had heard, seemingly afraid that they might enter the room at any second. Hot tears came seemingly from nowhere, streaming down my face like a sudden rainstorm cascading over a waterfall into an ocean. There were so many emotions running rampant through my brain, flooding my entire body by their sheer magnitude. I was left with a feeling of having been violated, a sense of standing stark naked before the world while it bore witness against my soul. When I spoke again, it was in a much lower key.

"You're just trying to destroy what Tyree and I feel for one another. How can you call yourself a mother, and then seemingly take pleasure in causing other people pain, especially when it comes to the happiness and well being of your own child? What about Tyree and what *he* wants from life?"

"What my son wants is irrelevant. He will be involved with someone of my choosing and approval, not that of his own. Tyree will have a young lady possessing the proper breeding and decorum, not some street urchin from a background riddled with violence and bloodshed.

But all of that is beside the point. Whoever he ends up with in life doesn't include, nor should it concern, you, my dear. The only things you need to worry yourself about at this moment, is the continued freedoms of your mother and grandmother. I'm not certain if your grandmother knows anything about the improper use of her social security number, but I do know that at her age and disability, the last thing your grandmother needs is for her only daughter to be put on trial for attempted murder."

"Tyree," I called out, moving toward the library.

As I blinked in an effort to clear the water from my eyes, Ms. Dickerson stepped in front of me to block my path.

"Pull yourself together before my husband and son come back into the room. After that, I want you to leave here, Paris. Thirty days from now, I don't ever want to see your face in this building again," Ms. Dickerson summated.

The smile Ms. Dickerson extended to me was not that of warmth, but of a vicious triumph. When the doors to the library flew open, Ms. Dickerson looked as beautiful as she had when Tyree and I first arrived. I can't say the same for myself. Both of my eyes were red, and there was a black streak of mascara running from my face down the front of my dress, its discoloration leaving a stain deeply embedded in the material. Tyree and his father hurried out to the living room, each looking from Ms. Dickerson onward to me. Right away I could see they both already knew something was terribly wrong.

"Lyn Dickerson, what in the world is happening in here?" Mr. Dickerson demanded to know as he came to stand by the side of his wife. "We thought we heard raised voices."

"No, we didn't think that," Tyree corrected. "We heard somebody shout."

"I want to go home," I heard myself say.

It was like someone else was using my body to say words independent of my control. As I glanced toward Ms. Dickerson I realized that, in a way, the statement couldn't have been any truer. I walked around her and began to head toward the exit. Before I could leave, Tyree rushed over to me and wrapped his large, strong arms around my neck and shoulders. I could see by his pleading stare that Tyree wanted to know what had happened, but at that moment, all I could do was cry on his chest without uttering a word.

"You want to go back home?" Tyree parroted in disbelief, wearing a frown as he eyed his mother and father, then looked at me again. "But we were supposed to go out tonight, and now you're telling me that you'd rather go back downstairs to sit all alone inside your apartment. What gives here, Paris? And why are you crying like this?"

"No, what I'm saying is that I'm going home. I'm leaving here, moving out of this building to go back and live with my grandmother.

I've recently learned that she needs me there, maybe now more than she ever has before. Knowing you, and dating you has been nice and everything, but it has come to an end. Goodbye, Tyree."

"See what I mean," I heard Ms. Dickerson say as I broke away from Tyree, then rushed past them all, moving swiftly toward the exit.

I ran into the foyer, through the front door without closing it behind me, and out into the corridor.

"Didn't I tell you she was just the type of girl who was going to do that to you, son?" Ms. Dickerson reminded. "The kind who'd spend your money and then move on to a better prospect, the next sucker or another free meal who just happened to mosey along? Good riddance to bad rubbish is what I always say."

Edward Nubian James

BOOK TWO

Edward Nubian James

CHAPTER 1

"If you would only put the gun down so we can talk about the situation rationally, I can explain all of this to you, baby. She don't mean nothing to me, just a piece of ass that's all..."

It's funny, but that's all I can remember Joseph saying to me before I lowered the gun, his .38 caliber, down to my side then pointed it toward the ground.

"What would really make me feel better is for you to pack up your belongings and then go."

When he punched me in the face I didn't feel the blow as much as I heard the sudden thud of it. The gun slipped free from my hand and I found myself staggering backwards in circular motions. My eyes instantly became swollen, transforming into tiny slithers from which I could no longer see. Only light filtered through them, my vision now reduced to shapes and shadows of movement. Time seemed to flicker off and on as I passed into and out of consciousness. But I knew that I could not allow myself to pass out completely, knew that if I fell asleep for a moment too long, the rest I took would surely become my last. My arms groped aimlessly in the air, reaching for anything I could use to regain my bearings and steady myself so that I'd be able to find the exit to our bedroom.

As an excruciating pain traveled downward from my skull and extended throughout the entire length of my spine, blood began to gush from a cut above my forehead where the ring Joseph wore had broken the skin. For a moment I became completely blinded by a shroud of crimson. A shove, which seemed to emerge from nowhere, caused me to fall backwards and I came crashing down against the worn carpet with both of my arms reaching upward as if in prayer. He leapt atop my chest with his legs straddled crosswise my waist, then wrapped his hands around my neck so tightly that I felt a vessel in my jugular vein snap, felt its artery actually pop and implode from him exerting pressure.

When I awoke from the nightmare my eyes were as swollen as they had been fifteen years ago, only now with the tears of its memory. How many nights must I travel down this same river? When will these knells from my past finish haunting me with their melodies of loss and regret? For me, sleep is not slumber but rather a sentence without pardon that I serve each night. May God offer rest to my soul, for I am weary and effete, like a child lost in the snow who cannot find his way back home. Some people say that home is where the heart is, but my heart is where my home was, where my children are...

◊ ◊ ◊

Living in New York City helps me to keep pretty much to myself. To the neighbors around here I'm just a woman with a job, just another face blended into a sea of people who walk the crowded streets every day back and forth between their places of employment and their homes. I can't stay at any job for too long, never more than a year or so, because when tax time rolls around employers start asking too many questions. These days, since everyone and everything is connected via the Internet and is tracked by a giant network of computers, using my mother's social security card is becoming a riskier and riskier thing to do with each passing year. The first and last year that I tried to file for a tax refund with my mother's card was when I'd been without a job for a very long stretch. After I'd gone into a local Jackson Hewitt office down on Main Street and said that I was her, the man whose desk I was sitting in front of took one look at his computer screen, took another look at me, then said that I looked fantastic for a sixty-year-old woman. He told me that he wouldn't call the police if I left his cubicle right then and there. After I asked him to return the social security card that I'd just handed him, of course, he just stared at me like I was crazy and kept it. The attempt itself was more than stupid, and I should have known better.

When I packed a suitcase and left my children with my mother fifteen years ago, it had all seemed like a kind of forced vacation from which I'd return someday. After years of moving around from place to place in a state akin to sleepwalking, going from living on the streets of Manhattan to residing in an efficiency apartment, it finally dawned on me that I could never have any physical involvement with anyone from the life I left behind in North Carolina. Even if I had written a letter to my children using an assumed name or mailed it without using a return address, anyone could trace the parcel back to the area from which it was mailed.

For years after I'd left Paris and Derick with Big Mama, I used to think that I saw one or both of them whenever I'd catch a glimpse of small children frolicking at a playground or walking with their grandparents on the streets. I thought those illusions had ceased altogether until about two months ago, when I was coming home from work and saw a young woman shopping with a man. As I watched the couple climb in the back seat of a limousine, I heard the woman calling out the name Tyree, and I imagined that she'd be around the same age as my Paris. The woman was so beautiful that I suddenly found myself blinking back tears, all the time thinking that I wouldn't know what my own daughter or son looked like even if they were standing right beside me. Sometimes during the night, when I'm only a breath away from sleep, I keep reminding myself that I had no choice in the matter, that I did what was necessary to preserve the life of my only son.

For me the fourth of July was merely another holiday, one that I hoped would pass by quickly without a lot of questions from coworkers about how I'd end up spending the long weekend. Unlike most of the staff here in Doctor Meagan Ultra's private practice, I have no family with whom to share special occasions and, although I know everyone here means well when they invite me out to cookout after cookout, I really would rather just be left alone to perform my duties here as the receptionist and allowed to fade quietly into the background.

Dr. Ultra is an attractive woman, in her early forties and of mixed race, most likely a combination of African American and European decent. She has an athletic build similar to my own now that I've lost the weight I'd been carrying around since childhood, only her figure is due to a well-balanced diet and exercise, while mine altogether can be attributed to a lackluster appetite. My weight loss has left me with a voluptuous, hourglass figure that most men like and other women seem to either admire or resent. Even at my current age of thirty-seven, many of the men I attract are oftentimes half my age. These days I don't use much makeup at all, though my youthful appearance has made for many an awkward situation whenever I've had to diffuse a crush or puppy love mistaken for the real thing.

Approaching my desk at a brisk pace was Dr. Peter Parker, a general practitioner who shared office space here with Dr. Meagan Ultra since she'd relocated her practice back to her birthplace of New York City. As I watched him draw closer, I could feel myself developing a headache. With sandy brown hair and blue-green eyes the man is certainly attractive enough, and if I didn't think that Black men were the sexiest things ever placed upon God's green earth, my body would probably want to give him and his gym toned body the correct time of day. However, at this point in my life, men are the last things on my mind or agenda. I've been working in this position for the last eight months now, and never a week goes by that the man isn't asking me out on a date or requesting that I join him for a cup of coffee after work.

"Morning, Barbara. You're really looking good today," Peter greeted before taking a sip from one of two Styrofoam cups he held in his hands.

I could see steam rising above both rims as he placed a container before me, resting the cup down on my desk before he continued speaking.

"I figured that if Muhammad won't come to the mountain, then I must move the mountains for Muhammad. Since I couldn't find him and you're much more attractive, I decided to move one for you instead. Bringing you java isn't exactly the same as moving heaven and earth, but it's a beginning. Now how about grabbing some lunch with me later today?"

I glanced from my white blouse to my gray pleated skirt, and even though I knew Peter couldn't see the fashionable split running from my hipbone down to its fringe while I sat behind a large oak desk, I pulled the cotton material over to conceal more of my thigh regardless. He was looking at me the way he always did, with an expression that seemed to ask, *"What time will dinner be served and are you one of the items on the menu?"*

At the age of thirty-five he was as handsome as he was spoiled, but since I worked for Dr. Ultra and not for him, I wasn't too concerned about jeopardizing my job security by staving off his advances. For the most part I just ignored him or played dumb, pretending not to know who or what he was talking about. Though Peter was becoming more and more aggressive in his desire to develop a personal relationship with me outside of work, I couldn't risk losing my job nor could I claim sexual harassment without drawing a lot of unwelcome attention toward myself.

'Saved by the bell,' I thought to myself as the telephone began to ring.

I quickly thanked Dr. Parker without responding to his invitation, then put on my headset and clicked the button to answer the call.

"Offices of Doctors Meagan Ultra and Peter Parker, this is Barbara speaking. How may I direct your call?"

"Hi, this is Pamela Gardner, a patient of Dr. Parker. I'd like to make an appointment with you to see the doctor next week."

"Ms. Gardner, believe it or not, you have perfect timing."

"Well, that's good to know, but whatever do you mean by that?"

"Nothing, nothing at all really. What time would be good for you, Ms. Gardner?" I asked with a sigh of relief.

Chapter 2

As Ebony sat alone in a popular, family owned Italian restaurant only two blocks from her place of employment, she glanced outside the large plate glass window in front of which she'd been seated to see that Peter Parker was about to enter the same establishment. It was noonday and, as a result, the dining room and bar was already becoming crowded, so as Peter strolled into the eatery and began scanning the room for a place to sit, Ebony held up her menu high enough to conceal her face. She was desperately hoping that he wouldn't recognize her from the outfit she was wearing and then come over to ask if it would be okay to join her for lunch. When she peeked around the menu to see where Peter had gone, he was already pulling out the chair situated opposite from her.

"May I sit here with you, pretty lady, to join you for lunch and keep you company since we're both flying solo today?"

"Damn!" she mumbled under her breath.

"Pardon?" Peter asked.

"I said ham," Ebony lied. "Ham is what I'll order for lunch when my guest arrives."

"Oh. Well, I'll just sit here with you until she comes," Peter said as he pulled out the chair opposite of Ebony's and seated himself at the table, not waiting for an invitation or protest from her.

"She's here," announced a tall stranger who appeared seemingly out of nowhere.

Neither Ebony nor Peter had seen him approaching the table; one minute there was no one, and then suddenly the stranger was towering above the two of them. The thirty something African American male was standing directly behind Ebony's chair, holding onto its back as though he'd assisted her with being seated.

As Peter rose he began to stare at the lean athletic figure wearing an aquamarine tie and gray mesh suit, taking in his dark eyes which shown like black onyx amidst a sea of white pupils surrounded by an almond shape. His hair was locked in auburn dreads that flowed down his back like a horse's maim, and if Peter didn't know better, he could have sworn that he'd seen this guy somewhere before, perhaps

173

on television or in a movie. The man was so stunningly handsome that even Peter was gazing at him with a sense of admiration.

Ebony literally jumped as she heard the sound of a baritone voice ringing above her head. Feeling his fingertips touching her shoulders and back she looked up, wearing a look on her face that bore a startled and somewhat frightened expression. She watched as the handsome stranger came from behind her, strolled to the opposite side of the table, and claimed a seat in the chair that, only moments before, had held Peter's bottom securely on its cushion. Not that she knew what to say to the man in the first place, Ebony opened her mouth to speak but found that no words would come out. She could only listen mutely as the man continued.

"Sorry I'm late, darling, but traffic in the City is a mother. Who's your friend?"

"Ahh…he's, ahh…," Ebony stammered, using words that were as perplexing as her expression.

"Hi, I'm Doctor Peter Parker. I'm one of the two physicians that Barbara keeps in line. And you are?"

"Herman."

"Nice to meet you, Herman."

"No, Doctor, I said that I'm *her man*. And if a brother didn't know that you two just worked together on a platonic level, I'd be getting some kind of jealous. The last man who kept hitting on my Barbara here got his ass kicked. But that was another time, another story, and a completely different situation. That guy wasn't merely a coworker like you and Barbara are, now was he, honey?"

"Oh my, look at the time," Doctor Parker said first then looked down at his watch second, not even bothering to read it. "I need to be getting back to the office."

"But you just arrived and you haven't even eaten yet, Peter," Ebony pointed out. "Why don't you join me and a-hum…me and…"

"Nubian. Nubian Prince," the stranger announced with his hand extended toward Peter.

"Now I know where I've seen you!" Dr. Parker proclaimed in a voice that was nearly a shout.

He shook Nubian's hand with such excitement that, for a moment, Ebony wasn't sure if he was ever going to release hold of it.

"You're that model that Calvin Klein uses," Peter continued, "the one in all those magazine ads and television spots."

"I guess that would be me."

"Listen, my man, I didn't mean to," Peter said without finishing his sentence as he turned to look at Ebony. "Barbara, if I'd only known about the two of you being together, I would have never done…"

"Would have never done what?" Nubian said as he rose from the table wearing a frown.

Nubian's build loomed large and muscular, even though the clothing he wore looked to be tailor-made with a relaxed fit. Standing side by side, Ebony could see that Nubian made Dr. Parker's physique seem like that of a child standing next to his father. Nubian stood well over six feet and weighed every bit of two hundred pounds, his entire stature nothing but ripples and arms yielding massive curves. There was no body fat anywhere to be seen on this man.

"Nothing. Never mind, dude. I gotta' go! See you back at the office, Barb. Bye for now," was all Peter sputtered before making a beeline for the exit.

Peter darted out the front entrance and disappeared as quickly as he'd arrived.

"I've never seen the man move that fast before, not even during an emergency at the office," Ebony explained as she reached for her water glass then took a long sip, laughing before she drew in a deep breath with which to speak.

"Well, I saw what *you did* when you yourself saw the man enter the restaurant. Then, when the guy came over here and sat down with you, the expression you made with that pretty face of yours was priceless. It didn't take much to see that the man was interested and you were not, so I thought I'd do my Samaritan thing for today and save a damsel in distress."

"Well, thanks."

"Most welcome," Nubian said as he picked up her menu and started to scan through it.

"What are you doing?"

"Reading," Nubian explained without looking away from the menu.

"I know that, but why are you doing it here instead of where you were seated before?"

"Because you and I will be eating lunch together," he said, and then winked. "You didn't think I was getting rid of him to let you dine here alone, did you?"

"Yes, I did."

"But I wanted to tell you about myself, and it would be sort of silly for me to shout to you from the bar. So, how about it? Have lunch with the guy who saved your life."

"Saved my life?" Ebony countered with skepticism, shaking her head back and forth while she considered the idea of not dining alone for a change.

"Yeah, I might as well have. The man wasn't about to leave you alone, not even if you'd used this menu to fan him away. Oh, but you couldn't have done that, now could you? Not since you were using the menu to conceal your face in the hope that you'd somehow become invisible and Doc wouldn't see you."

"Are you finished?"

"Almost. In *my* book, what I just kept from dining here with you for lunch constitutes me saving you from at least being bored to death."

The laugh Nubian made was loud and sincere. Ebony looked at him with a genuine affection, happy about the fact that at least for the moment…at least for an hour…she would not be alone.

"You've given me a reprieve from his advances, so for at least that much, I do owe you a thank you, Nubian. Please, have a seat and join me for lunch."

"Don't mind if I do, Barbara. So is this your treat or mine?"

"Let the Dutch have the treat and you pay for your own meal, Nubian."

"Okay, but the next one will be on me."

"And what makes you so certain that there'll ever be a next meal between you and me? I don't even know you."

"But that's what this lunch is all about, Barbara, me getting to know you, and you me."

"Nubian?"

"Yeah?"

"Shut up and order something," Ebony countered as she flagged down a waitress.

Nubian just smiled as though he knew something that she did not.

CHAPTER 3

It had literally been years since Ebony had gotten dressed up to go out on a date. She didn't have much from which to choose when it came to evening wear, so she settled for a dress that she'd bought at an estate sale several months prior, a black crepe with a strapless back and long flowing train.

Big Mama had always been superstitious about wearing the clothes of a dead woman; however, to Ebony, the act seemed woefully appropriate considering her current position and circumstances. Most of the time, living day to day without both mother and children in her life, Ebony oftentimes felt less alive than anyone buried six feet underground ever could've been.

As Ebony stood before the mirror applying a coat of mascara in her last step preparation for going out with Nubian, tears came to her eyes when she realized that her children were no longer children anymore; but rather, they were now full-grown adults. There were so many years lost among them all that had never been shared, years that could never be recovered.

Wiping her eyes to see that the waterproof makeup she wore indeed held up to its promise, Ebony accentuated her gown by putting on a pair of pearl earrings that belonged to her mother, and then lastly, swept her hair upward into a bun to pull the entire look together. Just as she'd pushed the last bobby pin into her hair to hold the style in place, the doorbell rang. The look of admiration that showed prominently upon Nubian's handsome face let Ebony know without a doubt that she looked good.

"Let me tell you something, Barbara, when I met you in that restaurant two days ago, I said to myself, 'This is one good-looking woman.' Well, I was wrong. You're just plain gorgeous!" Nubian gushed, he himself looking as fine as could be in his black tuxedo and gray cummerbund.

Without stepping inside her apartment, Nubian held out his hand as Ebony grabbed a beaded purse. She locked her door, took hold of the arm he was extending to her, and walked with him to the parking lot. Nubian opened the passenger side door of his Lexus and helped her inside before walking around the car and climbing behind the wheel.

"Thank you, Nubian. Where are we going tonight?"

"We're going to a party that one of my clients is hosting, and then afterwards, out for a quiet dinner and some coffee. How does that sound?"

"That'll be fine with me."

'What on earth was I thinking?' Ebony thought to herself as she and Nubian were riding in the car across the Staten Island Bridge, moving rather slowly due to a small fender-bender several feet ahead of them. 'Going to a party with a bunch of strangers will only serve to promote a lot of personal questions about my work history and family background.'

In her head she rehearsed the new background that she'd created for herself. Everything that she was, the person she'd been for so many years previous to now was all gone. Ebony Hightower existed only as a memory inside her mind. Now there was merely Barbara Hightower, the birth name given to her mother rather than to herself.

It was an identity Ebony stole and had devised an entirely new history about, one she hoped could not be traced back to her past life in North Carolina.

"So, Barbara, you've never told me anything about your family," Nubian announced as he turned on the wipers, clearing drops of pelting rain that were falling hard against the windshield.

Ebony hadn't brought a wrap or overcoat, and hoped they'd arrive at their destination without her getting drenched in the only evening gown she owned.

'Was Nubian studying her or was it merely her imagination at work?' Ebony wondered.

"Well, Nubian, there really isn't much to tell you about. I'm an only child," Ebony said knowing that, at least so far, that bit of information about her past was true.

From this point forward there'd be nothing but lies coming from her mouth.

"You can't hail originally from New York City, not with the slight accent I hear in your voice."

"I didn't realize I had one," Ebony stated while the feeling of being trapped in a confined area began to engulf her thoughts. "I'm originally from out west. I worked in a beauty…"

"No, let me guess. Given how radiant you look tonight, you probably worked in a beauty shop at one time. Am I right?"

"No, at a waste disposal plant," Ebony lied.

'Damn, I almost slipped up and told him the truth about my having worked for a salon, but if that waste disposal answer doesn't throw him off track, then nothing will,' Ebony thought to herself. 'I'm not even sure how I got that one outside of my mouth without laughing first. That image will probably be the only thing he remembers tonight about me, or our date.'

"You're joking?"

"No, I'm not. Do you see something wrong with that? Not everyone can be a model or superstar like you," Ebony blurted out before she caught herself.

His questions were making her nervous, causing her responses to become sarcastic.

185

Without missing a beat, Nubian dismissed her comment with one of his own.

"No, actually, I was going to ask you if you knew anything about the mechanical workings of a disposal. Mine is on the fritz again, and even though I've called maintenance to come out and repair the unit, I still like to try my hand at fixing things around my apartment myself."

"Nubian, please forgive that dis' about your being a model slash superstar. That was an unfair dig and I apologize for it."

"Apologize for what, calling me a superstar? The statement itself isn't even half true, but I'd hardly say it was an insult," he laughed as they turned into the parking lot of a high-rise apartment complex.

The dwelling made the one bedroom apartment in which Ebony lived look like a shoebox by comparison. Even the lobby area was bigger than some of the units she'd seen several months ago, when she'd first moved into the Sanford Arms.

The ballroom that Nubian and Ebony entered was even more opulent than she could have ever imagined. There was a live jazz band playing on stage, while an ornate crystal chandelier hung eloquently above each laced tabletop. Ebony looked down at her gown and realized that what the other women were wearing must have been designer-made and not something off the rack, yet Nubian held onto her hand as though she were the only female in the room. He made her feel pretty when...for so long...she'd felt nothing, made her feel wanted when...for so many years...she'd felt forlorn. They strolled past a dinette where Toni Braxton sat next to a man with whom she had costarred in a video, and they continued on to another table near some palm trees. The trees surrounded the dinette to form a semicircle of privacy. Nubian pulled out a chair for Ebony and helped her to be seated before he sat down himself, beaming at her before he spoke.

"I'm glad you decided to allow me to take you out tonight. When I saw you in that restaurant, before that man from whom you seemed to be hiding came along, you looked as though you'd lost your best friend."

"Not exactly my best friend, but something close to it," Ebony admitted before she could stop herself, realizing that...for some reason...her guard was uncharacteristically down and that she was talking too much.

"Now, that sounds interesting. To whom were you so close and lost?"

As she gazed back into eyes that seemed to be probing her for a response, Ebony tried hard to suppress an overwhelming fear that Nubian could sense something phony about her. The smile that felt so warm only moments before had taken on the appearance of skepticism. 'No, Ebony, you have practiced this background and given it to employers and coworkers alike, so much so that you know it by heart,' she told herself. 'You've told the story about why you relocated here to New York City a million times by now. Since the lies I tell are the life I'm living, telling it again should be nothing more than mere recitation. Just remember to keep a real person in mind when you describe people, be able to visualize anyone about whom you're speaking so that what you say is always consistent. And, if all of the above fails, start answering his questions with another question.'

With quick precision Ebony mentally reviewed the fictitious details of her past, and then managed to smile before she spoke.

"To make a long story short, I broke up with a boyfriend quite some time ago."

"What story? You still haven't told me one. I guess the breakup was kind of rough on you, though, huh?"

"No, actually the breakup was something that I needed to happen, something that came along far too late. For a very long time afterward I literally avoided human contact, probably due to some form of depression related to being alone."

"If you were feeling down because of loneliness, then I don't understand how avoiding other people came into play. What brought you out of that state of mind?"

"Being by myself all the time made me realize that life was passing me by, so I packed up my bags and moved here to New York, a place that I'd always wanted to visit. My experience here has been quite amazing," Ebony explained, remembering how difficult it was to get a job without having a reference.

After moving here from North Carolina fifteen years ago, she had lived in an abandoned building for several months before she became a volunteer at a homeless shelter, a place where she could take a bath and get a steady meal. Using their address as her own, she'd gone down to the local social security office and nervously applied for a card using her mother's maiden name. There were many days when she would wonder about how her children were doing in school, and would speculate about whether Big Mama had read to them at night like she used to do whenever Derick or Paris couldn't sleep.

"Are you okay, Barbara?" Nubian inquired, breaking the trancelike state that seemed to envelope Ebony like the folds of a security blanket. "You seem to be a million miles away from here."

"In a way, I guess I was," she mumbled.

Though her mind ached with the torment of losing her mother and children, never did she feel regret for the actions that saved the freedom of her only son, Derick. Her screams were of a silent frustration that could never be spoken aloud. And since she couldn't answer Nubian's question with the complete truth, Ebony decided to move on to another rehearsed lie.

"When my mother remarried and left Los Angeles for good, I ditched the boyfriend, moved here, and got a job in a doctor's office. I've been doing that type of work ever since."

"So what's up with this ex-boyfriend of yours? What did he do for you to have given him the axe?"

"Back then, I weighed a lot more than I do now, and that was a problem for him. Some time later I came to realize that it was he who had the problem, and no matter how much I weighed, our relationship was never going to work out. His temper was off the hook and it was a situation that we...*that I*...didn't need to live with or be in any longer."

"Yeah, I know the type. So do you ever hear from him?"

"No, it has been years since I've seen him, and I'm sure that I'll never hear from the man again. He must be a world away from here by now."

"I'm sure you're right about that, Barbara."

"I know I am."

CHAPTER 4

The humidity in North Carolina had finally succumbed to the onset of a fall breeze. As Barbara Hightower…better known to her daughter, grandchildren, and friends as Big Mama…walked around her home, she began to raise the windows in the living room. A cool zephyr was causing the long arms of the weeping willow trees on the front lawn to sway, and she wanted the same tranquility of nature, the sweet smells of autumn, to flow throughout the house as she fetched her ritualistic morning cup of coffee.

Since Paris had moved back into the house a couple of months ago, every morning before heading out to her first class at the university, she'd make Big Mama a large pot and then pour a cup of java into her grandmother's favorite mug. Derick had already left the house long ago, leaving for his job earlier in the morning at around six o'clock. So, after opening up the panes and pouring some milk and sugar into her cup, Big Mama plopped her ample body on the red velvet couch situated across from a matching love seat. Much like the sofa inside the living area, most of the furnishings in the home had been acquired from garage sales. Although the articles were well worn, each piece was still quite comfortable and looked very attractive against its backdrop of soft eggshell-painted walls. A coffee table with a scuffed leather top and long Jacobean legs made of white oak sat on a handsome faux Persian rug. Their placement in the room caused the home to take on a mellow, comfortable atmosphere indicative of the entire dwelling.

Just as Big Mama picked up the remote from the coffee table and clicked on the twenty-seven inch television situated atop a small cart in front of it, the telephone began to peal. She muted the sound of the set and reached for the receiver.

"Hello," Big Mama answered with great irritation at being interrupted just when she'd gotten comfortable. "How are you this morning and who the hell is this?"

"Mama, it's me. What's wrong? Is something going on with the children?"

"No, not exactly. And they aren't children anymore, Ebony.
These days Paris and Derick are as grown as you or me ever were at
those ages, with the drama in their lives to prove it."

"I know, Mama. I know they're now both young adults and not
the youngsters that I remember," Ebony said in a voice that was as
melancholy as her mood had suddenly become, "so you don't have to
keep reminding me of that every time I refer to Derick and Paris in
that way. No matter how old they get, no matter where they go, those
are *my* children and, to me, they always will be. Does my age make
me any less *your* little girl?"

"I suppose not, but that's not what you and I need to be
discussing. I'm so glad you finally called, because we've got some
trouble brewing."

"What do you mean, Big Mama?"

"Ebony, where are you? In what city and state are you living?"

"Now you know I can't tell you that, Mama. You can never know
where I am because, if you ever do, that would make you an
accessory to harboring a fugitive."

"Let all of this come to an end and come home, Ebony. My not having known where you were living for over a decade hasn't made me any less guilty. For years now I've been taking care of my grandbabies as if they were my own children, and for years I've lied to them, telling them that I didn't know whether their real mother was dead or alive. I've told Derick and Paris how much you loved them yet, in the very same breath, I've led Paris to believe that you left her a trust fund in the event of your death. She thinks you left her money to help pay for her college education and tuition when, in reality, you call me every few months and tell me where to pick up funds at some Western Union location from a sender using an assumed name. For fifteen years you and I have lived in a web woven by complicated lies, lies that have only served to keep you apart from me and away from your own children."

"Lies, yes, but all that I've done has been for the sake of my two kids being able to grow up together, living in a home under the care of someone who truly loves them, even if it meant that I couldn't be around to see it happen. If I had stayed to face charges of shooting the father of my children in his back, of putting Joseph in a coma that will eventually lead to his death, do you honestly believe that the authorities would've permitted me to stay with you and the children? Do you honestly think that they would have allowed me to retain custody of two impressionable ten and seven year old adolescents? No, they would've split up both my kids and sent them to live in foster homes while I served time in prison."

"We could have at least tried to deal with the situation together as a family. But instead of doing that, what did you do? You shot a man, and then dropped his kids off at my house, promising to come back for them. Then, nearly a year and a half later, you called me on the telephone refusing to return to North Carolina, nor would you tell me where in the world you were living. You never even tried, Ebony. You never even tried to own up to what you did to that man. Now, I know that Joseph was a drug-pushing bastard. I know he was cruel and abusive to you, but you could've explained that to the courts, to a judge, or to a jury. If you had attempted to stop running a long time ago, then this situation with Paris that I need to tell you about may never have arisen in the first place."

"What situation, Mama? I'll tell you what the situation was back then. I was just as wrong for staying in an abusive relationship as Joseph was for being the abuser."

Ebony was yelling into the receiver without realizing it. She had come into the office early to catch up on filing some paperwork, so neither of the doctors, any other employees, and none of the patients would be in for at least another fifteen minutes.

"Mama, I was as sick as Joseph himself was, but I didn't realize it until it was far too late. He beat me and still I stayed with him, sending my seven year old daughter the message that it was okay for a man to bludgeon a woman until she bled. And what message did I help give to Derick, my only son? Was growing up in a household such as that going to teach him what manhood was all about? I don't think so! Thank God he doesn't remember what happened on the day his father was shot. A child of ten years should *never* have to relive such an event of violence and mayhem."

"You never would tell me about what happened that day, and even though Derick was with you at the time of the shooting, he has no recollection of the events. What *did* happen, Ebony? Why did you

197

shoot Joseph and let that whore you caught him sleeping with escape? If it had been me holding a gun, hers would have been the first ass that got blown away."

"And that's just my point, Mama," Ebony continued without answering the question her mother had posed. "Between the damaging testimony that his mistress would have given to the police and a courtroom full of jurors, coupled by my having been charged with the attempted murder of both her and Joseph, the only choice I had left *was* to run away and hide. I was a Black woman who was the girlfriend and mother of two children from a known drug dealer. Joseph was the one dealing drugs, Mama, not me. I had no funds to speak of and would've been assigned a court appointed lawyer, one who wouldn't have given a damn about keeping me out of prison, much less saving my children from being split apart from each other by Social Services. And don't forget, Big Mama, back then, you were in the process of healing from a hip replacement surgery. If the police hadn't been so concerned about attempting to learn my whereabouts, there isn't a doubt in my mind that the authorities would've taken both Paris and Derick away from you based on your ill health and perceived inability to care for my kids. The only reason none of that occurred is because the press was coving the story and the police were under great public scrutiny. No one would dare take grandchildren away from an elderly woman who'd already suffered a great loss and gone through so much, not when a prosecutor had a reelection to win and such publicity surrounded the spectacle of his or her case. We just got lucky, Big Mama, if you can call my being ripped asunder from the only people I've ever loved and who have ever loved me, good fortune."

"Who in the *hell* are you calling elderly? I'm still in my prime, just got laid last week! But I digress. That's not what we need to be talking about anyway. We have to deal with the situation I mentioned to you earlier, and we need to do something about it before it's too late."

"But I thought you said that Derick and Paris are fine."

"Derick is fine; Paris is dealing with some issues. But it's *you* who's the one that's in trouble, not either of them!"

"What makes you say that, Big Mama?"

"Ebony, where are you?"

"I already told you. I can't tell you that information for your own sake."

"Well, how about I tell you then. You're living somewhere in New York City," Big Mama said as she listed to Ebony make an audible gasp.

She gave her daughter a moment to compose herself before she continued.

"Answer my question, Ebony. Are you or are you not living somewhere in the state of New York?"

"How in the world do you know that? I called you using a calling card. It can't be traced by those Caller-ID systems. Tell me how you knew that, Mama!"

"I *am* going to tell you, but you can just stop yelling in my ear cause that shit hurts! Since I know where to start looking for you at, I'll make a special trip up to New York and, after finding your behind, will plant my foot squarely between the cheeks of your ass. Let Big Mama tell you something, baby girl. You will never grow too old to get a spanking if you start disrespecting me," Big Mama explained as the ringing in her left ear began to subside.

Big Mama paused to take a sip of her coffee, noting with irritation that it was now cold before she resumed speech.

"I have my hearing aid in this morning, and thanks to you, now it feels like somebody is beating down on a jungle drum inside of it."

"Big Mama, stop with all the jokes and sarcasm and tell me what's going on," Ebony pleaded, this time being careful to keep her tone in check.

"Okay, I'll make a long story short. *Your ass is in trouble!* Paris started dating some guy who has rich parents. From what I understand, these people are loaded and have real estate holding in places all over the world. Anyway, the boy liked Paris something awful until his mother found out. To get her son away from our Paris, who apparently doesn't come from a proper and wealthy enough lineage to satisfy these people, Ms. Dickerson hired a private detective to dig up dirt on our family and, as a result, he stumbled upon you. They tracked you down because the woman knows that I'm retired, but then she found out that someone was using my identity and social security number."

201

"How is Paris? Is she okay? And does that mean the authorities know who and where I am?"

"Well," Big Mama said with a sigh, "Paris is just heartbroken. Ms. Dickerson told her that she believes the person using my identity and social security number is you, and then insisted that Paris not see her son any longer. She demanded that Paris stop dating him without ever explaining to the boy the real reason why. Ms. Money-bags said that if Paris didn't do exactly as she was told and move out of their building, an apartment complex where Paris not only had a lease, but also where Mr. and Ms. Dickerson, and their son all have units, the police were going to pay you and me a little visit. And believe me when I say that it wasn't going to be a social call. So, after all of that happened, Paris moved back in here with her brother and me. We decided not to tell Derick what was going on since the boy has a temper and would probably go over to their penthouse and start cussing people out. The situation is volatile enough without his intervention, and they'd only have had him arrested anyway. Like we don't already have enough problems to deal with as things stand. But I'm telling you, Ebony, that woman is a stone cold bitch cast from an original mold! When it comes to having money and going on power trips, Ms. Dickerson is as dangerous as they get."

"Oh, my God," Ebony called out with tears brimming her eyes. She tried hard not to cry, but the water that began to fall was out of her control. At that moment, a man wearing a uniform passed through a service entrance. He walked into the office carrying a large bouquet of flowers in his arms.

"Flower delivery for the Barbara who has no last name," the youth announced as he began to stare at Ebony, probably wondering what in the world was the matter with her.

He was obviously in his teenage years, and was a dead ringer for Ron Howard when he played Richie Cunningham on the 1970s sitcom, *Happy Days*.

"The gentleman who sent these said I could find the person to whom they belong working in this department. He didn't have a last name to give our agency, so I'm hoping there isn't more than one Barbara who works here."

Ebony held the receiver away from her mouth and stared at the flower arrangement in awe, taking in the bouquet of calla lilies towering above red and yellow roses with green baby's breath surrounding their sculpture, standing tall and regal within their housing of a solid crystal vase. Her tears suddenly subsided, and she seized the moment to take a breath and compose herself before she replied to the deliveryman.

"I'm the only Barbara that works here. Who are these from?"

"Here's the card that accompanied them," the young man answered, passing to Ebony a cardstock embossed with gold and green lettering.

The card simply read, *'Not even the beauty of these can compare to the one who receives them.'*

For the first time that day and since a long time ago, a smile creased Ebony's lips. She reached under her desk to retrieve her purse from one of the drawers as the young man standing before her began to shake his head in a negative predication.

"No, Ma'am, thank you. Everything has been taken care of. A very generous tip has already been included with this delivery. You have a nice day," was the last thing the boy said before walking away.

It wasn't until Ebony heard the faint call of her real name being yelled through the receiver that she raised the phone back to her ear again.

"Ebony Hightower, are you listing to me? This is serious! If that woman is mean enough to blackmail my grandbaby, don't think the bitch isn't dishonest enough to turn you over to the police anyway. She's probably just waiting for her son to get involved with someone else before making a move. I know Paris is still a virgin, but you would think that her vagina was made of solid gold the way the boy has been acting. For the last eight weeks he keeps calling or coming over here, trying to get Paris to change her mind and date him again, but she won't see or even talk to the man. I'm not sure whether she truly believes that it's you who's been using my identity and social security number somewhere in New York or not, but what I do know is that the girl is in love. She cries herself to sleep almost every night, especially if Tyree has either dropped by or telephoned."

"Tyree..." Ebony said aloud to herself, thinking back to when and where she'd first heard that name before. "No, that couldn't have been them who I saw. It would be too incredible of a coincidence for it to have been my baby climbing into the back of that limousine."

"Limousine? Ebony, what in the hell are you mumbling about?"

"Nothing, Mama…nothing at all, I guess."

"Well, all I have to tell you is to be careful. You need to watch your back, relocate, and then start looking for another job. Since you can't use my identity any longer to find employment, what are you going to do?"

"Does Ms. Dickerson truly believe that I would allow her to get away with threatening my daughter? I'll tell you what I'm going to do. I'm going to destroy that woman!"

"Ebony, there is nothing that either of us can do. Those people have money and lots of it. How could we possibly contend with all of the resources that that family has at their disposal and command?"

"Ms. Dickerson has made a serious mistake in judgment. She threatened the child of a woman who has nothing to lose. But it is not *my* family who will be doing the suffering. I'm going to use all of the resources *at my command* to make certain of that."

"What resources are you talking about? Forgetting for the moment that you're wanted by the authorities, you don't have the kind of money it would take to deal with those people."

"No, I don't, but my husband will."

"Husband? What in the hell are you tripping on, Ebony? Your ass isn't married."

"No, I'm not married yet, Big Mama. But believe me when I tell you that I will be, and I will be very soon."

CHAPTER 5

"Today was a pretty good workout for us, Nubian, considering that I haven't seen you here in a while."

I turned around at the familiar sound of my workout partner, Brad. Brad was also a model, and even though he was around thirty-five years of age, yearly visits to his plastic surgeon kept him looking more like he was twenty-five. His broad shoulders, long legs, and ash blonde hair got him the attention of honeys from multiple cultures.

A couple of years ago, we'd chatted after doing a few photo shoots together, only to discover that we belonged to the same gym. Since then, one of us would call the other to spot while we lifted free weights whenever we happened to be in town at the same time.

"Yeah man, I know. As of late I haven't had much time away from work, so I've been limiting my workouts to home and spending what time I have left with my new lady friend."

"Okay, say no more," Brad said as he dried his hair with a white towel. "I should have known that a female was somewhere in the picture."

"Man, you don't even know the half of it," I said as I reached into my gym locker and pulled out a pair of khaki pants, sliding them over the black silk boxers I wore.

Brad and I both finished getting dressed, and then decided to sit in the club's lounge area, just chitchatting and catching up on each other's lives as we sat on a plush leather sectional. Since I didn't give Brad much of an opportunity to interrupt, we were really just talking about my life and newfound happiness with Barbara Hightower.

"I'm telling you Brad, man, this girl is like three women all rolled up into one. Depending on our plans or her mood, Barbara is constantly evolving, going from plain looking to attractive, from stunningly beautiful to voluptuous, as if she was playing the role of a centerfold with the sexual appetite to match. When we were together the other night the girl almost ate me alive. It's like she hasn't had sex in years, something that would be ridiculous considering her beauty. Whenever we're together the woman acts like she's using me to hone her erotic skills to an exact science. Not that I'm complaining, mind you, but she wears my ass out! I couldn't ask for a better lover."

"God, does this girl have a sister, because she sounds like my type? So what happened man, did you two do it on a table or something?"

"Barbara lives in this one bedroom apartment near Manhattan. I'd taken her out to dinner and, after we got back to her place, I'm not sure who made the first move. All I can remember from that point on was our undressing each other. A moment or two later she was in my arms, ripping off my clothes so feverishly that a button popped off my shirt and nearly hit me in the eye. Our lovemaking was something primal, something with its own rhythm, flowing with the music of our bodies as they danced in an animalistic ritual. In the morning, over a breakfast of scrambled eggs, bacon, and toast, we just talked. We talked about all that we had done, and all that we'd like to do together in life. Sometimes I think that she saved my life, saved me from being the kind of player and flirting bastard I'd been with so many other women in the past. There have been times in my life so painful that I didn't think I could share them with another living being. But when I started talking to Barbara and shared with her some of the stories from my childhood, it was as if she understood my pain. She placed her head upon my shoulder and we wept together. At times I've felt as though I could tell her anything.

I've had countless women fall in love with me, but this time I think I'm the one who's been hit hard. I like the way she makes me feel when I walk into a room, the way other men stare at her, wishing that she were with them instead of being by my side. I've taken her to some of New York's finest restaurants, but Barbara would rather prepare a home-cooked meal or whip up a picnic lunch so we could dine out by a lake. When I've suggested that we go to a club, she counters my offers by proposing that we instead go to a gospel play or take in a Broadway show. When we're out in public it's like I'm the only guy who matters to her, the only man she seems to notice walking along the streets.

Just the other day we went for a ride in Central Park, drawn by horse and carriage. Throughout the entire ride I kept thinking to myself that it must be illegal to feel this much happiness. The weekend before last we drove to the mountains and rented a cabin. We couldn't keep our hands off each other. Before we ever got inside it, Barb and I made love right there in the woods. That night she prepared a salad and grilled flank steaks marinated in soy sauce, serving them with garlic potatoes, and a selection of the perfect red wine to compliment the meal."

"Nubian my man, this Barbara sounds too good to be true. It almost sounds as though the woman is studying you…becoming your cook, your lover, and best friend all wrapped up into one sexy little package."

"You just don't know the half of it, Brad. During the six months that we've been dating, she's become all that to me and so much more."

"Sounds like you've found one that you'd better hold onto."

"Thanks, man. Actually, I was thinking along those very same lines. You feel me on that one, Brad?"

"Word?"

"Word."

CHAPTER 6

As Tyree sat at a corner table in a crowded restaurant, he could see his mother approaching the booth in a style and gait that was definitely all her own. She was dressed in a silver chiffon dress adorned with translucent beads. White alligator shoes with an eggshell tint covered her feet, while an elegant diamond necklace in the shape of a heart dangled around her neck. As people turned to stare as she walked past their table, Tyree had to admit to himself that his mother was indeed a striking woman, one with the carriage of an aristocrat.

"Hello, my dear. You must be early," Ms. Dickerson pronounced as she leaned over to allow her son to kiss her cheek, then sat down opposite from him.

"No, mother, actually you're late as usual."

"Am I?" she asked with an exaggerated frown of concern before looking down at her watch in a dismissive gesture. "Maybe you're

213

right. So, anyway, how do you like my new dress? It's an original gown from Maurice Fuqua."

"You look beautiful as always, mother. However, I didn't invite you to lunch to talk about what you're wearing. I want to know what you said to Paris that caused her not to want to see me anymore."

"Are you still harping on that Paris kick? What is it with you and these street urchins you drag home for your father and me to meet? How should I know why the girl doesn't want to see you anymore?"

"Because you were the last person who spoke to her right before she decided to end our relationship. What did you to talk about once Dad and I left the room?"

"Tyree, that was more than six months ago. How am I supposed to remember what I said to the girl? You asked me to keep her entertained while you and your father talked over some business, and that's just what I did."

Before Tyree could respond, a waiter approached them and placed two menus on the table.

"Good afternoon sir and madam. What can I get you both to drink?"

The voice Ms. Dickerson used to respond left no mistaking that she was indeed ticked off.

"What, are you blind as well as stupid? Can't you see that we're in the middle of a conversation? Now go away until you're sent for!"

"I'm...I, I'm sorry, madam and sir," the man stammered as he backed away from the table and scurried off in the direction of the kitchen.

When his mother resumed the conversation as if there had never been an interruption, the embarrassment Tyree felt was tangible.

"Your going out with that girl was a mistake in the first place; a big mistake!"

"Who are you to tell me that dating Paris was a mistake? She is a decent woman. You probably scared her away by flashing our money and making her feel inadequate or unworthy of dealing with our family."

"Damn straight, that that girl and her family of misfits are unworthy of us and you! For goodness sake, Tyree, those people are poorer than the dirt that you and I trample on. And you want me to socialize with filth? I don't think so!"

"Mother, Paris and I share the same interests. We have the same ideals and values."

"Yeah, and?"

"And I love her."

"The girl dumps you and now you're in love with her. Are you crazy? You're smart, you're handsome, and not to mention, rich. You can have any woman that you please. Why waste time on an opportunist?"

"The fact that Paris dumped me should prove to you that she isn't after our money."

"The only thing that proves to me is that she's also an idiot," Ms. Dickerson explained as she made eye contact with the waiter and waved him back over to their table.

Tyree studied his mother as she smiled at the young man genially before she ordered.

"While we're glancing over our menus, bring us two glasses of your best aged merlot."

Chapter 7

Ebony sat on the couch in her living room wearing a cream-colored blouse and black wraparound skirt. As usual, her thoughts were occupied by Nubian Prince, about all the times they'd spent together and the many experiences the two had shared in such a short period of time.

She was trying to decide what to prepare for dinner when the telephone rang. Ignoring the ring, Ebony went into the kitchen and grabbed a bottle of water from the refrigerator. She listened as the answering machine picked up and heard Nubian's voice.

"Hi, Barbara, I just wanted you to know that I'm madly in love with your voice and didn't call to speak with you; but rather, I just wanted to hear your machine. Now that I think about it, I wonder if it's the machine that I might be in love with. But seriously, Barb, if you want to do dinner tonight, I'd certainly like to take you out or just share your company for a while. So call me. Take care for now. Nubian."

Ebony walked back into the living room, depressed the rewind button on her machine, turned up its volume, and listened to the message again, this time trying to read in between the lines of his words. She realized that Nubian had just told her for the first time that he was in love with her, that he wanted to share a meal together, but if she'd already eaten, then his merely being in the midst of her company would suffice.

"It won't be long now," she said aloud to herself.

There were footsteps behind Ebony as she ran into the forest. Her hair began to blow wildly as a sudden gale rose, and in Ebony's mind, the locks seemed to crunch as loudly as the leaves beneath her feet. As she squinted, straining to see through the thick brush engulfed in the darkness of night, blood began to flow from the ring cut above her brow and her vision became blurred. She listened intently as the sound of feet trampling fallen branches and thumping against the ground grew louder in volume, indicating to all her senses that Joseph was approaching her from behind with a greater speed than she was moving.

"He's going to catch me," was the last thing Ebony thought before she awakened to find that Nubian was standing over her.

Ebony literally leapt off the sofa with a start before she realized that she was not in the woods; but rather, she was in the comfort and security of her apartment. Nubian grabbed her by both shoulders before she could run away from him, holding her firmly until she focused to see that it was he and not this stranger named, Joseph, standing beside her in the living room.

"Nubian?" Ebony questioned with uncertainty, hearing his voice from a distance that seemed to emanate from far, far away.

"Yeah, it's me, Barbara. Sorry to swing by your apartment unannounced like this, but I left a message on your machine about our going out to dinner tonight. Since you hadn't called me back to decline my offer, I just assumed that you could make it. I decided to drop by and wait for you here while you finished getting dressed. Are you all right, Barbara? When I walked up to the door of your apartment I heard you screaming. I tried the door and it was unlocked, so I came on inside."

"Why are you calling me that? My name is Ebony," she said without thinking, then brought both hands up to her mouth while making an audible gasp.

"Ebony? I thought that your name was Barbara Hightower. It isn't?"

"No, ahhh…Yes, it is. My middle name is Barbara and…"

"And what?" Nubian asked as he released his hold of her shoulders then took two steps backwards, giving Ebony room to either lie back down on the sofa or run away from him.

She looked as though she wanted to do the latter of the two.

"No, that isn't true, Nubian. My name is Ebony Hightower. The reason I haven't told you that before now is because I changed my name to free myself from my past and of the abusive boyfriend that I mentioned to you when we first met. I'm honestly sorry to have lied to you about that," Ebony apologized with an earnestness that loomed sincere.

"Bar...," Nubian began, but then quickly corrected himself. "Ebony, you know that you don't ever have to lie to me, don't you?"

"I should know that."

"Then you should also know that I wouldn't allow anyone to ever harm you again."

Ebony was completely unaware of exactly when Nubian had placed his arms around her. All she knew was that the tears falling from her eyes were making his cashmere shirt look a darker shade of gray than it was when dry. They stood there together, each remaining perfectly still in the same spot for well over twenty minutes, both securely entwined in the arms of one another until the entire room became gloomy from the setting of the sun. As her teardrops subsided and she forced herself to relinquish hold of the raw fear that the nightmare had incited, Ebony also released hold of Nubian. She walked over to the windows and drew down each shade one by one. Nubian clicked on the lamp situated atop a coffee table nigh the couch, illuminating the interior of the living room.

"See Ebony, not a single monster or a Joseph anywhere to be found inside the whole room. I must have scared them all away."

221

For the first time since his arrival Ebony smiled. She strolled over to Nubian, took him by both hands and pulled him down with her upon the sofa. She sat in his lap, wrapped both arms around his neck and shoulders, and kissed him.

"I'm sure you must have done just that, Nubian."

"I want to do that for you forever, Ebony. I want to protect you from the world, want to love you until your heart overflows and can't hold anymore. What I'm saying is I want you, Ebony. I want you to be my wife."

"But you don't even know me, Nubian. You don't know anything about me. Your learning my real name for the first time today should tell you that."

"I know that I love you. And even though you haven't said it to me yet, I believe that you love me, too. I can feel it. Marry me, Barbara?"

"See what I mean? You just found out that my name is really, Ebony, and you're still referring to me by the lie I told."

"Okay, then. Marry me, Ebony, or whoever you are, because I'm in love with the both of you."

"But you don't know anything about me; you don't know Joseph or the troubles that being associated with me could bring to your life. You know nothing about my past, so how could we realistically plan on building a future together? I've thought of marrying you, Nubian, perhaps even planned on doing so. But you're such a wonderful person and have been so good to me that I can't go through with it. I can't drag you into my personal problems. I thought that I could do just that, but I can't. There's got to be another way for me to handle this situation."

"Look, I don't know about any situation other than your being as stubborn as hell. What I do know is that I will let no one, and I do mean *no one* ever hurt you again, Ebony. You are my woman and you'll soon become my wife. I don't know what this Joseph person did to you, but as my wife you will want for nothing...not emotionally, materialistically, or when it comes to your physical protection. In fact, if it'll make you feel any better, I'll hire an around-the-clock security team to make certain you feel protected and secure."

"I'm poor, Nubian. I have no money whatsoever to contribute toward a marriage."

"You're rich in what I want in a woman, wealthy in all the ways that it counts the most. Do you think I just want you because of your body? Ebony, there are a lot of women who have nice shapes. Do you think that I want you because of where you work, what you drive, or how much income you net at the end of the year? I know plenty of beautiful, rich females who would love to marry me and secure their future by having a baby, then hire a high-priced divorce lawyer to help them build their own personal wealth.

When we first met you didn't even know who I was, which in and of itself, is rare. Given my looks and salary, I have never in my life dreamed of having to beg someone to marry me," Nubian said as he stood up, pulled Ebony to her feet and knelt down before her upon one knee, "but you, I will beg. You, Ebony Hightower, a poor woman with a past of obvious domestic abuse, I will beg to marry me. You, a woman with an outward beauty that surpasses most pageant winners and an inward comeliness that radiates to the surface; yes you, just a poor girl from California or wherever, who has stolen the heart of a man that many affluent women have attempted to slay and have lost. You, Ebony Hightower, have placed a very rich man down upon one knee to beg you, *and only you,* to marry him."

"Love has been lost to me for a very long time, Nubian. I wouldn't know where to start."

"Ebony, do you want to get married in a large church or a small chapel? Because *you are* going to be my wife, so stop vacillating and just admit it."

"Okay, Nubian, I'll admit it," Ebony responded as she again found herself blinking back tears.

For the first time in over fifteen years she realized that the impossible had actually happened, that she'd been a part of two miracles occurring in the span of a day. Ebony was in love with a man whom she trusted.

CHAPTER 8

The entire office was talking about the forthcoming wedding of Barbara Hightower to the handsome model and accomplished businessman, Nubian Prince. Someone had leaked the story to the press and an article had appeared in the New York Times commenting on the mysterious woman named Hightower, who had passed on an interview and the opportunity of having her picture appear in their newspaper.

After Ebony had told Dr. Megan Ultra about her pending engagement, then handed in a two-week notice of resignation, the following three weeks were filled with hectic preparations for the wedding. Invitations were sent to over two hundred people, all friends or family members of Nubian, whom Ebony herself had never met or laid eyes on before. Nubian had hired a professional fashion consultant to help Ebony pick out her gown and his suit, and after careful consideration, she and the consultant decided on an exact reproduction of the dress that Princess Diana wore when she married

Prince Charles. The only amendment to her outfit was that Ebony chose to add long white gloves, an enhancement that complimented the gray waistcoat and pinstriped trousers in which Nubian himself was to be adorned. Nubian had a friend by the name of Brad that was to be his best man, while the consultant coordinated with a few of the invited guests who volunteered as bridesmaids for Ebony.

Ebony had given her approval of the people the consultant had arranged for the wedding and, just after she'd hung up the receiver, the telephone rang again. She thought that it was probably the consultant calling her back, this time to tell her something in reference to the reception since they hadn't spoken much about what to serve. Ebony shifted slightly to make herself more comfortable on the sofa in her living room, picked up the cordless from the coffee table, and turned it back on.

"Hello, again, Rodney," Ebony greeted in a foregone conclusion. "Don't bother to say a word because I can guess as to why you're calling me right back. Anything you decide to serve at the reception is fine with me. As long as Nubian likes it, just go ahead with whatever preparations you think best."

"Miss Hightower," a male voice with an obvious Parisian accent called out.

The utterance caught Ebony completely off guard.

"I believe you're mistaken as to with whom you're speaking. This is Nubian, Sr., and I'd like to meet with you before you and my son are wed."

Every ounce of blood drained from Ebony's face and she was at an utter loss for words.

Several months ago Nubian had explained to her about how his mother had been killed in a car accident when he was only ten years old. Nubian had missed the bus that day and needed a ride to school. Since his dad had already taken the limousine to the office, Mrs. Prince decided to drive him there. After having dropped him off at his second period class, she decided to take an unfamiliar route back to the house via a shortcut she'd seen their chauffeur take. She had lost control of the conveyance and skidded off the road into a ravine. Because of a massive head trauma caused by the accident, Mrs. Prince had been rushed by a medical helicopter over to a nearby hospital, where she was treated but later died from her injuries, leaving behind a husband who became a widow and single parent all in one tragic day.

Ebony had been reduced to tears after Nubian told her the story, expressing to her the deep-seeded guilt he still held inside because his mother had given him a ride to school that day. Nubian felt that her death was, at the very least, indirectly due to him missing his bus and then asking her for a lift. Although the losses Ebony had suffered were private ones about which she never spoke, she and Nubian had both held each other all night long, comforting one another amidst their grief and pain.

Once Nubian had grown up, moved out of the family mansion and bought a condominium of his own, Mr. Prince retired and relocated to Europe where he currently resided. Neither Nubian nor Ebony thought she would meet or speak with him until the day of their wedding. Obviously, she and Nubian were both wrong in that assumption since the man was on the other end of the telephone.

"Mr. Prince," Ebony called out, not wanting her voice to register how taken aback she was. "What? What...a surprise. What a nice, surprise."

"Thank you, Miss Hightower. I think you and I should have a chance to become better acquainted before the wedding of you and my son takes place next week."

"I'm not certain how much time there will be before the ceremony; however, I'll certainly make time to spend with you, provided of course, that Nubian isn't around when we meet. I'm superstitious about the groom seeing his bride on the day they're to be married."

"I understand that completely. My wife, God rest her soul, shared that same belief and tradition. Be ready in an hour. There will be a car waiting outside your apartment to pick you up."

Ebony hesitated before she spoke.

"You're...you're in New York right now, at this very moment?"

"Yes. I'll be staying here at the Plaza until the day of the event, and then I go back to Paris the following morning. I'll see you in an hour, young lady," he said before breaking their connection.

Exactly one hour from the time they spoke, a silver and gold limousine pulled up in front of the building. Instead of the driver getting out of the vehicle, the passenger side door sprang open automatically. After Ebony climbed inside a spacious cab, she watched in awe as the door closed by itself just as magically as it had opened to allow her entry.

Mr. Prince was a distinguished looking man, his height and visage the very likeness of his son. The hair atop his head was a mixture of salt and pepper, and he had a jet black, neatly trimmed mustache beneath an aquiline nose. Ebony summed up her appraisal of Prince Sr. by noting that he wore a wing-collared, white silk shirt with a wool suit displaying colors of chestnut and brown.

"Very nice to meet you, young lady," Mr. Prince said before taking a sip from a crystal glass he held in his hand. In the rear of the limo, near the backseat was a fully stocked mini-bar from which he reached over, picked up an identical goblet, and passed to Ebony a martini.

"I thought that we could enjoy a cocktail together, and make a toast of good fortune for the impending marriage between you and my son."

"Thank you, Mr. Prince," Ebony said as she reached for her glass, raised it in a toast with his, and took a sip of the sparkling beverage.

She didn't drink alcohol often and certainly was no expert, but she could swear that the martini he'd made for her was nearly perfect.

"Mr. Prince, I'm very appreciative of your gesture, though you didn't have to be so extravagant as to come and pick me up in a limousine. I certainly would have caught the subway to meet you at the plaza."

"For you, those days are over, Ebony. So just sit back and enjoy the ride to our destination. What purpose does money serve, if not to make the lives of those you care for and love more comfortable?"

"I actually don't know what to say, Mr. Prince."

"You will," he announced just as the car stopped in front of a large jewelry store.

The doors opened and Mr. Prince stepped out, walked around to the opposite side of the vehicle and assisted Ebony in climbing outside the car.

"What are we doing here, Mr. Prince?"

"We're picking out my wedding gift to you and my son," he explained as they walked through the entrance of the posh establishment.

Dozens of clerks were busy assisting patrons. A striking young woman wearing a simple but elegant black dress similar to the one Ebony wore dashed from behind a counter and almost tripped over a potted plant as she greeted them just inside the door.

"Hello, Mr. Prince," greeted the saleswoman. "I was told by the manager to be expecting you and a guest to drop by. How may I be of assistance to you this afternoon?"

"My future daughter-in-law and I are here to select a ring for the ceremony. I'd like to know what original pieces you have available for us to choose from."

"Original?" Ebony repeated as if she'd heard him incorrectly.

"Nothing but," Mr. Prince answered as they moved beyond the first display room into an adjoining private showroom.

Ebony couldn't believe her eyes as they took in display cases holding shimmering teardrop earrings, emerald tiaras, diamond bracelets and multi-carat rings. Mr. Prince smiled as he watched her eyes grow in amazement. He held out his arm for Ebony to take hold of, and led her to a glass case lined in black velvet.

"Mr. Prince, I appreciate all of this, really I do. But I wouldn't dream of purchasing something of this magnitude for myself."

"That's good, because you're not the one who'll be buying it. This will be my gift to both you and Nubian, to commemorate a union that will last a lifetime or until death do you part. How does the second ring from the left suit you?"

Mr. Prince pointed his finger down at the display case and indicated for Ebony to look at a diamond so brilliant, that she almost couldn't see the gold ring and setting in which the jewel was mounted.

Its glare caused her to blink several times more before she found the words to respond.

"All I can say is it's as big and beautiful as I myself was at one time."

"Given your athletic figure now, I could not have guessed that you were ever full figured. But, I myself, like a woman with a little girth to her," Mr. Prince said as he handed Ebony a credit card.

Ebony, in turn, gave the card to the clerk. After the card was processed and approved, the saleswoman returned it back to Ebony instead of passing it to Nubian's father.

Because her eyes had become misty from the sight of her engagement ring, it took Ebony a moment or two to see that the name *Ebony Prince* was embossed on the front of the card. Her voice and face both held a perplexed mien.

"Mr. Prince, what is this?"

"That card is your new wardrobe, and anything else you need to purchase before and after the wedding. The fashion consultant assigned to help you with the wedding preparations will also assist you with decorating your new home and getting your "Pretty Woman" makeover. In other words, shop until you drop."

"What new home?"

"The one my son just bought for you last week. Nubian owns a small realty agency that he had working day and night until they located an estate for the two of you. Actually, the business is a faltering mom-and-pop operation that he acquired for the sole purpose of closing it down at the end of the year to reap the tax benefits from.

During the interim, Nubian put them to work on finding you guys a home he thought might befit your tastes. The estate is already furnished, although I'm sure you'll want to make your own imprint upon the house. Most women don't feel like a house is a home unless they themselves furnish or redecorate it."

Her head felt as though it was spinning, and all Ebony could do to keep her balance was to look around. She thought of a story that she'd read to Derick and Paris when they were children, the one about a prince who had fallen in love with a lonely girl to whom he later became engaged. That innocent fable had influenced and shaped her life in ways that she could have never predicted.

"I don't know what to say, Mr. Prince. To be completely honest with you, all of this is just a bit overwhelming."

"A simple, merct, will be sufficient enough. Do not deprive my son of showing you how much he loves you. If my wife could have only lived to see how our Nubian has grown up to become such a fine young man. If only I myself could continue to express the love I hold in my heart for her...My son is a fortunate man to marry someone who seems as beautiful on the inside as she appears on the outside. I can tell you right now that if my wife had survived to witness this event, she would have liked you very much, just as I myself do now that I've met you."

Ebony studied him for a moment, then nodded and acquiesced.

"Okay, Mr. Prince. Thank you for the ring, the wardrobe, and credit card, but most of all for such kind words."

Mr. Prince examined the showcase once more, turned to the clerk who had stepped away to give them some privacy, and waved her back over.

"We'll take those teardrop earrings to go along with the ring."

"No," Ebony protested with a nod of her head. "Thank you, Mr. Prince, but buying that in addition to the ring is much too expensive. Those things cost a fortune."

"We'll take them," Mr. Prince insisted, ignoring Ebony as the clerk punched in a code on an electronic panel to disable an alarm on the case.

The saleswoman took out a small key, unlocked the display, and removed the ring and earrings. Mr. Prince took the ring from the clerk then slid it onto Ebony's finger.

"I would say that's a perfect fit. That, in and of itself, must be a sign of events to follow."

"You really think so, Mr. Prince?"

"Of course I do, young lady."

"I pray that you're right."

"Why wouldn't I be?"

"Oh, no reason, Mr. Prince," Ebony hurriedly announced, thinking to herself that she'd spoken just a little too quickly to have sounded believable.

She wondered if she looked as paranoid and nervous as she was actually feeling.

"I guess I'm experiencing some pre-wedding day jitters," Ebony explained, this time modulating her tone as she reminded herself to speak at a normal pace. "I just don't want anything to go wrong."

"What could ever go wrong, Ebony? My son loves you very much."

"And I love him, too, sir," she heard herself reply with a smile, knowing deep within her heart that she meant every word from the depths of her soul.

CHAPTER 9

The wedding between Nubian Prince and Ebony Hightower took place three weeks later at the Union Baptist chapel. It was an event to behold. At the prompting of the minister performing the ceremony, the slender, mysterious woman who stood by the side of an aristocrat pronounced the words, "I do." After Minister Thompson declared them man and wife and instructed for Nubian to kiss his new bride, Ebony quickly lowered her veil before anyone could take a photograph of her face. She and Nubian strolled away from the alter walking hand and hand. They then left the church and headed over to their wedding reception being held in a ballroom of the Plaza Hotel.

When Ebony and Nubian left their guests to embark on their honeymoon, there was a limousine parked outside the hotel. The chauffeur held open the door as they climbed inside the vehicle. He then hopped inside the car himself and took the newlyweds on a thirty-five minute drive over to a neighborhood in Manhattan that Ebony had never seen before. She watched in awe as they entered a gated community situated on Long Island Sound. The limousine pulled up to a handsome brick mansion that was a pale red color. As the driver brought the limo to a stop along a semicircle driveway at the main entrance, Ebony could see that the building was turreted on either end, and, through age, had acquired a mellow patina that complimented the evergreens surrounding the extensive grounds. She and Nubian stepped from the car, strolled up a flagstone path, and entered an unlocked abode. With each step she took further into the dwelling, Ebony found that she was becoming more and more awestruck. The foyer was huge, and frankly, looked more like a reception area. Situated directly beyond the vestibule was a mahogany staircase leading up to the second floor of the house. The living room was to the right of the stairwell. To the left of the stairwell was a long hallway that continued past the family room and led into the kitchen. The left wing of the home was also where the library and formal dining room were positioned, both chambers containing more square footage than the entirety of her apartment.

"You're not surprised, are you my love? My father must have told you about this house being my wedding present to you."

"Yes, he did, Nubian. But never could I have imagined such a magnificent dwelling. This isn't a home, it's a palace. Believe me when I tell you that I've never seen anything like it, never in my entire life."

"Does that mean you're going to keep me then, that you're happy with both your new husband and the life that we shall build together here in our new home?"

"Yes, I'm going to keep you and, yes, I'm very happy," Ebony emoted as she turned to Nubian, embracing him as they stood at the threshold of the library.

He enveloped her in his arms and kissed her passionately, never relinquishing his hold as they turned again to look into the room.

"Good. To me your happiness is all that matters. I love you very much, Ebony Prince."

"I'm going to have to get used to my new name."

"You're going to grow accustomed to a lot of things, most importantly, to me sleeping in our bed every night. I must confess to you that I snore."

"Okay, then, let me confess to you that I probably snore louder. See, we're a perfect match," Ebony proclaimed with a hearty laugh as Nubian joined her in jollity.

"Just like bread and butter, baby."

"Yes, darling, like bread and butter."

Two weeks after he and his new bride celebrated their honeymoon in the confines and seclusion of their new home, Nubian Prince was having a busy afternoon at work with no end in sight to the day's events. The photo shoots had been a whirlwind of location after location, taking them from Central Park to the streets of Manhattan. All day long he had worn nothing but a pair of boxer shorts while two beautiful models held onto each arm.

As the photographer told the models and crew to take a ten-minute break so that he could remove film from his camera and reload for another shoot, the cell phone in Nubian's gym bag rang, so he dashed from the set to answer it.

"Yeah?"

"Nubian, is this you?"

"Well, now, that depends. Is this my wife or my girlfriend calling?"

"It had better be both if you know what's good for you."

"Hey, baby. What's up?"

"Could I come down and meet you at the set?"

Nubian hesitated for a moment, then frowned.

"Why Ebony, is there something wrong?"

"No, but it's really important that I see you."

"We're going to be working until the sun goes down and then move into the studio to complete the shoot. How about I meet you at home and we can discuss it then, rather than you making the trip all the way down here?"

"No, I want to see you now."

"Okay, Boo, whatever you want. You can come down, but I can't promise you that I'll be able to speak to you exactly when you get here. We can chat in between the times the crew is setting up shots. We're filming on a section of Fifth Avenue that has been cordoned off from the general public, so I'll have someone leave you a pass at the gate so you'll have access to our location. Go into the den and look at the calendar on my desk. The exact address is written down on the planner."

"Okay, then, I'll see you in about an hour."

Sixty minutes after Nubian had pressed the end button on his cell phone, Ebony pulled into the area of the shoot, driving a twenty foot stretch limousine. She climbed from behind the wheel wearing a full-length mink covering a formfitting, strapless evening gown that was auburn with gold undertones.

With the clicking of her high-heeled shoes, which perfectly matched the ebony hue of her coat, several crewmen turned their heads to stare at her shapely figure when she strolled by them. As the guard who was posted at the barricade escorted her onto the closed set, Nubian saw them approaching and began walking towards the twosome. He was wearing a terrycloth bathrobe knotted at his waist.

"Ebony," Nubian pronounced in a questioning tone as he glanced toward the parking lot with an awkward stare.

He hugged his wife then allowed the security guy to move away before continuing.

"What the hell are you doing behind the wheel of that car? For goodness sake, we have a driver for that sort of thing."

"I didn't feel like disturbing him or waiting until he was all dressed up in that stuffy uniform. I was ready to leave, and so I left."

"The man is on salary, Ebony. He's paid very well to drive you wherever you need to go. Get used to that, and let Davis do his job. Taking the car to drive down here by yourself could be perceived as an insult, indicating to the man that his job, one in which he takes a lot of pride, is an unnecessary task."

"Oh," Ebony said as his statement settled in, bringing to her mind a new clarity and awareness. "I didn't think of it like that. I guess I still have a lot to learn."

"No problem at all, baby. Just call the man whenever you need to take the limo, okay?"

As a cool zephyr moved though, Ebony pulled the collar of her coat closer around her ears.

"Nubian, aren't you cold, standing out here dressed only in a bathrobe and some drawers?"

"Yeah, but it comes along with the nature of the job. It's all par for the course, ergo, I'm used to it. Now what was so important that it couldn't wait until I got off work and came home?"

Before she got an opportunity to answer his question, the director came over and ushered Nubian to a woman holding a black case. The woman indicated for Nubian to take a seat down in a director's chair, and began applying his makeup. Fifteen minutes after the artist was finished, Nubian was herded back to the set, posing as the photographer began taking roll after roll of film. When the bulbs stopped flashing and the shutter ceased its clicking, Ebony had to refocus several times before she could see that Nubian had stepped offstage and was approaching her.

"Nubian, is that you? Those flashbulbs are positively blinding."

"Yes, it's me, the one and only. Now, what do you want to talk to me about? You pregnant?"

"Negro, please! No, I'm not pregnant."

"Not yet, anyway, but we can work on that. So, then tell me, what's on the mind of the woman with the beautiful face?"

"I want a job."

"A job?" Nubian questioned, wearing a perplexing frown. "Why would you want one of those when you just quit your receptionist position? We sure as hell don't need the money."

"It's not about the money. It's about me, and how I'd like to spend my time during the day. You work, don't you?"

"Yeah."

"We have plenty of money, don't we?"

"Yeah."

"Then why don't you quit your job so we can spend more time together? After that, you can stay at home with me all day long, and we'll have more time to travel and make that baby you were talking about."

"Hell, no, I won't be quitting *my* job!"

"I don't blame you, baby, and neither will I."

"That's not the same thing, Ebony. I'm self-employed. My wife doesn't need to work for nobody."

"I couldn't agree with you more, so that's why I've come up with a business plan."

"A business plan?"

"Yeah. Let me have that realty company you own, and I'll run it myself. That way I'll be working for me and not for anyone else."

"That piece of crap of a company? You don't have a realty license, and even if you did, that place is losing money out the behind. At the end of the year, I'm going to close it down and use it as a tax right off."

"You won't need to do that if I can turn it into a profitable entity. And I'm not planning on personally selling houses, so I don't need a realtor's license. I'll just run it and be in control of the day-to-day business operations."

"Do you really want to do that? The business is like a graveyard. I had them find us our home because the few employees who still work there didn't have anything better to do with their time. Larger firms that have more sellers and property listings to offer their potential homebuyers are wiping all of the smaller and independently-owned businesses off the map. I bought the place due to its dwindling profits. I knew it was losing money and believed it would be a good tax right off at the end of the year."

"Then my running it can't hurt anything, now, can it?"

"You got a point there, baby. I guess it wouldn't hurt anything to let you run it."

"Then can I have it?"

"Anything for you, Boo. And, by the way, I meant for that to rhyme."

"Thank you, Nubian."

"Don't thank me. You have me wrapped around those pretty little fingers of yours, and you knew that I was going to say, 'yes,' now didn't you? Be honest."

"I love you, Nubian," Ebony announced wearing a sly grin.

"Love you, too. Goodness, all of this newlywed sweet talk is probably going to give us both cavities," Nubian chortled.

CHAPTER 10

Ebony spent the next three weeks researching the day-to-day operations of the realty company owned by Nubian. She'd even subscribed to some online business courses over the Internet and was taking several classes remotely from a local community college. Exactly one month later she scheduled a meeting with Clark Garrison, the chief operating manager for their real estate firm.

As she sat down in his office, Ebony took in the unpleasant face of a large man positioned behind an antique oak desk. He looked to be in his early fifties, was completely bald on the crown of his head, and had brown hair with gray streaks on either side his temple. Last evening during dinner, Nubian had explained to her that Garrison was single and had never been married. Sitting face-to-face with him now, Ebony was certain that Garrison's bachelorhood most likely stemmed from issues dealing with his weight, or perhaps, the lack of a likeable personality altogether.

"Good morning, Mr. Garrison. I'm Ebony Prince and we're going to be working together to see if we can make this business profitable again."

"Yes, I know exactly who you are, Mrs. Prince. You're the boss's wife, and now you think you're going to come in here and start telling me how to do my job when I already know what I'm doing. You have no realtor's license, no administrative background, nor any business education of which I'm aware. In fact, no one knows anything about you other than you've recently married the owner of this company and that, in and of itself, Mrs. Prince, does not qualify you to make business decisions pertaining to the daily operations of this firm."

Ebony sat silently for several moments, studying the man before she spoke.

"I'd like a cup of coffee, Mr. Garrison."

Without responding to her request, he buzzed the receptionist and asked Brook Logan to bring in two cups of black java, then turned to Ebony wearing a scowl.

"Let me tell you something, lady, I'm in charge of running this real estate firm and if you have any designs of putting me out of this position and running the company yourself, your husband can explain to you that I have an ironclad employment contract. If I'm terminated for almost any reason, I get a hell of a severance package which, in layman's terms, means that this establishment will undoubtedly be out a lot of money. It would be far less expensive for both you and your husband that I remain employed here."

Someone knocked on the closed office door and Mr. Garrison instructed the indistinguishable figure beyond the glass to come inside. Brook entered the room carrying a tray that held two cups of steaming hot coffee, and placed the Styrofoam containers before them on the desk. She was an attractive woman with blonde hair who looked to be in her mid-twenties. Just as she was about to ask if either of them needed anything more, Ebony watched as Mr. Garrison rudely sent her away with a dismissive wave of his hand.

"Mr. Garrison…"

"What is it, *Ebony?*"

The sound of his voice pronouncing her first name was like someone taking their fingernails and scratching them across a chalkboard, but she held her temper and emotions in check.

"Maybe I have been too forward in thinking that I could run this business. Perhaps what I'll do is take a hands-off approach. If I observe any problems requiring improvements to be made, then we can take a vote, and your last word will be considered law."

"I think that would be very wise, Ebony. Now, if there's nothing further, I do need to get back to work and earn my keep around here. You can let yourself out. Just close the door as you leave."

When Nubian arrived home later that evening, Ebony mentioned to him the meeting she had with the operations manager of their realty company.

"Look, baby, I don't see why you want to get involved in that business anyway. And you're one hundred percent correct; the man had no justification to speak to you that way. But he was right about one thing, Ebony. Whoever hired him before we bought the company gave the man an employment contract that's virtually irrevocable. It's more cost conservative to keep him employed there rather than not. Besides, you're the one who asked for this headache. I myself had planned on selling that business and writing his salary off as part of the losses."

"Nubian, what do you mean by an almost unbreakable contract?"

"I mean that nothing work-related can get the man fired, not even a lack of his performance on the job. Sad, isn't it? When the previous owners gave him that contract, the business was much more profitable and robust."

"I see. Nubian, would you do me a favor?"

"What do you want now, Mrs. Prince? Don't tell me that since Mr. Garrison won't let you be in charge, you now want some additional part-time employment to accompany your new full-time job," he chortled.

"No, I want you to call Garrison at home and tell him you're cutting his salary by twenty-five percent starting the first of the month."

"I couldn't do that even if I wanted to, Ebony. Like I said before, the man has an airtight contract that won't allow me to amend or suspend his salary, not without me paying heavy penalties to him in the form of a severance package."

"I didn't ask you to actually do it. I merely want you to make the threat of doing so. Then, when you finish your shoot tomorrow afternoon, come into the office and meet with him to discuss the matter further."

"What will an empty threat do but to antagonize your working relationship with the man?"

"Nubian, I'm not asking you to do anything but make the call and meet with Mr. Garrison tomorrow afternoon. I'll handle the rest of it from there. I promise."

"Okay, but I hope you know that you're making an even worse enemy of the man. Based on the meeting you had with him earlier today, he'll think that I'm just trying to be spiteful toward him because of the way he treated you. How do you expect to work with the man at the agency under those circumstances?"

"I don't."

In the morning Ebony called to arrange a second meeting with Mr. Garrison at twelve-thirty in the afternoon, scheduling it with his secretary during a time when he would normally be out to lunch. At twelve forty-five, when she walked past Brook's desk and into the adjoining office, Ebony could tell by the sour expression on his face that Garrison was hungry and not at all happy to see her. Compared to the blue silk skirt with white blouse that she was wearing, the disheveled appearance of Mr. Garrison's suit, despite its obvious high quality and look of expense, made him seem somewhat like a homeless person in need of a hot meal.

"I see that you went home last night to complain about me to your husband. Well, it's not going to work, sister. I'll sue his ass for all it's worth if he attempts to cut one penny of *my* salary!"

"No, I didn't do any such thing. In fact, I think my husband is being a complete ass about the situation. We have plenty of money and can afford to pay you twice as much as you're getting now. The man is merely being cheap, and is trying to get something for nothing. And if he cuts your salary one iota, then you should sue his ass!"

The unmistakable look of surprise on his face was exactly what Ebony had been expecting. She pulled the chair away from his desk and wheeled it around to the opposite side, taking a seat beside him. She then removed the large handbag hanging from her left shoulder, placed on his desk, and waited for him to speak first.

"Why on earth would you side with me against your own husband?"

"Because I know what it's like to work hard for a living. I was a receptionist when Nubian and I first met. One of the reasons why I came here to work with you is because Nubian didn't want me to continue being employed anywhere after we were married. My current work situation at this realty company is sort of a compromise to that."

"Like I told you before, I run this agency and am not about to relinquish the reigns to you or anyone else."

"And why should you? As you stated so clearly and adeptly just the other day, what do *I* know about running a realty company? You're the boss around here, and if I were you, I wouldn't allow anyone to push me around, not even my husband. He's just a man, not God! Who is *he* to tell *you* that you're worth twenty-five percent less of your hard earned salary?"

Ebony paused to allow him a retort.

"You're damn straight about that!"

"Would you like something to drink?" Ebony asked as she reached over and pressed a button on his telephone, buzzing for Brook to come into the office. "I don't know about you, but I'm a bit thirsty myself."

When she instructed Brook to bring in two glasses half filled with ice, Mr. Garrison frowned. Once Brook had come and gone and they were alone again, Ebony reached into her handbag and pulled out a bottle of scotch. She poured herself a small shot, but filled his glass up to its brim.

"I think I'm starting to like you, lady. Just as long as you keep in mind who's really running the show around here."

"Yes, I do know who's running things in this office, Mr. Garrison; although, I can tell you with all certainty, that my husband does not," Ebony explained as she watched him down his drink in one long gulp.

She quickly refilled his glass before he resumed speaking.

"Look, Ebony, your husband won't be pushing *this* guy around. I've already made a call to my lawyer and he's poised to file a lawsuit if need be. As long as I'm doing my job around here, the man doesn't have a legal leg to stand on."

"That's true, but let me tell you something about my husband, Clark. He doesn't take anyone seriously. Unless you show Nubian that you mean business, the man will walk all over you and won't even think twice about it. You've got to show him that you're serious about your threat of filing a lawsuit, yet, at the same time, you really don't want to have to go through with it. With the kind of resources at his disposal, Nubian could reduce or cut off your salary altogether, then keep you in the courts fighting legal battles for many years to come. You'll eventually win, but think of all the money you'd have to disburse to an attorney in pre-paid legal fees. Any way you look at it, that scenario would ultimately be a, lose, lose, situation for you both."

"Yeah, you're right about that. Pour me another one, sister. I have to put something in my stomach until I can leave here to grab myself a bite to eat. To tell you the truth, I'm hungrier than hell right now."

Ebony did so without hesitation, never once refilling her own glass.

"That's why you need to show my husband how upset you truly are about his attempt to pilfer a quarter of your salary. Prove to Nubian that you aren't going to just lie down and take such a betrayal without putting up one hell of a fight!"

"And just how am I supposed to do that without suing the man?"

After a very long period of silence, Ebony looked away to make certain that the door to his office was completely closed before she resumed speech.

"Last night my husband mentioned that he was coming into the office today to speak with you further. He plans on telling you that he won't be changing his mind or backing down from his decision, and that effective immediately, your salary will be cut by twenty-five percent. But believe me when I tell you that it doesn't have to end that way. I have an idea which could bring you both to a swifter resolution and avoid a long, drawn-out legal battle."

"How so? Exactly what do you have in mind?"

"Like I said before, show Nubian that you're no one to take lightly. He thinks your talk about filing a lawsuit is all a big bluff but, when he gets an eyeful of your new attitude and demeanor, then he'll know for certain that you mean business."

"I still don't understand what you expect me to say or do that could help the situation any."

"When my husband comes in here to speak with you later today," Ebony said before a prolonged pause.

Garrison nodded to indicate to her that he was paying close attention.

"Cuss his ass out!" Ebony exclaimed.

He looked at her wearing a somewhat puzzled expression.

"Are you serious? Your husband works out and is an extremely muscular man. He doesn't look like the type that would take a lot of mouth from anyone."

"He is also a very rich man who can't afford to go around hitting people. With his physical size alone, not to mention all the money he makes, if Nubian went around doing that sort of thing he'd go broke

261

from tying to settle lawsuits before they ever went to court. Besides, I'm not suggesting that you hit him. Just be loud and kick over a few chairs. Pick up your computer and monitor, and throw them against the ground hard enough so that they smash into a million pieces."

Garrison's eyes widened before he replied.

"You think I should do that? Lady, are you crazy?"

"No, I'm not. However, my husband will think that you are. He'll know you're so upset that you could...and would...do anything to prevent him from stealing your money. Nubian expects you to accept his demands and to do so quietly, but don't. When my husband comes in here later this afternoon, show him that you're willing to so some real damage, in your office as well as in a court."

For several moments Garrison remained silent in deep contemplation, watching Ebony intently as she sat quietly beside him.

"Are you sure about all of this? The man *is* your husband after all, so why would you of all people encourage me to go to such extremes?"

"Look, all of the damage you inflict can easily be repaired in a couple of days, and I'll take care of that myself. I'll place whatever restoration costs there might be on a credit card account that Nubian set up for my personal use, so he'll never see the bill. I've thought this situation over very carefully and, in the long run, I'll be doing Nubian a favor by keeping you both from a legal confrontation that could last for many years to come. This firm would never survive the process of a long, drawn-out litigation. As you might already suspect from my husband attempting to cut your salary, there won't be any more of our personal funds sunk into this business unless it somehow turns profitable again. If he's fighting you in court without a qualified person to run this agency, then everybody loses...including us."

A smile of conspiracy crossed the lips of Clark Garrison.

"You really are an interesting lady, Ebony. I admire your style. Care to join me in one last drink?"

"Clark, I thought that you'd never ask."

They raised their glasses together in a silent toast before each took a sip.

CHAPTER 11

At two o'clock when Nubian entered the office of Clark Garrison, it took him only a moment to realize that the man had been drinking. He extended his arm to shake hands, but Garrison simply stared at him with contempt then began using language so foul, that all Nubian could do was to blink his eyes without responding. It was after his mouth stopped moving that Garrison went berserk. He kicked over his desk, causing the computer and monitor to come crashing to the ground, turned over several tall filing cabinets that were lined in a row against the wall, then opened up one of the drawers and threw a lit match inside it to set the paper folders ablaze.

When Brook Logan came into the office to see what had caused the loud crash, Nubian quickly sent her back outside, but not before he instructed her to grab the fire extinguisher hanging on the wall in the hallway.

Taking the extinguisher from her, Nubian quickly doused the small flames. For several seconds more both he and Brook stood near the wall, watching in awe as Garrison continued with his rampage of destruction. In a desperate attempt to call someone, to contact anyone for help or assistance, Brook raced over to the telephone lying on the floor and picked it up, but before she had a chance to dial an outside line, Garrison ripped the cord from the wall.

A small group...a mixture of customers and the ten other employees who worked there...formed a small congregation at the threshold of Garrison's office, each watching in horror as he continued his reign of demolition. Clark was so caught up in the fever and excitement of his havoc that he never noticed as two uniformed police officers parted the crowd and entered what was left of his office.

"I'll show you whose salary to cut, you modeling bastard!" Garrison cried out before he picked up a six-foot potted ficus plant.

When Garrison turned around to face Nubian and Brook, his eyes suddenly focused on the two officers who had their weapons drawn and trained on him. Looking from the police officers over to the television cameras, news crew and reporters who had all come to stand at the side of office spectators crowding the entranceway,

Garrison drew a look of bewilderment across his face. As the cameraman rolled film when the authorities moved in to handcuff and arrest him, the only thought left in his mind was how they could have arrived on the premises so quickly. The answer came to him as he was being led off the property and placed in a squad car waiting outside the building.

Standing across the street, watching from a distance away was Ebony Prince. While she waited for the signal to change from "DON'T WALK" to "WALK," Ebony reached into a small brown bag, withdrew a donut, and began eating it. When they made eye contact with each other, she simply waved goodbye to Garrison and continued to eat her food.

"That bitch set me up! Ebony Prince did this to me! No judge in the world will uphold my employment contract after this episode, and that's just what she'd banked on. That woman planned this whole thing, set up this entire situation just so she could have my job and run the realty agency herself. God, how could I have been so stupid to not see this coming? I know how…the whore got me drunk!"

When Ebony had first started working at the realty company, several of the employees there had treated her with indifference, acting as though she were an interloper to be tolerated, but not to be taken seriously. However, after the footage of Clark Garrison's arrest appeared on the national news and they learned he had to post a ten thousand dollar bond to stay out of prison, his fellow coworkers had all fallen right into line and now looked on Ebony as a force with which to be reckoned. The scuttlebutt around the office was that Garrison had gotten into a head to head confrontation with the owner's new wife and lost. No one knew for certain what had actually transpired between them because there was a restraining order placed on Garrison ever setting foot on the property again. As a requirement of the charges against him being dropped, Garrison had to agree to never return to the agency again, not even to acquire any of the belongings he'd left behind. After Ebony cleared out his office, she packed up his belongings and sent Garrison a check for six month's salary along with the contents of his desk, and then took over the space as her own.

Two weeks after Garrison had been fired and Ebony was completely moved into his old office, she called for a mandatory meeting of all employees. As the group of ten agents filed into the conference room and took their seats, Ebony followed them and sat down at the head of the table. Brook Logan knocked on the closed door, entered, and placed a box holding ten tall cups of coffee on the table. She was about to leave when Ebony stopped her departure.

"Logan, would you please stay for this meeting?"

"I don't know how to take shorthand, Mrs. Prince. If you use the recorder, I can certainly transcribe the minutes and then put them on CD or diskette for you. If also you need a hard copy of the meeting, I could print it out from that."

"No, that isn't it at all, Brook. I'll need you as a participant in this meeting. Now, please take a seat," Ebony instructed, then turned to face the other ten men seated with her at the table.

Ebony motioned for the person sitting closest to her to move down one chair. Brook alighted herself beside Mrs. Prince, all the while wearing a look of surprise on her face.

"I called this meeting to inform you of some changes that I'll be implementing throughout the agency. According to our latest sales figures, for several months now we've been losing money rather than making profits on real estate commissions. Our competition is increasing its market share by giving customers deep discounts off their commissions or by offering them a written guarantee to purchase the homes they themselves can't sell to other buyers. Obviously, since we haven't made sales projections for three consecutive quarters, we can't afford to do those same things and stay competitive with them. So, from this point forward, we're no longer going to try."

Mr. Parker, an older gentleman in his late fifties who had been at the agency since the original owners founded the firm, was the first one to speak.

"What do you mean that we're not going to try any longer? Are you going to fire us, too, then close up shop around here?"

Ebony looked at him and then nodded in the affirmative.

"Yes, Mr. Parker, we're going to close up shop in a sense. Our records show that seventy-five percent of our revenue has been generated through the sale of real-estate, fifteen percent through the management of miscellaneous properties, and the remaining ten percent from consulting fees charged to customers wanting us to research about an area to which they might relocate. All of that is about to change."

"Our business practices are about to change in what ways?" Brook asked at a slip of her tongue.

Brook cupped both hands over her mouth from allowing the thought to escape her mind and move beyond her lips.

"I apologize for that, Mrs. Prince. I didn't mean to interrupt, or to…"

Ebony looked at her and smiled before she continued.

"You didn't interrupt at all, Brook. That's a very good question that I was just about to answer. Effective as of today, we will no longer be in the business of selling real estate."

There was an audible gasp heard throughout the room.

"That's crazy," someone said under his breath.

"I would have to agree," echoed Mr. Parker.

Parker stood up from his chair to emphasize the confusion and frustration growing among the entire group.

"How the hell are we supposed to feed our families if we stop doing something that constitutes seventy-five percent of our revenue?" Mr. Parker demanded to know.

Ebony stood up with her gaze fixed so intently on him that the others in the conference room seemed to fade from her sight.

"Swear once more in my presence and you won't have to worry about the source of your salary from this company, because you'll be out looking for another job. Now, take a seat, Mr. Parker."

For several moments longer, his eyes remained fixated on Ebony as though they were at a standoff in the old Wild West. The tension inside the room began to rise as the other employees waited to see what was going to happen next. Slowly, Parker averted eye contact with her and sat back in his seat. From that point forward, he remained completely silent while Ebony continued.

"From now on we will no longer sell properties; we will procure them. We're going to purchase apartment buildings and town homes in key markets, renovate those dwellings, rent them out, and then manage the properties ourselves."

"Mrs. Prince, implementing such a restructure plan would take capital," Brook offered, wearing a somewhat perplexed expression, "capital which you've already indicated we don't have."

"We have something better than capital, Brook. We have an almost unlimited line of credit...a lifeline for us, a noose about the neck for others."

"So how do we go about making this transition happen, Mrs. Prince?" asked an employee named Craig.

Before she responded to his question, Ebony noted that Craig appeared to be in his early twenties and was dressed in an attractive dark gray suit.

"I've rehired an attorney that the former owners of this agency have used in the past, who'll be handling the paperwork and legalities of this venture. As far as the rest of you are concerned, I'll be dividing you up into two distinct teams, one who'll be in charge of property procurement, while the other oversees their day-to-day management. I myself will be handling the renovations, pricing, and all development locations. Brook will be my executive assistant and second in command. If you need anything to assist you in doing your jobs, you may contact her first and me thereafter."

Again the room filled with whispers until Brook spoke to interrupt the murmurs.

"Excuse me, Mrs. Prince, but you want us to get in contact with Brook who?"

"Brook Logan," Ebony replied before adjourning the meeting.

Brook sat silently and waited until she and Ebony were the only two remaining in the conference room.

"Mrs. Prince, I'm certainly flattered, but I'm not qualified to be in that sort of position. For goodness sake, I'm only the secretary around here."

"And why do you think you're not qualified, Brook?"

"Because I have no training or experience in that kind of position; I've got no realtors license, no nothing."

"Do you have a brain?"

"Of course I do."

"Then you can, and will, learn. In the past when one of our salesmen sold a property, who typed the invoice, filed it, and followed the paperwork from closing through escrow?"

"I did, but..."

"And who updates our web pages with the current list of sold properties, and the ones that are still available for purchase?"

"Well, I do, but..."

"And when one of the realtors calls in sick, who handles our clients until he returns to the office to finish closing on the sale?"

"I do."

"Brook, you do all the legwork around here, while the men in this firm make a commission and take the credit for it. To date, you've been performing these duties without a license. However, I plan to do something about that starting today. Your salary will be increased by fifty percent so long as you maintain passing grades in the classes that I've scheduled you to take."

"Classes?" Brook parroted. "What are you talking about, Mrs. Prince?"

"While we're both learning the ins and outs of this business, you will take two afternoons per week to attend school and pursue your realtor license."

"I've been out of school for a very long time, Mrs. Prince. I don't know if I can."

"Brook, you can, and you will, do it. I see your talent even if you yourself do not, and as of today, attending those classes will be part of your job requirement. As incentive for you to follow through with these courses to their conclusion, your salary will be increased by fifty percent as long as you maintain a passing grade."

"I don't know what to say, Mrs. Prince. I don't know how to thank you."

"When the time comes, you will. Now let's get to work on acquiring those properties, shall we?" Ebony said as she climbed to her feet.

Brook stood up also, following behind her as they walked out of the conference room.

"Whatever you say, Mrs. Prince; whatever you say, indeed."

CHAPTER 12

Friday afternoon Ebony scheduled a meeting with Conner Davis, a corporate real estate attorney whose name she'd gotten from Nubian. Conner had worked for the previous owners of the realty agency that she and Nubian owned, and he was now representing Nubian in several other business ventures. He was a good looking, athletic man who appeared to be in his late twenties. On this particular day he was wearing a suit that matched the shade of his green eyes.

When Conner walked into her office, he glanced at the slim, provocative figure that rose to greet him and right away he assumed that Ebony was, or had been, a model at one time herself. The gray suit she wore hugged every curve of her body, and her hair, a shade that had turned dark honey from its exposure to the sun, complimented her high cheekbones and caramel complexion. Her beauty was a distraction that Conner had not anticipated.

"Hello. Nice to meet you, Mr. Davis," Ebony greeted as she came from around her desk, took his hand in hers and shook it.

Ebony motioned for him to sit down then reclaimed her seat behind the desk.

"Conner, the reason I asked you here today is because I need you to discreetly acquire some properties for me."

"Certainly, Mrs. Prince. Which real estate holdings should I procure?"

"I need you to obtain properties in Cincinnati, Philadelphia, New York, and Los Angeles. But first I want you to buy a warehouse located across the street from an apartment building in Raleigh, North Carolina, that has recently been put on the market. These are maps and a list of addresses."

Ebony picked up a small stack of papers from her desk and passed them to the attorney. Before Conner spoke his eyes widened.

"Mrs. Prince, you don't want to buy these properties. According to the maps you just handed me, rental properties owned by the Dickerson Corporation are already heavily entrenched in these neighborhoods. Trying to establish an apartment complex in the face of such stiff competition is financial suicide. We need to find some alternative locations, and from there we'll…"

"That wasn't a request, Conner. It was an order. The first property I'd like you to purchase is the warehouse in North Carolina."

"Are you kidding? The list price the seller is asking for that place is outrageous! By the time you finish renovating the property, creating individual apartments and get the interior ready for prospective tenants to move into, there may be no profit left. Even if that weren't the case, the Dickerson property is sitting right across the street from the one you want to renovate into a complex; and I'm telling you right now, they'd be fierce competition. They alone would dry up your business before it ever got off the ground. Other companies have gone up against that corporation and have lost. They've got the rental markets sewn up in those areas."

"I didn't ask you here to give me a second opinion. I called you to do the job that I need to have done. I want that warehouse, Conner! Now do your job and get it for me, or I'll find someone else who will. Then you may take your services to another family instead of doing business with mine."

"Yes, Mrs. Prince. I'll fly to North Carolina tomorrow morning, take a look at the property, and make a counteroffer to their asking price."

"Don't! I need that property and won't take a chance on losing it to someone else outbidding me."

"You realize that the warehouse is purposely overpriced. The owner doesn't truly expect to get his asking price."

"Yes, I realize that. Give the man what he wants and get me that warehouse, Conner."

"Okay, will do, Mrs. Prince," Conner acquiesced, all the while thinking about how low an IQ this woman must have.

◊   ◊   ◊

In six days Ebony was the owner of the warehouse, and in six months the property was transformed into lush, pre-furnished apartments that could easily rent for over a thousand dollars a month. Ebony and Conner sat in her office pouring over the books to review their business expenditures, and discussing how to recoup the cost of renovations.

"Mrs. Prince, when do you want the grand opening of the North Carolina property to occur?"

"It's almost Christmas now, Conner, so how about having the grand opening on the first of December. We'll allow that to be the debut date around the country for every property whose renovations have been completed and is ready to be occupied by tenants."

"I say we wait until sometime in the New Year, perhaps at the beginning of January or February. Right now most people are caught up in all the hustle and bustle of spending money on gifts rather than thinking about moving into a new place."

Without replying, Ebony pressed the intercom button and asked for Brook and Craig to meet her and Conner in the conference room. Once they were all seated at a large oval table, Ebony looked from Conner, to Brook, and then to Craig before she spoke.

"I know that you're all aware of the fact that we have bought, built, or developed properties via renovation that are in the vicinity and in direct competition with the Dickerson Corporation."

"May I talk freely, Mrs. Prince?"

"Certainly Brook, and that goes for the rest of you also. I want everyone to speak your minds freely."

"We are in debt because of buying, building, or renovating our rental units while the Dickerson Corporation is operating on pure profit alone," Brook explained.

"They're making money while we're trying to pay off our creditors," added Conner.

"How are we ever going to compete with them?" asked Craig. "Their company is already so heavily entrenched in the marketplace."

"We are not going to compete with them, Craig. We're going to put them out of business," Ebony explained.

Both men took one look at each other and suddenly the room filled with boisterous laughter. Brook merely glanced silently from one man to another, and then back at Ebony before she spoke.

"Mrs. Prince, how do you think that we could ever accomplish a feat like that?"

"Have you ever watched any of the nature programs on the Discovery channel?"

"Yes, Mrs. Prince, but what does that have to do with anything?" Brook inquired wearing a perplexed frown.

Conner and Craig had regained their composure and were both listening intently, waiting to see what the nutcase was going to say next.

"When a vulture sees an injured prey that's oftentimes much larger than itself," Ebony continued wearing a serious mien, "it waits until the creature is bleeding and almost dead before it swoops down to peck at and consume its remains. We're going to bleed each and every one of the Dickerson properties until their profits start dying off. After that, we're going to swoop down on them and consume the remains of their businesses before they ever realize what's happening."

"And just how are we going to do that?" chimed in Conner, his face drooling with skepticism.

"Starting with the property in North Carolina, we're going to have a grand opening at each one of our properties simultaneously. If the Dickerson units are renting for a thousand dollars a month, we'll rent our units to tenants with approved credit for seven hundred dollars a month, given one stipulation...the offer is good for the first six months and, after that, is subject to increase at anytime subject to the current market price in that particular neighborhood. We're going to hold a grand opening contest at each property that will air on radio and television stations; anyone signing a three-year or more lease is eligible to win a rent-free apartment for the first year. Oh, and Brook, once we adjourn here today, I'll need you to start publicizing our contest immediately. I've already hired an advertising firm who's in the process of pulling together the final details of our campaign. You'll be working very closely with them until we get this project rolling full steam ahead."

"If the rent is subject to being increased, then why would anyone take a chance on signing a three year lease with us?" Conner asked.

"Because of human nature, Conner; because most people can't resist the opportunity of getting something for nothing, even if it's subject to being taken away sometime in the future."

When Ebony brought the meeting to a conclusion, everyone in attendance filed out of the conference room one by one, each thinking silently to themselves that the boss's wife was going to destroy the

business before its competition ever got a chance to do so.

CHAPTER 13

Three months after they held grand openings all around the country for each property in close proximity of the rental units owned by the Dickerson Corporation, Conner Davis stormed into Ebony's office unannounced.

"Do you realize we're losing money left and right?" Conner asked in a tone that was almost a shout.

He tossed a stack of papers on her desk and stood in front of them as Ebony sat in silence.

"People are moving into our units like flies because by comparison to everyone else, the rent is damn near next to nothing," Conner continued in exasperation as his face flushed. "We could easily get over a thousand dollars a month for apartments going for almost half that much. When is this madness ever going to end? Are you even the least bit aware of just how much money we're losing each month?"

"I know exactly how much we're losing, Conner," Ebony replied in an utterance so calmly spoken that Conner stared at her for several moments after she'd stopped talking, certain that she had to be a madwoman.

"How much longer do you intend to keep this up? We can't continue to allow people to move into our properties, and charge them only a few hundred dollars a month."

"When the Dickerson Corporation decides to drop prices for their units then our strategy might change but, until that point in time, keep advertising the contest and continue charging the reduced rental fees."

"Your plan is not working, Mrs. Prince. The Dickerson's could care less about our driving this company into the ground ourselves. We're getting plenty of business that once belonged to them, but all of it is coming at a hefty price. Our units are filling up with their old tenants while we are drowning from losses from which we may never recover. I know that you've pumped a lot of money into this development, but against such heavy competition, we should cut our losses and think about selling off these properties. After a few more weeks of losses like the ones we're experiencing now, we'll no longer have a choice anyway. Pretty soon we'll *have* to declare bankruptcy to pay off our creditors, if for no other reason than to keep them from filing lawsuits and going after your personal property."

"Things will never come to that, Conner."

"You just wait and see, Mrs. Prince!"

Exactly one week later, Ebony got the break she had been anticipating. The intercom rang and Brook announced that someone without an appointment was here to meet with her.

"I'm rather busy at the moment, Brook," Ebony explained, then thought to herself that if this was another urgent message of doom from Conner Davis, she was definitely not in the mood to hear it. "Who's here to see me?"

"The gentleman said his name is Mitchell Dickerson. He was visiting one of his properties in the area and decided to drop by to see if you might be available."

For an instant her heart started to beat more rapidly, and Ebony found herself beginning to panic. What if he and his wife had discovered that it was she, the same fugitive whose daughter Lyn

Dickerson had forced out of her son's life, who was attempting to drive their family out of business? Then she thought to herself, if they learned who I was and had turned me over to the authorities, the police would be here now instead of Mitchell Dickerson.

Trying to calm the sound of alarm in her voice, Ebony instructed Brook to show Mr. Dickerson into her office. Before they entered the room, she stood up and smoothed out a noticeable wrinkle from her navy skirt and matching blazer. After Brook departed and as Mr. Dickerson approached her desk, Ebony could see that he was a well-dressed, handsome man in his mid-fifties, who was in very good shape. His eyes were positively striking, holding flecks of brown and gray in each iris.

"Hello, young lady. I'm glad you were able to see me on such short notice."

"It's my pleasure, Mr. Dickerson. Please, sir, have a seat and make yourself comfortable," Ebony said invitingly, before sitting down herself.

There was something about him that reminded her of Nubian's father.

"To what do I owe the pleasure of your visit?" Ebony inquired.

"I'm on my way to the airport to join my wife in Alaska where we'll have a week of skiing and some needed relaxation. However, to be frank with you, I was checking on one of my properties here in New York and decided to drop by and size up my competition. I thought perhaps your husband might be working here today, but I didn't realize until just now that you were the person running this division of his enterprise."

"Yes, that is correct. Nubian has many obligations with respect to his modeling career and stays extremely busy; therefore, I'm handling the day-to-day operations of this agency."

"I see. Well, your company is about to become engaged in a bidding war," Mr. Dickerson said congenially.

His smile faded and he leaned forward, watching Ebony with intense scrutiny. When Mitchell spoke again, there was a menacing quality to his tone.

"Beginning next month, we're going to offer all potential tenants competitive rates. I thought you and I should discuss what fees would be reasonable, so that we could agree to charge similar rental costs.

Doing so would be in the best interest of both of our companies, unless of course, you'd rather put your properties up for auction and sell them to me."

"Mr. Dickerson…"

"Please, young lady, call me Mitchell. And by what may I refer to you?"

Once more, the same panicky feeling came over Ebony and she wondered if her forehead might be shining from the perspiration she could feel developing across her brow. It only took her an instant to regain her composure and continue speaking.

"You may call me Barbara, but, to tell you the truth, Mitchell, I doubt very seriously if you could afford to buy my properties even if they were for sale, which of course they aren't."

"Judging from the rates you're charging your tenants, you can't be making much of a profit, if you're earning one at all, which makes your holdings worthless on the open market."

"Okay then, Mitchell, for the sake of this argument let's say that my business is faltering, I'm not making much of a profit, and I can't realistically compete in the marketplace with your company. Since we're assuming all of this is supposedly the case, please tell me exactly why you're in my office proposing that we negotiate to raise our rental fees," Ebony questioned skeptically, speaking in a tone that required no response.

"You are way out of your league, young lady. For lack of a better description, you are merely a neophyte that has no idea what she's up against."

"Oh no, I know exactly who my competition is. It is you and your wife that are the ones who don't know with whom *you're* dealing!" Ebony announced in a raised voice, speaking from the heat of their exchange.

Immediately, she regretted having talked so much and abruptly decided to bring their conversation to an end.

"Mitchell, I have a busy schedule this morning and really need to get back on track. Thank you for stopping by."

"You really should reconsider my offer to either raise your rental rates or contemplate selling off your properties to the Dickerson Corporation. Otherwise, I'm afraid that you're going to turn your husband into yet another unfortunate casualty who battled with my company and lost. The bankruptcy courts are littered with our so-called competition, companies that refused to agree to our offer to by them out."

"Mitchell, it is *your* company that decided to lower its rates in order to compete with mine, not the other way around."

"We are heavily entrenched in our markets. If you insist on going up against my company, young lady, you will surely lose."

"The Dickerson Corporation charges the people to whom they rent twice the rates that I do, all for properties that are older units as opposed to mine which are completely new dwellings."

"Who the hell do you think you are, a pair of supermodels playing house?"

"I see you've lost the accent and that the family resemblance to your wife is starting to show. Now if you wouldn't mind, Mitchell, get the hell out of my office and take your harassment somewhere else!"

"What exactly is that crack about my wife supposed to mean?"

"You'll find out in due time, Mr. Dickerson. All in due time," Ebony promised as she rose from her seat.

She walked over to the door and opened it wide enough for Mitchell to get the hint that she intended for him to leave her office immediately. Mr. Dickerson got up, followed her over to the exit and paused at its threshold.

"You're beginning to make some very serious enemies. If you value your business at all, then I would suggest you discuss my offer with your husband and you both mull it over. I'll be back in New York in the next couple of weeks."

"That sounds like a threat, Mitchell."

"Merely, a few friendly words of advice. Now you have a good day, Ebony."

"Why did you call me that?" Ebony asked quickly, her words riddled by a panic that she hoped was not apparent.

"Just referring to you by the nameplate resting on your desk," he replied wearing a frown that deeply creased his forehead. "For now, I bid you *au revoir*, Mrs. Prince."

After Mr. Dickerson departed her office, Ebony sat back down and contemplated in total silence for a very long time. Her extremities were literally shaking as she picked up the telephone to dial the corporate law offices of Conner Davis. When he answered, she was certain that he could hear the palpable strain in her voice.

"Conner, do you recall me asking you to gather information on the banks doing business with the Dickerson Corporation?"

"Yes, I've collected that info, and I'm awaiting your direction as to what to do with it."

"I need you to identify who Lyn and Mitchell Dickerson's personal banker is, locate his or her branch office, and set up a meeting for me to meet with both a supervisor and the district manager."

"Will do, boss, but what reason do I give for you wanting to meet with these people?"

"Just explain to them that Nubian Enterprises is interested in opening up several accounts with their organization and we are in need of advice on expanding and developing our future investments."

CHAPTER 14

The flight from New York City into the Juneau airport in Alaska took nine hours with just one stopover in Seattle. Mitchell Dickerson walked up to the car rental counter and a young man in his early twenties greeted him with a courteous, 'Hello,' then asked how he might be of service.

"Yes, my name is Mitchell Dickerson. You should have a car reserved in my name."

"Just one moment, Mr. Dickerson," the clerk said before turning around to retrieve a set of keys.

The clerk asked to see some identification, promptly handed Mitchell the car keys, then instructed him to walk around to the side of the building and look for stall number five. Mitchell found the Land Rover, hopped inside it, and embarked on the forty-five minute trek to the bed and breakfast where he and his wife were lodging for the week. As he drove through the capital city, moving along its narrow winding streets, his cell phone rang.

"Hello, Mitchell Dickerson speaking."

"Hello, Mitchell dear. How far are you from the cabin?"

"Lyn Darling, I'm almost there. Are you in our suite or off shopping somewhere?"

"I'm actually getting dressed for lunch. I bought a stunning outfit from the ski shop next door, a beige pantsuit with a cashmere lining. The lodge has just opened a new restaurant on the premises, so I'm going downstairs to try out the cuisine. How did your meeting with Mr. Prince go?"

"I never met with him, but I did see his wife. She's a strikingly beautiful woman, although, at the same time, she has somewhat of a strange demeanor. I can't put my finger on it at the moment; however, there's something about her that's vaguely familiar, as though I've met her before at a social function or elsewhere."

"Cut to the chase, Mitchell. Are they going to stop this bidding war and raise their rental fees or not? We have people moving out of our properties in droves, complaining that we're charging them way too much while our competitors are renting out their units at almost half our asking price. We can't continue to suffer these kinds of losses much longer. Those people are bleeding us to death. And in case you've forgotten, Mitchell, your wife likes to shop. So, you need to do something and do it soon, because I don't intend to give up one iota of the lifestyle I'm accustomed to living!"

"I'm almost at the lodge now, so I'll meet you for lunch and we can discuss how my meeting went with her then. But I can tell you right now that you're not going to like what I have to say. The woman is as stubborn as they come with all the money and backing she needs to justify her being that way. In other words, Lyn, we've got a fight on our hands. When I was in the office trying to reason with Mrs. Prince, it took everything I had within me not to loose my temper. And something else happened when I spoke with her, something rather peculiar."

"And what was that, Mitchell?"

"A couple of times when I mentioned your name, it actually seemed to irritate the woman. I'm sure Mrs. Prince didn't think I took notice of how oddly she was behaving, but I did. You don't know her by any chance, do you, dear?"

"I don't think so. What's her first name?"

297

"Well, she said her name was Barbara Prince; however, the plate on her desk read Ebony Prince. I suppose that one or the other is her middle name. So do you know her? Have you ever run into a Barbara Ebony Prince or her husband at some social event?" Mitchell asked.

He waited for his wife to respond, but she never said anything more. It was then he realized that their connection over the cellular network had been broken. Mitchell wondered exactly how much of the conversation his wife had heard before they were cut off. Instead of calling her back, he decided to just wait and meet with her in the dining room at the lodge.

The restaurant on the premises of the bed and breakfast was large and crowded with noontime diners. When Mitchell walked inside and approached the hostess, she immediately told him there weren't any tables available and there would be at least a forty-five minute wait.

"Look, Miss, my name is Mitchell Dickerson and I..."

The hostess cut him off before he could complete his sentence.

"Oh, I'm sorry, Mr. Dickerson. I didn't recognize you at first. Of course, we always have a table available for you, sir. Give me one moment and I'll have one of the busboys clear off an empty booth for you."

"That won't be necessary, Miss. I'm joining my wife here for lunch, so I'm certain that she already has a table and is seated somewhere in your establishment. Just find out where she is and I'll dine with her."

Two minutes later Mitchell was pulling out a chair and being seated down across from his wife. The waiter, a man who was a nonstop talker and who also appeared to be gay, greeted them at their table.

"Hello, my name is Dwayne and I'll be your waiter for the afternoon. I love your outfit, Ma'am. Did you buy it from the ski shop next door?"

"Yes, as a matter of fact I did, and now I'd like to order the..."

"I thought you had," Dwaine continued without pausing to listen to her order. "They're always carrying the newest fashions from all over the country. Anything you buy there will cost an arm and a leg to own, but I suppose that's the price you pay for fashion, isn't it? We've gotten quite a bit of snow for the season and since the ski shop can fix you up with anything you might need, from the best clothing to free-rider skis, you're guaranteed to want for nothing and you're free to simply have a good time."

When the waiter finally stopped talking to take a breath, he noticed the impatient expression upon Lyn Dickerson's face. He took both of their orders and scurried away in direction of the galley.

"Okay, Mitchell, tell me more about how your meeting went with this Barbara Prince person," Lyn requested, listening to him speak without interrupting.

By the time he finished speaking, their meals of veal chops and lobster tails had been placed on the table before them. Using both utensils, Mitchell cracked open a tail, dipped its contents in a garlic-butter sauce and silently studied his wife, allowing her an opportunity to think before she spoke.

"Mitchell, dear, here's what we need to do. Since Prince Enterprises is offering its dwellings for almost half less than ours, we need to not only match their offer but also remodel all of our units as well. I'll hire a corporate interior designer who'll make the apartments and extended-stay condominiums that Prince Enterprises is leasing to people look like the inside of a barnyard in comparison to ours."

Mitchell frowned at his wife's proposal.

"Lyn, how on earth; no, *where* on earth do you think we're going to get the hundreds of thousands of dollars we need to renovate our units, especially when we're currently experiencing a decline in new tenants? Besides that, there's nothing wrong with any of our properties as they stand. The exterior of our buildings are well maintained. The lawns are all professionally manicured and the grass is cut or fertilized twice a week. The interiors of most of our real estate holdings are as lavish as can be, with the rental fees reflecting prices for that standard of living. We have only a select few properties that are more reasonable and are a step down from those prices, with our building in North Carolina being one of them. In a word, Lyn, we *don't* have the funds to implement your ideas."

"Mitchell, our private stock holdings are worth millions, and our corporation has *always* been on friendly terms with Wachovia Bank.

If we pool together all of our resources as a family…yours, mine, and the trust fund that we set up for Tyree when he was just a baby…that total would comprise one hundred percent of our stockholdings and interest in the Dickerson Corporation. We can get a loan against a percentage of our holdings as collateral, and make the remainder of our stock a public offering."

"Lyn," Mitchell called out in a surprised tone, blinking several times in disbelief at her suggestion, "if we make our real estate holdings public, we open ourselves up to the risk of a hostile takeover."

"Not if we only make a public offering of forty-five percent of our company available for trade on the open market. We'll keep the controlling fifty-five percent interest of our stock in family hands. The money we'd make from selling shares to the public is what we'll use to pay off our mortgages and the new loan."

"But doing something like that would require perfect timing. What if we didn't sell enough stock to pay back the loan to Wachovia? We'd be at risk of the bank foreclosing against the controlling interest of our stock, stock that we'd *have to* put up as collateral in order to secure a loan from them. In other words, in a worse case scenario, the bank would own our company while the rest of our stock would be up for sale to the general public."

"That would never happen, Mitchell. We have a wonderful history with Wachovia and our joint ventures in the past have made us both much wealthier from that union. The bank would have no reason not to grant us an extension of the loan if we needed one. The loan *will be repaid* and our units will have a lavish makeover. Then, once we've forced Nubian Enterprises into bankruptcy like we've done to the rest of our competition in the past, we'll be able to substantially raise the rent on each property and charge our tenants whatever we want. All of our units will be transformed into living suites for the elite."

"Lyn, the penthouse where we reside in North Carolina is indeed opulent but, if we renovate that entire structure, there is no way the people who currently live inside our building will be able to afford the kind of rent that you're proposing we charge them."

"And?" she asked as she stabbed her fork into the last piece of veal on her plate. "Mitchell, with progress, you have to break a few eggs. The ones who can't afford to pay what we're eventually going to start charging them for rent will simply have to move out, paving the way for those like us who can."

"Yes, but what about our elderly tenants such as Miss Johnson in 103? She has been living in our building for years now and is on a fixed income."

"Mitchell, that woman isn't your responsibility. However, your son, Tyree, and I are. Worry about your own family and let Miss Jefferson..."

"Her name is Johnson," Mitchell interrupted to correct her.

"Whoever," Lyn Dickerson said in a dismissive tone as she retrieved a cloth napkin from her lap and wiped her month. "Let her own family find the assistance she might need. That's what organizations such as the Salvation Army, the United Way, the YWCA, and YMCA are for. As for our own family, I'll be damned if Barbara Prince or Nubian Enterprises takes another dime or tenant away from me. In other words, do you want to contact our personal banker or should I?"

Mitchell released a sigh of defeat before he spoke.

"I'll call the bank in the morning, but let me warn you of this, Lyn. If we don't pay our loan on time or are not granted an extension once the note is due, *damned* is what *we* just might be!"

CHAPTER 15

Ebony had just stepped from the shower when Nubian entered the bathroom and snatched a towel from the hammock. Every time she reached for the towel in an effort to dry herself off, Nubian playfully pulled it from her grasp, holding the cloth high above his head.

"Nubian, give that back to me before we're late for this dinner party you want us to go to so badly. And why are you still standing around here in your boxers, anyway? You took a bath before I did, so you should already be dressed. For goodness sake, the drive alone will take us twenty minutes to get there and it's almost a quarter of seven now."

"I was waiting for you to get out of the shower, baby," Nubian said seductively.

He slapped Ebony on the rear with the towel and then held it out for her to take. She quickly grabbed the terrycloth from him, dried herself off, wrapped the towel around her, and strolled into the bedroom. Nubian followed her and grabbed Ebony from behind.

"Ebony, you've been working late almost every night. I know that you're trying to rebuild the agency, and you know I fully encourage you in that endeavor, but now it's time for you to work on your husband some, baby. I need you, too."

Ebony pulled the end of the towel tucked between her cleavage, unwrapped the cloth from around her waist and allowed it to drop to the floor.

"So why are you still talking rather than doing something about it?" Ebony asked her husband in a seductive voice. "Take off those boxers and use some sign language."

Using one hand Nubian pulled Ebony into his arms. With the other he found the curve of her back and began stroking it softly, allowing his fingertips to gently caress her up and down along her spine.

"Baby, your body is absolutely beautiful."

"Tell me something that other men haven't already said," Ebony instructed as she began grinding her body into his.

"I could call you a hoe if you like," he joked.

"Nubian, it would take more than a hoe to garner the attention of, hold onto, and then tame a man like yourself. A man with your might and muscle needs a woman who can bring him to his knees, someone who'll slap you around a little bit until you're feeling all giddy from the inside out. And in case you haven't noticed it yet, I'm all of that and so much more. By the time I'm finished with you tonight, you'll be screaming out my name in several different languages. After that, I'll need for you to run downstairs and fix me a ham sandwich, because *I will* be hungry!" Ebony assured him.

She pushed Nubian down on the bed and straddled him as though he were a horse that she was about to ride.

"Oh, and Nubian…"

"Yes?" he inquired in a husky tone, his body burning with a desire that, to him, almost felt tangible.

"I'll like some mayo on that."

The dinner at the Chancellor estate was a glamorous, black tie affair with rooms filled by well-known models, politicians, and corporate heavyweights. The house held twelve bedrooms and had a second floor that seemed to overlook the entire city. A maid who answered the door led Ebony and Nubian down a long hallway with hardwood floors, directing them into a large ballroom where there was a fireplace that extended far beyond the ceiling up through the second level of the spectacular mansion. The room was filled almost to capacity by the other guests, and was decorated with marble tables, antique mirrors, and bookshelves holding rare porcelain figurines. Wingback chairs covered in silk, with colors ranging from pale blue to soft amber, stood next to white walls with a satin finish. Catherine Chancellor was seated at a backgammon table with the mayor of New York City. However, once she noticed that Nubian and Ebony had come into the room, she rose and walked over to greet them.

Catherine Chancellor was an attractive woman who appeared to be in her late forties. As Ebony studied her blonde hair, which had a trace of gray at its roots, she couldn't help but think that there was a cautious aloofness to Catherine's demeanor. Since she'd been married to Nubian and had come to meet some of his friends, Ebony decided that this particular air of confidence and carriage was something uniquely belonging to the rich and elite.

"Nubian, I'm so glad that you both could make it," Mrs. Chancellor emoted.

Catherine then turned and scrutinized Ebony from her head down to her toes.

"I've been dying to meet the mysterious woman who finally had what it took to capture the heart of this elusive bachelor," Catherine proclaimed. "Nubian, this woman is absolutely beautiful. I can certainly see why you'd want to take her off the market."

"It's very nice to meet you too, Mrs. Chancellor. Thank you very much for the compliment," Ebony greeted.

As Ebony continued speaking, she could feel herself blushing with a rosy hue.

"I'm sorry that Nubian and I are so late. Something came up at home and we had to take care of it immediately."

"Judging by the flush of your cheeks and the grin on your husband's face, I wish I could say the same for myself."

Ebony looked at her in surprise. Mrs. Chancellor merely chuckled and resumed speaking.

"I'm not going to apologize for being blunt, because your husband should have warned you about me and my mouth before now. I'd introduce you to my own husband, but darn if I can find him in this crowd. I've been searching for the man for the last hour and a half. Anyway, you folks go ahead and mingle while I greet some of the other guests. Have fun you two; well, not too much fun."

"That woman is a trip," Ebony said while they watched Mrs. Chancellor meander through the crowd and disappear. "And I like her."

"Yeah, she's great," Nubian agreed as he turned in the opposite direction.

He stopped a waiter who was passing by and grabbed two glasses of champagne from a tray carried by an older gentleman. Nubian handed a goblet to Ebony before he resumed speaking.

"But if you want to see a real trip, then wait until you meet Mr. Chancellor. He's a very nice man; however, he's also an extremely eccentric one. He has some kind of foot fetish. So, if you ever meet him in person, just keep an eye on where his hands go and where your shoes are."

311

"Ahhh…okay, I'll do that," Ebony assured him, wearing a frown. "My goodness, there are nothing but wall to wall celebrities in here."

"None more beautiful than you, baby."

At that moment Ebony saw Mitchell Dickerson heading straight toward them, approaching as he held the hand of an oriental woman who was walking a few paces behind him.

"Good evening, young lady," Mitchell greeted Ebony, looking from her to Nubian, and then on to his wife. "Lyn, dear, this is Nubian and Barbara Prince."

"What the hell are you both doing here," Lyn Dickerson interrogated with sarcasm, "following my husband and me to see what you can copy about us next?"

Nubian looked at Mr. Dickerson with fury in his eyes, and he had to calm himself before he was able to speak.

"Look, man, this is a social event, and my wife and I didn't come here to argue with you people."

Lyn Dickerson ignored Nubian and leaned closer to Ebony.

"Just remember what my husband told you last week," Lyn warned. "If you're looking for trouble, my dear, you've certainly found it. Consider your asses forewarned!"

The Dickerson's both turned around in unison and walked away. For several moments longer Nubian just stood there, watching the couple from behind as they blended into the crowd and then vanished from sight.

"What in the world was that all about?" Nubian inquired wearing a perplexed expression. "Did Mitchell Dickerson call you sometime last week?"

Before Ebony could respond to either one of his questions, a cellular phone rang, prompting Nubian to ask her yet another.

"Is that yours or mine?"

"Mine," she said thankfully, glad that his questioning had been interrupted by the ring of her unit.

She fished around inside a small, black beaded purse draped casually over her shoulder and retrieved her phone from a side compartment. Ebony turned on the cell and brought it to her ear.

"Hello?"

"Mrs. Prince, this is Conner Davis. Sorry to call you this late in the evening, but I thought you'd want to know this information as soon as possible."

"No, it's fine that you called, Conner. Go ahead. What is it?"

Ebony could see that the expression on Nubian's face had changed to one of curiosity.

"Mrs. Prince," Conner continued, "I contacted the people at Wachovia and attempted to set up an appointment for you to meet with both the branch manager and the agent who handles accounts for the Dickerson Corporation."

"Conner Davis is calling you at this hour?" Nubian quizzed without really expecting her to respond to his rhetorical question. "Is everything all right?"

Ebony told Conner to hold for a moment, cupped her hand over the receiver, and then looked up at Nubian.

"Everything is fine, baby. Conner is just working on some new investments and wanted to update me on how things are coming along. Since there are so many people in here talking, I'm going to step into the hallway so I can hear Conner a little better. Go ahead and mingle with some of the other guests, and I'll catch up with you in about five minutes or so."

"Okay, baby, you and Conner knock yourselves out for now, because once we get back home later tonight, that sweet ass of yours is going to be mine all over again," Nubian pronounced.

He watched Ebony from the rear as she began to saunter away. Sensing that Nubian was observing her from behind, Ebony threw an extra swagger in her walk as she moved in seductive steps from his view into the corridor.

"Okay, Conner, go ahead. When is our meeting scheduled?"

"There isn't going to be a meeting, Mrs. Prince, not if you're seeking an investment partner. Since the bank currently maintains several corporate accounts with the Dickerson family, the branch manager explained that a partnership or venture of any kind with us would be a direct conflict of interest for them. In a word, they aren't interested in hearing any proposal we have and will not meet with you *ever.*"

"Conner, what's the name of the branch manager?"

"His name is Darrin Stevens. He's working in a dual capacity while the original manager at that particular branch is on maternity leave. In reality, he's their district manager for all of the banks here on the East Coast. Without scheduling a time through his secretary to meet him, you'll never see the man face to face. And like I stated to you earlier, he won't be giving us an appointment in the first place. I'm sorry, Mrs. Prince, but I've exhausted every reason and resource. The man is simply unwilling to meet with you."

"Thank you for trying, Conner. By any chance, do you have Mr. Steven's office address on hand?"

"Yes, as a matter of fact, I do. Not that it will do you any good to have it, but here it is. Stevens works out of an office at their corporate suites in North Carolina. The address is in downtown Raleigh, at 420 Fayetteville Street Mall."

"Thank you, Conner. Have a good night."

The next day Ebony caught an early flight into the Raleigh-Durham International Airport. From there she hailed a taxi to 420 Fayetteville Street Mall.

Wachovia was housed in an enormous building, standing squarely between Salisbury and Wilmington Streets, which ran parallel with each other. The Fayetteville Street Mall sat sandwiched between the two and was actually a street itself once. It had been completely paved over with ornate bricks to make a walkway, with stores and office buildings situated on either side.

When Ebony entered the Wachovia Building, it was filled with dozens of people bustling around, each moving to and fro. She approached one of three receptionists seated behind a long marble counter.

"Hello. How may I help you today?" asked a middle-aged woman.

"Hi. I'd like to see the district manager for this region, a Mr. Darrin Stevens."

"Do you have an appointment with him?"

"Yes, I do," Ebony lied. "It was scheduled several weeks ago,"

Ebony thought about making a mad dash for an elevator going upstairs, but for one, she didn't know the floor on which his office was located and, for two, there were a pair of uniformed guards allowing or denying entrance to board the cars. People who weren't wearing either a permanent red badge with their picture embossed on it, or a temporary green badge that was hanging prominently from their clothing were all turned away and sent back to the lobby area to see a receptionist. The receptionist who assisted Ebony picked up her telephone and spoke into its receiver.

"What is your name?"

"It's Ebony Prince."

The woman repeated the name and then lowered her voice so low that Ebony couldn't hear what was being said next. When she hung up the telephone, Ebony could tell by the expression on her face that whatever she was about to say certainly wasn't going to be good news.

"His secretary has no record of an appointment made for you to see Mr. Stevens."

"There must be some kind of mix-up in the communication between our respective offices. If I could see Mr. Stevens for just a few moments, I'm certain that I could straighten out this entire matter."

"Mr. Stevens is a very busy man, and *no one* sees him without first having an appointment," she explained in finality.

One of the other receptionists seated next to her tapped the woman on the shoulder. When she turned her head in that direction to answer a question, Ebony reached across the counter and snatched a green badge from a wicker basket. With hurried steps Ebony moved away from the desk and walked to its end, taking a position behind a tall potted plant. After pinning the badge on her silk blouse, Ebony saw a large group moving in the direction of the elevators and joined them, centering herself in the throng.

"Oh, goodness," Ebony called out just as the elevator began its ascent. "The receptionist told me on which floor Darrin Steven's office is located and now I've forgotten. Can someone press the number one so I can go back downstairs to the lobby and ask?"

"His office is located on the thirteenth floor," volunteered a woman dressed in a beige blouse and tan jacket similar to the one Ebony was wearing.

Ebony thanked her as a Caucasian man wearing an emerald green suit pressed the control panel button for the floor she needed.

When the elevator stopped and the doors opened, both Ebony and the man wearing the green suit exited at the thirteenth floor. He allowed her to leave the car first and followed as she approached a desk where a young woman was seated.

"Hello," Ebony greeted with a warm smile. "I'm here to meet with Darrin Stevens."

The secretary frowned before she spoke.

"Yeah, but you didn't have an appointment to see him. How did you get past our security guards to make it upstairs?"

"Yes, that's what I'd like to know, too," chimed in the man whom Ebony had just been on the elevator with.

Ebony turned her head and met his gaze.

"I don't believe that she or I were speaking to you," Ebony explained to him as a matter of fact before she herself frowned. "So do you mind going somewhere else and finding some business of your own to get into?"

The man merely grinned, walked past them both, and then entered the office located directly behind the desk of his secretary. When he closed the door, Ebony could see that the nameplate hanging on the portal read *District Manager*. Ebony swallowed hard before she could find the words with which to speak.

"Who was that?"

"That was the man with whom you claim to have an appointment," the secretary explained with a sneer and an audibly irritated voice.

Before Ebony replied, she leaned so closely in front of the secretary that the woman could actually smell the spearmint on her breath.

"Inform Mr. Stevens that I'm a reporter from the local CBS television affiliate preparing a national broadcast feature pertaining to him, and the alleged misappropriation of funds reported to us by a previous employee. It would be in his best interest to speak with me now, unless he'd rather tune in to our broadcast later tonight. Tell him to watch the Six O'clock News and then again in the morning for our sunrise show."

The secretary lost her sarcastic demeanor, quickly picked up the telephone, and spoke into the receiver. She got up and went inside his office, closing the door behind her. Two minutes later both she and

Mr. Stevens emerged from the room. Only this time the secretary offered Ebony a cup of coffee while Stevens himself ushered her inside his large paneled office wearing a polite smile.

"My secretary explained to me that you're a reporter doing some kind of story. With which one of our previous, apparently disgruntled, employees have you interviewed? Who would make such ridiculous accusations?"

Darrin Stevens was a thin man in his early fifties, with a guileless face and soft blue eyes. He was seated behind an enormous desk, peering at Ebony above the rim of wireless glasses.

"Mr. Stevens, my name is Ebony Prince."

"Yes, I know who you are. I recognize you from the news. Never miss one of your broadcasts. Now, which one of my past employees are we talking about?"

A chuckle slipped from her mouth that Ebony couldn't stop in time.

"Mr. Stevens, I own rental properties that are a subsidiary of Nubian Enterprises."

"Wait just a minute. Are you the person who had Conner Davis calling me to set up an appointment?"

"Yes, I am."

With eyes that had suddenly turned cold, he rose from his chair and stood erect.

"This meeting is over. For one, I don't intend to lose the Dickerson account because I'm in bed with their competitor and, for two, I don't enjoy being lied to or tricked!"

Ebony remained seated.

"Is that why you never miss one of my news broadcasts?"

This time it was Stevens who guffawed.

"I'm here because I'd like to become a stockholder in your bank," Ebony continued.

"How much stock are you interested in purchasing?"

"A lot..."

"When you say a lot, exactly what dollar amount are we talking about?"

"I have a cashier's check with me. I'll allow it do the rest of the talking for me!"

CHAPTER 16

For several months Ebony watched via detailed reports from Conner Davis as one by one, all over the world, each property owned by the Dickerson Corporation underwent extensive renovations and reconstruction. As she sat in her office pouring over her own portfolio of recent acquisitions, she decided that now was the perfect time to make her move. Her eyes filled with water as she realized that today was the beginning of the end...not just for the Dickerson Corporation, but for her own marriage as well. The first call she made was to the studio where Nubian was shooting an ad for IBM. When he came on the line she could barely speak, her emotions constraining her throat and allowing sound to emerge only as a whisper.

"Nubian?"

"Yeah, it's me baby. How's everything going?"

His voice was like a warm blanket wrapped all around her. Despite its perceived warmth, Ebony found that she was literally trembling. How could she explain to him that he was never going to see her again, at least not as a free woman?

"I'm going to have to leave town for a while," Ebony pressed on. "And I don't know exactly how long I might be gone."

"Where are you off to now, to buy another property for the realty company?"

"Yes, something like that," Ebony said, trying hard not to go into any details.

The last thing she wanted Nubian to do was follow her back to North Carolina. What she had to do there, she needed and intended to do alone. Eventually, in time Nubian would find out the truth; however, she didn't want to be the person who told him about her past. Yes, not being honest with him was an act of betrayal of the man she vowed to love, honor, and cherish until death do them part, but perhaps betraying him in this way would help Nubian forget all about her and allow him move on with his life. In time she was certain that he would give up on their marriage and set out to find someone new, a woman who was more worthy of the abundance of love that he'd showered upon her every day of their married lives.

"Even though you haven't gone anywhere yet, I miss you already," Nubian gushed. "When will you be back?"

"I'll miss you too, Nubian," Ebony said as she fought back sudden tears. "More than you could ever imagine."

Nubian was instantly alarmed by the tone of her voice.

"You sound funny, baby. Is anything wrong?"

"No, Nubian, nothing much; just that time of month, I guess."

"Okay, well, you have a safe trip and hurry on back to your husband. Maybe you haven't realized this yet, but I need you and appreciate your being a part of my life. I love you more than any woman I've ever known, Ebony Prince."

"If anything were to ever happen to me, just remember that I love you, too, Nubian. I love you very, very much."

"I couldn't bear to ever lose you and I won't, so don't even think like that Ebony. These days flying on an airplane can be a safer means of travel than driving a car, especially with all of these nuts on the streets exhibiting road rage. You'll be just fine, baby, just you wait and see."

"And the same holds true for you, too, Nubian. Just *you* wait and see."

"Then we're both in agreement, I see. That's a switch," Nubian teased.

They talked for ten minutes more before Ebony ended their conversation. She buzzed Brook over the intercom.

"Yes, Mrs. Prince?"

"Brook, I need you to contact our public relations guy and tell him to stop advertising our contest immediately. Then I want you to get Conner Davis on the phone for me."

"Sure thing, Mrs. Prince. I'll get started on doing both right away. Is there anything else you'd like me to handle for you?"

"Yes, just one other thing. I need you to call my travel agent and get a one-way ticket from LaGuardia to Raleigh, North Carolina. I'll need my flight to arrive there later this afternoon."

"Are you leaving early to go home and pack some clothes, or shall I have the limo driver just bring whatever bags you might have already packed to the office?"

"I'm not taking any luggage with me, Brook. Booking the flight will be quite enough, thank you. As of today, you'll be in charge of this agency for an indefinite period of time."

"I hope you don't mind my saying this, Mrs. Prince, but you sound funny. Is everything alright?"

"In time it will be, Brook. Please let me know when you have Conner on the line," Ebony requested then clicked off the intercom.

Five minutes later Conner Davis was on line two.

"Hello, Mrs. Prince, how might I be of service to you this morning?"

"Conner, I need to make you aware of some of my recent acquisitions, as well as some organizational changes in the structure of management around here. I'll be taking an indefinite leave of absence and, while I'm away, Brook Logan will be in complete charge of this agency. She has recently completed training and, from my understanding, will be awarded her reality license within the next few weeks. Also, I'll need for you to double the rent on each and every one of our units. If you receive any complaints from our tenants, please refer them to the clause in the contract they signed, the one stating that their rent is subject to increases in line with the current market rates of their respective neighborhoods."

"Wow, I never thought I'd hear you say those words, not before we were out of business and in bankruptcy court. Are you taking a vacation with Mr. Prince?"

"No, I'll be away on sabbatical by myself. Also, I need to let you know about some recently acquired properties."

"Which properties have you recently acquired, Mrs. Prince?"

"The Dickerson Corporation."

There was a long, stunned pause followed by silence on the opposite end of the telephone, and Ebony wasn't sure if there was still a connection.

"Conner? Conner, are you there?"

"Yes, Mrs. Prince, I'm still here. But what on earth are you talking about?"

"Recently the Dickerson family borrowed a huge sum of money from Wachovia Bank. In the contract they signed, there was a clause that stated their loan could be sold to other investors associated with the bank as long as the interested parties were majority stockholders of Wachovia."

"If any of this is true, Mrs. Prince, then how do you know about the details and terms of their loan? Besides, you couldn't even get an appointment to meet with anyone over there. That information is privileged, intended only for the bank or its officials. No one other than an employee is allowed to have access to those files."

"No one other than the bank employees or a majority stockholder, the latter of which, Nubian and I became several months ago. I know what I know about the terms of their loan, because it was *I* who made certain that the Dickerson Corporation gained approval to borrow those funds...approved to borrow the money at a price, of course. I purchased the account from Wachovia and, according to the agreement that Mitchell and Lyn Dickerson signed, if they miss one payment...just one...then I'd have the right to either extend the due date of the note, or to foreclose upon the loan and take controlling interest of their stock. According to my estimates, most or all of their capital is currently tied up in reconstruction. The stockholdings they made public have been met with lukewarm reception from day traders and their net asset value is way down, probably due to the increased competition in their rental markets."

"Oh, my God," Conner exclaimed with an audible astonishment that could be heard across the line, "they no longer owe the bank anything. They owe you the money!"

"Their first balloon payment is due by five o'clock today. Guess what my answer is going to be when their lawyer calls to ask the bank for an extension?"

"Up until now you've done all of this covertly. I'm supposed to be your lawyer, and you've been keeping *even me* in the dark as to what you've been up to. How will the bank explain not giving them an extension of their due date?"

"When you and I finish talking, I'm going down to the North Beach branch of Wachovia Bank. As we speak, I'm having Brook book me a flight out of LaGuardia but, before I go, I'll make certain that no one from the bank will extend the terms of the Dickerson's loan or explain to them why it was declined. Twenty-four hours from now Nubian and I will own controlling interest of the Dickerson Corporation. In other words, by this same time tomorrow, their

331

company will be mine. Later today, I'm flying to North Carolina and delivering the bad news to them myself. Then, just like they told my daughter to do, I'll give them thirty days to get the hell out of my apartment building!" Ebony blurted out in a heated fervor, without ever taking a breath between her words.

"Are you certain you don't want to try to work things out with the Dickerson's rather than taking over their company? The interest you'd make on their loan would be a substantial amount. Is what Lyn did to Paris really worth your throwing away all of those potential profits?"

"Conner, what Lyn Dickerson did to my daughter was unconscionable and is *the only reason* I ever did any of this. And since I've been doing all of this for Paris, then yes, all of it has been worth it. I'll protect my children until I'm a breath away from sleep and the very life leaves my body."

"You're risking everything you have by doing that. But if you've already made up your mind, then there's nothing I can say to change it."

"You're absolutely right, Conner. *I have* made up my mind and there *is* nothing you could say to change it."

"Will you need a ride over to the airport, Mrs. Prince, or are you having the limo come by and pick you up? I'd certainly be glad to give you a lift."

"Thanks anyway, Conner, but I don't need a ride. Nubian had a shoot today and so he took the limousine, but I'll just take the subway to the bank. From there I'll catch a taxi over to the airport. As I said before, Brook will be in charge here while I'm away, so if you could just keep an eye on her for me and offer any assistance as needed, I'm certain she'll appreciate your help during my absence."

"Okay, then, very well; whatever you say, Mrs. Prince."

"Thanks much, Conner. Goodbye for now."

The last two calls Ebony had to make were the hardest of them all. First, she telephoned Big Mama to say that she was finally coming home and to prepare Paris and Derick for her arrival. Her next call was to the Raleigh Police Station, in which she stated that she was turning herself into the authorities for the attempted murder of Joseph

Morgan, an attack that was committed over fifteen years ago upon the father of her two children.

CHAPTER 17

After Ebony had completed her call to the authorities in North Carolina, explaining that she would be voluntarily turning herself over to them within the next twenty-four hours, Brook knocked on the ajar office door and gave Ebony information for about an electronic ticket, explaining that all she would need to do was to show her identification at the airport.

"Since you'll be running a little short on time this afternoon, I thought it would be easier for you if I handled buying your ticket this way, rather than me having a messenger bring over a paper ticket like I usually do," Brook explained.

"Thank you, Brook. Working with you has really been a pleasure," Ebony complimented with all sincerely before rising from her seat to give Brook a goodbye hug.

In preparation for the usual cool temperatures typical of New York this time of year, Ebony pulled on a wool coat over her hand-woven, floral print dress.

"I feel the same way about you, too, Mrs. Prince."

When Ebony exited the lobby area of the building, a blast of cold air caused her to pull the collar of her coat more closely around her neck and ears. She walked two blocks past busy pedestrians and people operating automobiles like they were professional racecar drivers. Even though she could see the entrance of the subway directly across the street, jaywalking was something that Ebony wasn't about to attempt in a million years, not on the traffic-ridden streets of the City. She strolled a few feet out of her way and waited at the crosswalk until the pedestrian signal indicated for her to walk.

She began to cross the street with a group of other people, all of them hurrying past her in an attempt to get to the warmth of their destinations, when she felt a violent shove from behind. The push sent her sprawling sideways into oncoming traffic, inside the portion of the intersection where drivers had a green light to proceed. A huge delivery truck sped directly toward her, but when Ebony attempted to run back in the direction of the sidewalk, one of her high-heeled shoes came off and instead she fell down in the middle of the street. The driver slammed down on his brakes and the wheels of his truck began to screech; however, its load was much too heavy and his speed way too great for the vehicle to slow down or stop in time.

As Ebony looked up in horror, she knew that there was only one chance for her survival. Curling herself up into the fetal position, she covered her head with both arms and rolled her entire body into a tight ball. For a moment the sky overhead went completely dark as though there had been a total eclipse of the sun. Time seemed to stand still as the truck passed directly above her, the roar of its engine drowning out the sounds of her surrounding world.

Then, as suddenly as it all had begun, Ebony could once again see the sky overhead. The sound of a roaring engine was replaced by the clanking of chains slapping against tires. Her ears were filled with screams of fear and excitement. Several people came rushing to her assistance and helped Ebony to her feet. A man climbed from behind the wheel of the truck, his face completely drained of color. He picked up her purse and the cellular phone that had fallen from it, and then held both of them out for Ebony to take. Groggily she stood up and inhaled several deep breaths, trying hard to regain her composure before she accepted the items from him. It took a moment longer for Ebony to remember that someone had pushed her out into the street. She was surrounded by what felt like thousands of men and women, all shouting or brushing off her clothing while asking her questions about what had happened to cause the accident. Ebony began to look around frantically, scanning the crowd for the culprit who had pushed her into the street in the first place, but it could have been any one of them. Pushing back the hands that touched her, Ebony moved away from the strange faces surrounding her, then turned and ran down the street into the distance.

When Ebony finally stopped moving, it wasn't until she was out of breath and could run no further. Now, she was in an unfamiliar part of Manhattan. She realized that she'd been on automatic pilot, racing blindly in various directions. Reaching into her purse, she found her cellular phone and dialed Nubian at the studios.

"Hello, this is Mrs. Prince. I need to talk to my husband."

"I'm sorry, Mrs. Prince, but your husband is out of the building while we're setting up for another shoot. Can I take a message and have him..."

Ebony turned off the phone, ending their connection without waiting for the woman to complete her sentence. She then dialed Connor Davis at his office extension. When his voicemail picked up, she hung up and tried his cell number. With each ring of the phone, Ebony prayed that it would be turned on and that Connor would answer.

"Hello, Conner Davis speaking."

"Oh, thank Goodness you answered, Conner!" Ebony gushed out in a wheeze.

It wasn't until then that she realized she'd been holding her breath.

"Hello, Mrs. Prince. Is there something you forgot to tell me when we last spoke?"

With a sigh of relief Ebony began to speak, telling Conner of the incident that had occurred back at the crosswalk.

"I'm *so* scared, Conner. I'm not sure what to do next. I tried to call Nubian, but he's off set and nowhere to be found."

"I don't like the sound of this at all. Why don't I come get you, and we can both go down to the police station and report to them what happened?"

"No, I'd actually rather report what happened to the authorities in North Carolina since I'm going there anyway. Just come and get me, then drop me off at the airport. I think someone intentionally pushed me in front of that vehicle, so it might not be safe for you to get anymore involved beyond that."

"Okay, then, tell me where you are."

"I'm not certain," Ebony said as she looked around, taking in her environment for the first time since she'd stopped running. Moving all about her was a cultural melting pot of African Americans, Asians, Caucasians, Europeans, and Hispanics. At a distance, standing directly to her left was a man whose face Ebony could have sworn she'd seen somewhere before. *My god, he must be the person who pushed me into the street and is now following me around to finish up the job.* The man appeared to be staring back at Ebony, but when he hailed a taxi and climbed inside it, she realized that he was the actor, Denzel Washington.

"Go to the corner and read the street signs, then wait for me somewhere near the intersection in a public area. Don't talk to anyone, and I'll be there just as soon as is humanly possible."

Ebony made her way toward the nearest corner where she could read the street names and an address posted on the front of a stone building.

"Got it," Conner replied after Ebony had relayed to him her exact location.

"I'm so sorry to be dragging you into this, Conner."

"You had no choice and I'm willing to help. Neither of us anticipated any of this happening, so we'll just have to make the best of a nasty situation."

At last Ebony began to calm down and feel a mild sense of security.

"Thank you so much, Conner!"

"Be careful and I'll see you very soon."

After speaking with Ebony, Conner Davis clicked off his cell phone. Then he dialed a telephone number in North Carolina that he'd called many times before. The woman on the opposite end picked up on its first ring.

"Is she dead yet?"

"No," Conner admitted. "I shoved her directly in front of a passing truck and she should've died then, but something must have gone wrong. I left the scene before I made certain she was dead. That won't happen again."

"You damned idiot!" Lyn Dickerson yelled into the receiver. "Can't you do anything right? I hired you months ago when that woman started building properties next to mine, and today you call me, telling me that that bitch is taking over my company. I've paid you very handsomely to keep me informed of her activities, and that sum is on top of the legal fees you already charge Nubian Enterprises."

"Yes, you do pay me well, but you never mentioned anything about murdering anybody until now."

"Look, Conner. I don't have time to hire a professional to do this job. That woman is planning on taking over my company come close of business today. I would love to do it myself, but I need Ebony Hightower Prince dead now! I promised you a quarter of a million dollars to get the job done, so do as you're told and make it look like an accident. After Ebony is dead, dealing with a grief-stricken widower will be a hell of a lot easier than asking for an extension of my loan from her. The death of that bitch will make all of our lives a whole lot less complicated, yours as well as mine."

"Don't worry about a thing, Ms. Dickerson. Next time I'll finish her off for good."

"You'd best make certain you do that, Conner. Because if that woman causes me any more trouble, you're the one I will hold personally responsible and both your lives won't be worth a dime. Do I make myself perfectly clear?"

"Yes ma'am, crystal clear. You can rest assured that Ebony Prince will be dead in a matter of hours."

CHAPTER 18

After speaking with Conner Davis, Ebony turned off her cellular. She glanced at her watch and felt grateful that there was still plenty of time to make it to the airport to catch her flight. Her anxiety ran high as a large woman emerged from around a street corner, howling like a banshee and complaining to anyone who would listen that her purse had just been stolen. Ebony hugged the side of the building to allow her ample body plenty of room to get by. Suddenly, for some reason, a vision of Ebony's mother flashed through her mind.

As she stepped further onto the sidewalk and peered around each corner of the skyscraper to keep a lookout for Conner, the crowd rushing past caused Ebony to be pushed back into the side of the building with an audible thud. The awareness of the soreness in her back was replaced by a nagging, elusive memory…something that she should have caught and paid attention to, but did not. As she studied the faces of the people passing by, she wondered who was trying to kill her and why?

A moment after the thought had crossed her mind Conner emerged from around the corner of a skyscraper and walked in her direction. Ebony rushed up to him and hugged him tightly. She hadn't realized that her face was tearstained until she pulled back and saw that his dress shirt was wet.

"Thank you for coming to get me, Conner."

"Not a problem at all, Mrs. Prince. It's actually my pleasure to do so," Conner said as he took hold of her arm and led her to the left.

"We need to go straight to the airport. I'm on Delta Flight 619 and I don't want to take any chances of missing it. Oh, please God, don't let there be any kind of delay."

They walked for several blocks in complete silence, moving in the same direction from which Ebony had just run. All of a sudden, a small child burst through the door of a shop they were passing. Both Ebony and Conner abruptly stepped back as the mother of what appeared to be a seven-year-old girl came barreling out of the jewelry store in pursuit of her daughter.

Within her mind the scene played like a movie in slow motion and Ebony was instantly transported back to the conversation she had with

Conner over the telephone. *'Are you certain you don't want to try to work things out with the Dickerson's rather than taking over their company? Is what Lyn did to Paris really worth your throwing away all of those potential profits?'*

"What Lyn did to Paris," Ebony repeated aloud without realizing it.

"What did you say, Mrs. Prince?" Conner asked congenially, as he held onto her arm to guide her steps.

"You weren't surprised when I mentioned to you that I had a daughter."

Her voice was filled with dread and unmistakable fear. It was becoming hard for her to breathe and Ebony found herself hyperventilating.

"You spoke her name before I ever told you what it was," Ebony continued. "How did you know that Lyn Dickerson had done something to Paris before I ever told you to whom I was referring?"

Conner's grip tightened around her arm until it became vice-like.

"And how did you get here in a matter of minutes to pick me up with all this noontime, rush-hour traffic?" Ebony demanded to know.

It was then that he started pulling Ebony at the elbow, herding her violently into a narrow alleyway immediately to the right of a jewelry shop. Ebony could not believe her eyes as New Yorkers continued to walk around them, going about their usual tasks completely oblivious to what must have appeared to be some kind of domestic dispute.

"Babe, please let me talk to you for a minute," Conner pleaded. "I don't care that you cheated on me with the milkman, just don't file for a divorce before we get a chance to talk it over."

The more Ebony screamed for help and attempted to garner the attention of passersby, the more she was ignored and stepped around without a second look given to her struggle. Conner dragged her closer and closer toward the passageway and, within moments, the two would be completely out of view from the public.

That's when she yelled out, "I don't care how much you want to pay me. *I will not* perform oral sex on you and Hugh Grant during broad daylight in some alleyway!"

The entire crowd moving around them came to a complete stop. Now everybody was staring at Conner and Ebony with keen interest. Some even moved into the alley to see if they could locate Mr. Grant.

Seizing the opportunity to escape, Ebony ripped free from his grip and made a mad dash into the jewelry shop. She grabbed the cellular phone from her purse and quickly dialed 911, only to realize that the battery, to her utter dismay, had drained completely dead. Conner followed her into the shop, reaching into his suit pocket with his eyes darting from left to right. *'He's got a gun,'* Ebony thought to herself.

All of the clerks were busy showing merchandise to customers except for one· who'd just completed a sale. Without a moment's hesitation, Ebony moved to a glass jewelry case and flagged the salesman down.

"Are you looking for anything in particular today, madam? Perhaps something for yourself, a special occasion, an anniversary, or loved one?"

"I'm looking for something special all right. Do you have another exit from this shop, some way to leave here by other than the front door?"

The clerk peered at her strangely then shook his head in the negative.

With menacing eyes, Conner approached the two of them while his right hand remained concealed, tucked securely inside the breast pocket of his suit. Ebony willed herself not to panic, to not pay attention to the hairs standing on end atop the surface of her flesh.

"No, there isn't another way of departure, at least not for the general public. There's merely a service exit around back that leads into our private parking area, reserved alone for the use of staff that are employed here. Is there anything else I can do for you, madam?"

Everything in the jewelry shop seemed and looked so normal, normal until Ebony peered over her shoulder to see that Conner Davis was standing nearby, listening to every word she spoke to the clerk. *'I've got to get out of here,'* she thought to herself. *'There has to be a way for me to escape without Conner plugging me in the back with a bullet. Obviously, he doesn't want there to be any witnesses, otherwise he would have shot me by now.'*

Ebony happened to glance down at the glass display case in front of her. That's when an idea came to mind. She asked the salesman if she could take a closer look at a diamond tiara that was worth six thousand dollars. When he unlocked the case and handed it to her,

349

she placed the ornate piece atop her head and started to walk toward the exit of the shop.

"Hey, wait just a second, lady!" the clerk called out to her. "You need to pay for that."

Ebony never looked back at the salesman, nor did she stop. Instead, she merely increased her stride and pace until she was sprinting towards the exit. As she stepped through two columns that held sensors in their towers, a bullhorn began to blast outside as the security tag attached to the tiara triggered an automated alarm system that notified the police of a burglary in progress.

Ebony stopped and waited at the entrance of the shop, standing still without ever stepping outside. Conner stood beside the clerk in total astonishment. Both men gaped with their mouths wide open in a speechless wonder. Patrons began to gather around to see what all of the commotion was about.

Feeling like an animal that was about to be trapped, Conner rushed from the shop and stood outside, watching helplessly from a short distance away. As he stood next to a tree and peered into the establishment through paneled glass, he could see that Ebony was being led further inside the jewelers by a pair of security guards who worked there.

"Miss, I'm afraid that you'll have to come to the manager's office and have a talk with us," commanded the taller of the two male guards.

Ebony glanced beyond the two men toward the front of the building, looking through the double glass doors of the shop to see that Conner was still standing outside, peering at her. Her attention shifted back to the security guard who had spoken.

"I'll have to come with you for what reason?"

"Because shoplifting is still a crime in this state," the shorter guard sarcastically explained.

Just then, the assistant manager of the shop came over, and for the first time Ebony realized where she was.

The woman looked at Ebony's wedding ring and immediately recognized the culprit.

"Mrs. Prince, how nice to see you again. What seems to be the problem here?"

"I saw something in the window I wanted and just had to have it. That's when I decided to..." Ebony began to explain before the salesclerk interrupted.

"That woman is lying through her teeth," the salesman interjected as he extended his index finger to point at Ebony. "She asked me if she could hold that tiara she's wearing, then rushed away without paying for it."

The manager, wearing a smile, corrected her salesclerk.

"Jonathon, obviously there has been some sort of mistake. Please shut off the alarm and telephone the police. Give them our password, and tell them this was only a false alarm and not to send a patrolman over."

"No, don't do that, Jonathon," Ebony protested, then extended both arms out with her wrists held closely together. "He is one hundred percent correct. I did steal it. Now for goodness sake, woman, call the police and have me arrested."

The patrons were all staring at Ebony in amazement. In turn, Ebony looked out into the crowd and extended both of her hands upward, gesturing in a plea to gain their support.

"Can you people believe this?" Ebony asked them. "Black men can't hail a taxi in this town to save their lives merely because of the color of their skin, but I walk into a jewelry store during broad daylight and try to steal something, and they won't even have me arrested for it."

If the assistant manager was becoming frustrated or irritated by the spectacle Ebony was creating, her demeanor and tone of voice never once showed it.

"I wouldn't dream of having you arrested, Mrs. Prince. I'm delighted that you found another piece of jewelry you liked. I'll just place the tiara on your account and send Mr. Prince a bill. Is there anything else you see in here that you want?"

Ebony sighed to herself in disbelief.

"Yes, I need a telephone."

"You need a what?"

This time it was the manager who looked bewildered.

"Can you please call me a taxi and have it pick me up at your service entrance around back?" Ebony requested wearing a look of impatience.

353

"Of course, Mrs. Prince, we can do that for you if you'd like."

"Thank you very much. Please, contact the taxi company right away, because I have a plane that I need to catch," Ebony said as she reached up and took off the tiara. "And here, you can keep this because the service and security in this establishment totally sucks!"

CHAPTER 19

As Conner watched Ebony speed away in the backseat of a taxi, his fury was beyond measure. He raced down the sidewalk in obvious irritation, heading back to where his car was parked. With apprehension, he turned on his cell and dialed Lyn Dickerson at her penthouse suite in North Carolina.

"Hello, Ms. Dickerson?"

"Is the job done yet, Conner?"

"No, ma'am, she got away again. But I know on what flight she'll be arriving this afternoon, so there won't be too much longer of a delay."

When Conner paused to let her speak, the obscene words coming from the opposite end of the connection were some of the worst he had ever heard.

"I'm sick and tired of hearing this shit, Conner! I want that bitch eliminated without anymore of your excuses by midnight tonight...or else."

"The job will be completed by then, Ms. Dickerson. I can promise you that. I'll see if I can get a ticket for the same flight Ebony will be on and..." Conner said before Lyn Dickerson interrupted, cutting him off in mid-sentence.

"Don't bother, Conner. I anticipated that you might bungle this somehow. I've arranged for our private jet to be waiting for you at the airport. My pilot will get you to North Carolina before her plane ever lands. You can arrange a reception for Ebony at RDU International. But let me warn you, Conner. This is your last chance to eliminate my problem before you yourself become one. So don't fail me again. Do you understand me?"

Conner started to say, yes, but before he could do so, he heard Lyn Dickerson slam the receiver down on the other end of the line. She had severed their connection.

Ebony climbed out of the taxi and found that she was almost paralyzed by fear. Pushing the terror from her mind in order to regain some semblance of control over her lower limbs, she began to walk briskly into the lobby of the airport. Her instinct was to run instead of ambulate, but she didn't want to draw undue attention to herself in case Conner had figured that she'd still try to make her flight to North Carolina. Once inside Terminal C, she found the Delta counter where a lone agent counted flight coupons.

"Excuse me, sir, but do you have an electronic reservation for Ebony Prince?"

As the clerk typed on his keyboard, Ebony could feel her heart literally pounding at twice its normal pace with each keystroke he made. It wasn't until he looked up from the computer screen and spoke that its rhythm relinquished an anxious reggae beat.

"Yes, ma'am, a one-way ticket going to Raleigh, North Carolina was reserved for you and is shown as paid in full. There is a stopover in Atlanta; however, you should arrive at your destination no later than six o'clock this evening."

'Thank you, Brook,' Ebony said to herself before she turned her attention back to the clerk and asked him another question.

"When is the flight leaving?"

"The plane is currently on schedule, so your flight should depart here at one o'clock. There is a lounge area around the corner and to the right. You may wait there until the plane arrives."

Instead of relaxing in the lounge area, Ebony located a telephone booth and called Brook at the agency. During the ride from the jewelry store a terrible thought had occurred to her. If Conner was attempting to murder her, only one person could be responsible and benefit from her demise…Lyn Dickerson. When Brook picked up the telephone, Ebony took a moment longer to glance around at the chattering travelers surrounding her. Once she made certain that it was safe for the time being, she placed her ear to the receiver.

"Prince Properties, Brook speaking. Hello? Is anyone there?"

"Brook, it's me," Ebony blurted out in a loud utterance, almost shouting from fear that Brook would think it was a crank call and hang up. "I'm in terrible trouble and I need your help. Someone is trying to kill me, and I need you to contact the police and send them to an address in North Carolina. Also, locate my husband and tell him that I'm on my way there now."

"What? Who would want to harm you, Mrs. Prince?"

Ebony could hear the alarm commingled with concern in her voice, but she needed Brook to avoid panic and remain calm.

"Please Brook, stay composed and keep a level head. There isn't enough time for me to explain everything right now. I need you to write down this address."

There was a moment of silence as Brook took down the information.

"Got it…I'll locate Mr. Prince and then contact the authorities."

"No, no, no. Call the police first and then find Nubian. This will all be a shock to him and in the beginning he won't understand any of it. I need you to make him listen. Tell my husband that I have family living there who are in need of protection. I must get to them to make certain that they're all okay."

"Who should I tell the police and Mr. Prince is living there?"

"My mother, daughter, and son."

Another moment of silence passed, more than likely because Brook herself was now in shock. Ebony scanned the room from one corner to the next and, with every passing second, her nerves grew more and more on edge.

359

"My plane leaves here in an hour and the battery on my cellular is dead, so I'm counting on you to make these phone calls, Brook. You might have to make several attempts to reach Nubian. Okay, now, if you've gotten all of that and are certain about everything I need for you to do, I really need to hang up and leave. For some reason I'm not feeling very safe where I'm at, and I have to get to a more populated area of the airport. *Please, please*, make these contacts for me, Brook, because it could very well be a matter of life and death."

"You can stop worrying about your family, Mrs. Prince. I'll make those calls as soon as we hang up."

A deep sense of relief sweep through Ebony's entire body.

"Thank you, thank you, thank you, Brook."

Just as Brook was placing the receiver on its cradle and broke their connection, two uniformed policemen walked into the agency.

"Yes, can I help you gentleman?"

The older of the two, a Caucasian man in his late fifties with an aquiline nose was the first to speak.

"Hello, ma'am, I'm officer Williams of the New York PD. Are you Ebony Hightower?"

At first Brook was frozen with apprehension and didn't know what to say, but she quickly rebounded and then smiled a wide, toothy grin before she replied.

"No, I'm not, officer. Is there anything wrong?"

"Is Mrs. Hightower here?"

"No one works here by that name."

"And what is your name, miss?"

They both looked at her accusingly, as though they thought she knew something more and was withholding information.

"Brook Logan."

"Look, Brook, we know that Mrs. Hightower telephoned a police department in Raleigh, North Carolina from this building because we traced the call back to here. Now, do you want to tell me where she is, or will I have to arrest you for obstructing justice?"

For the better part of a minute Brook furrowed both brows as she squinted her eyes, appearing to be in a state of deep concentration.

"Oh, you must be talking about Ebony Prince," Brook finally responded. "I didn't realize that her last name was Hightower. Let me see if I can locate her husband and put you in contact with him."

The plane was flying smoothly into the sunset at an altitude of thirty-nine thousand feet. A man with olive skin and an Italian accent was seated next to Ebony, trying to engage her in conversation. He was a handsome guy in his early twenties. From the way he was talking to her, as if she were a contemporary, it was obvious to Ebony that he hadn't guessed she was almost twice his age.

"My name is Marco Leone. I work for a website development firm, but in my free time, I sing in a rock band. I started the band myself when I was in college, and believe it or not, we just put our first CD up for sale on the Internet for worldwide distribution. Hey, you look kinda' familiar to me. Haven't I seen you on campus at St. Thomas Aquinas in New York State?"

"No, Marco. I'm sure that if I'd gone there, we wouldn't have graduated in the same year. I just have kind of a familiar face, that's all."

A flight attendant came down the aisle pushing a serving cart filled with refreshments and Ebony was appreciative for the distraction.

"Hey, if you'd like a beer just ask for a cup and some ice. I have a hot one somewhere in my travel bag," Marco offered.

He reached under his seat, groped around inside a purple backpack, pulled out a can of Budweiser, and held it out for Ebony to take.

"No thank you, Marco. Juice is all I want," she explained and then looked down at her watch, all the while thinking to herself, *'Fifty more minutes of this'*

When Delta Flight 1120...the exact airplane, crew, and most of the same passengers from its original flight number of 619, landed late at the Raleigh-Durham International Airport at six o'clock in the evening, Conner Davis was waiting with hand in pocket at gate twelve, watching keenly as each passenger disembarked. People were streaming out at a steady pace and his eyes were fixed on each and every one of them, following as they moved by him in an orderly procession. He was confident that there would be no way for Ebony Hightower Prince to escape, at least until he watched as the last person exited the plane and walked up the ramp. Wearing a look of

363

frustration, Conner ran down the ramp and boarded the plane. The only person he saw left on board was a flight attendant who was preparing to leave. When the woman peered up after putting away a serving cart, she saw him approaching and released a loud yelp, startled by the realization that she was no longer alone.

"Sorry to scare you, miss. I was looking for my sister who was supposed to be on this plane. Did you have an Ebony Prince registered?"

The woman placed both hands crosswise her bosom and drew in a deep breath.

"You gave me quite a fright, mister."

"Sorry about that, ma'am."

"No problem. Moving on…I'm not sure if your sister was aboard this plane or not, but if she missed it, then there are some other flights expected later this evening. We have two more connections coming in from Atlanta, both arriving here just before and after midnight."

'Damn, it!' Conner thought to himself. *'The bitch gave me the slip again. Ebony must have realized that I might be waiting here for her and she decided to catch a later flight.'*

CHAPTER 20

When his cellular phone rang, Conner pulled it from a pocket in the lining of his jacket and looked at the caller ID display with an overwhelming since of dread, fully expecting that it would be none other than Lyn Dickerson calling him for an update.

Instead, it was his longtime girlfriend.

"Conner, darling, I have some important news for you," she said in a breathless whisper. "I called as soon as they left me alone and I could speak to you without being overheard."

"Yeah, what is it?"

"Take down this address and do it quickly, before anyone comes back into the reception area," she demanded. "I may have to hang up abruptly, so don't take it personally."

After Conner jotted down the location, there was an extremely faint click on the phone line that went unnoticed by either of them.

"What is this for?" Conner asked.

"It's where Mrs. Prince is headed. A few hours ago she telephoned, telling me to call the police and have them sent to the address where her mother, son, and daughter reside."

"Brook, this information is important, baby. What took you so long to tell me?"

"Just when I was about to call you, two police officers showed up on the premises and started asking me a lot of questions. They wanted to know Ebony's whereabouts and I played dumb. When I realized they were becoming suspicious, I had to pretend to be helpful and to throw them off, I got in contact with Nubian Prince."

"You did what?" Conner yelled into the receiver. "Don't we already have enough trouble as things stand?"

"Look, Conner, I want the money that Lyn promised us as badly as you do, but those officers *made me* get in contact with her husband. As we speak, Nubian Prince and those policemen are next door in *my new office* having a meeting about where and how to find Ebony. It wouldn't surprise me one bit if, by the end of their conference, all of them begin their search somewhere in North Carolina. Once they run a check of her credit card, that plane ticket is going to rise to the surface like a dead man floating on water. If you intend to get rid of her so we can collect our fee from Ms. Money Bags, then you'd better do it quick, before these people start nosing around and spoil everything for us."

For a moment this new information threw Conner off and he didn't know how to proceed, but then he began to smile.

"I know just what to do. Thanks for the info, Brook."

"You're welcome. Just hurry back to the loving arms of the woman who adores you. That sounds like a song title, doesn't it?"

"Like music to my ears, baby. I'll be back in New York just as soon as I can. I love you," Conner said before turning off his phone.

Brook was about to replace the receiver when, for the first time, she took notice of a flashing red light next to the intercom button. The door to Ebony's office flew open, and Nubian bolted into the reception area with the two officers following him closely from behind. Their stunned expressions told Brook, without her ever having to ask, that the three men had been listening to her every word.

"My wife has been damned good to you, Brook, and this is how you repay her, by attempting to have her murdered for money or some other godforsaken reason?" Nubian yelled at the top of his lungs.

Nubian rushed over to Brook and grabbed her by both shoulders, shaking her violently while demanding to know the answer to one question.

"Where the hell is my wife?"

When the two officers pulled Nubian away from Brook, she swiftly snatched a piece of memo paper from her desk and promptly ate it. She made the move so quickly that none of the men could get to her in time to prevent her from swallowing it. An officer pulled both arms behind her back and slapped on a pair of handcuffs, while the other one read Brook her Miranda rights.

Paris, Derick, and Big Mama had all gone to bed at around eleven o'clock. Paris was in a deep sleep when suddenly her eyes shot open, awakened by the sound of a thud against the floorboards. Fighting the grogginess in her mind and the stiffness of her body, she glanced at the clock atop the nightstand adjacent to her bed and saw that it was approaching midnight.   There were muffled, unfamiliar voices emanating from the hallway through the closed door of her bedroom. Quietly, she got out of bed, slid her feet into a pair of slippers resting on the floor, and wrapped a violet housecoat around her silk negligee. With cautious steps she moved toward the door and pressed her ear against it, hearing bits and pieces of conversation coming from the opposite side.

"Now that we have the boy and his grandmother out of the way, we need to take care of the girl," Paris heard a female voice say.

Then a man began to speak.

"You want to kill her, too?"

"No," the female instructed.   "We can use Paris as bait for her mother."

As the heartbeat interior her chest began to pound harder and harder, Paris was now suddenly and completely awake, without the least trace of sleep remaining.

"Ebony will be coming here from the airport and when she does, what should we do next, Ms. Dickerson?" the man questioned.

"Then we can kill them all and make it look like an accident."

Paris had heard enough. When she realized that the voice in the hallway belonged to Tyree's mother, she backed away from the door as if it were a venomous viper, coiling its head so as to strike her. While walking backwards, Paris mistakenly bumped into a glass of water resting on the nightstand, sending the ceramic cup crashing to the floor in loud, shattering shards which broke into dozens of pieces. Moving swiftly, she raced back over to the bedroom door and locked it. Someone began twisting the doorknob, trying to gain entry, but Paris was not about to wait around and figure out which of them it was. Her brother and grandmother might already be dead or dying, and if she didn't go for help right away, she and her mother were surely going to become the next victims of the murderous couple standing on the opposite side of her bedroom door.

Paris went to her bedroom window and opened it, allowing a rush of frigid air to assault her face and practically nude body as she stared down at the ground from the second floor. With chattering teeth Paris crawled outside onto the window ledge. She was thankful for the fire escape leading to the ground and, moving with haste, she reached the earth in less than ten seconds flat. Just before she ran down the street,

Paris quickly glanced over her shoulder to see an unfamiliar White man and the silhouette of a woman, peering at her from the sill of her bedroom window.

Once Delta Flight 619 from LaGuardia landed at its stopover in Atlanta, something halfway between woman's intuition and a premonition caused Ebony to alter her flight plans. She exchanged her ticket at the counter and paid a hundred dollar transfer fee, then booked herself on a later flight set to arrive in Raleigh shortly after midnight.

When Delta Flight 2114 touched down on the runway of the RDU International Airport at a quarter past twelve, before she disembarked, Ebony peered outside her window-side seat and scanned into the darkness, searching for anyone or anything that looked suspicious. Under the illumination of nighttime spotlights, crew mechanics began to service and refuel the jet.

Ebony drew in a deep breath and prepared to deplane. She managed to stay surrounded by as many passengers as possible, walking into the terminal amongst the rest of the chattering crowd.

She moved through the concourse into the baggage claim area, past the carousels, and then outside to where several taxis lined the curbside. She didn't see anyone lurking about, but she also knew that both Conner and Lyn Dickerson were still out there somewhere, trying to make certain that she would never live to see another day.

Through the darkness and bitter cold of night, Paris ran as she never had before, sprinting down a deserted street directly centered on its dashed yellow lines. With each gazelle-like stride her legs pounded against the rock-hard asphalt, and she found herself growing weaker and weaker from an adrenaline induced exertion of speed.

When a pair of headlights rounded a corner from a side road in front of her, Paris thought perhaps this entire nightmare would soon end. She thought that until the flash of the headlights dimmed to reveal that the vehicle ahead of her was a stretch limousine. The car came to a screeching halt and the White man who had broken into her grandmother's house climbed out from behind the wheel. When Paris saw Lyn Dickerson leap from the back seat, she turned and ran back in the same direction from which she came; only this time, she lumbered toward home with legs that felt like lead weights. The tightness within her chest cavity was excruciatingly painful and, with every breath she drew, her lungs burned as if someone had torched her oxygen deprived body.

'If I can get back home and make it into the house before they catch me, I'll lock the door and call the police from there,' Paris thought to herself.

Without looking back to see where they were, Paris pelted the street with her footsteps, desperately trying to put all of her energy and concentration into getting home. When she finally arrived at the house, she attempted to open the front door, only to find out that it was bolted from the inside. As she turned around to head for the backyard, the Caucasian man was standing directly behind her, holding a gun in his right hand. He trained the weapon at her skull as Lyn Dickerson appeared from the darkness of shadows. Lyn drew a hypodermic from a pocket of the black dress she wore.

"We broke into your house from the backdoor, you stupid hood-rat bitch!" was the last thing Paris heard before Ms. Dickerson plunged a needle into the side of her neck.

As Paris felt the sting of its metal enter her skin, she could sense her body slumping toward the ground while she unwillingly slipped further into an unconscious state. Everything around her grew faint, and Paris closed her eyes for what she perceived would be the very last time. Her final cerebrations were of the prayer request that she'd made of God every Sunday since her childhood…that *He* would someday allow her to see her mother again one last time before death. Obviously, her most treasured desire would not be fulfilled in this lifetime; but rather, it would be inside the next.

With Ms. Dickerson walking by his side, Conner picked up the body and carried it back to the limousine. Lyn knew that Ebony would have only one place left to go. That place was to her, and when the time came, she intended to be waiting for Ebony with open arms.

CHAPTER 21

As Ebony rode down Highway 70 in the backseat of a taxi, speeding hurriedly towards her mother's home, minutes seemed to pass like hours. She had promised the driver an extra twenty-five dollars if he could get her there within fifteen minutes.

"The police should already be at the house by the time I arrive," Ebony said aloud to herself. "I don't care if they arrest me right there on the spot, just as long as I know that my family is safe."

The Iranian driver looked into his rearview mirror and began to stare at Ebony from his reflective view of the backseat. For the rest of the ride she sat back in her seat and remained silent, quietly contemplating until they pulled into Big Mama's driveway. She stepped from the taxi, reached into her purse and withdrew sixty dollars. Ebony was just about to pay the driver when she happened to glance toward the house and saw that the front door was ajar. He grabbed the bills and was preparing to drive away when she asked him to wait. The driver shrugged in a silent gesture to indicate that he would, and then placed his taximeter to standby.

'Perhaps they realized that I wouldn't have a key and before going to bed, decided to leave the door open so I could get in,' Ebony thought to herself, trying hard to keep the nagging sense of foreboding in her mind from growing out of control.

Temperature-wise the weather was freezing, and it immediately made her think of having left Nubian all alone back in New York City. Or, would he be inside the house too, waiting with the rest of the family for her arrival? In comparison to the last time she visited here over fifteen years ago, the building now seemed much smaller in stature, looked more rundown and nondescript than she remembered it to be. She climbed a small fight of stairs leading up to the entrance, then pushed open the door and walked inside without closing it behind herself. The living room was completely dark and when she tried turning on a lamp next to the sofa, the light didn't come on.

Like the release of water from behind a dam, panic began to flood her body and mind all at once. There were no signs of police activity inside or outside the home, no family members and no Nubian anywhere to be seen. In fact, the entire abode seemed devoid of sound and life altogether. Somehow Ebony knew that something, somewhere in the house was amiss.

Fear choked her as she moved from the living room through the kitchen, then down a long hallway leading to the bedrooms upstairs. Ebony was just about to enter the first bedroom she came to when she tripped over something and fell on the floor. Her fingers instantly became moist, and when she scrambled back to her feet, there was blood covering her hands, dress, and coat. Big Mama lay motionless on the carpet within a standing pool of blood, facing upright with a bullet wound in her neck. There was a geyser of crimson spraying upward from the wound like a fountain, making the floor slippery and wet to the touch.

Yowling out in a hysterical scream, Ebony knelt and listened to her chest but could not discern whether there was a heartbeat or not. Not knowing for certain if her mother was already dead or merely unconscious, she removed the terrycloth belt from the housecoat Big Mama wore and wrapped it firmly around her neck, trying to prevent anymore loss of blood. Ebony double-checked to make certain that

377

the makeshift compress wasn't tightened too tight or restricting her airflow, then moved onward into her mother's bedroom to retrieve a phone from the nightstand. Ebony listened for a tone, and then quickly dialed 911. The operator who answered told Ebony to stay with her on the line, but the cord wouldn't extend out into the hallway, and she had to go check on the whereabouts of Derick and Paris. So, after giving the woman their address and pleading for her to hurry up and send an ambulance, Ebony hung up the telephone rather than remaining on the line. She moved hastily in and out of every bedroom in the house, peering inside each of them one by one. When she couldn't find either of her children anywhere on the premises, Ebony dropped down on her knees and wailed out in a loud, inconsolable cry. The telephone rang again and, thinking that it must be the 911 operator or paramedics calling her back, Ebony composed herself enough to speak and picked up the receiver.

"Hello!" Ebony answered, her tone riddled by panic and stress.

The voice on the other end of the connection made Ebony's skin crawl.

"Hello, my dear," the woman greeted genially. "You and your daughter have caused me quite a bit of inconvenience over these past few years, but as you can see, all of that is going to come to an end very shortly."

For a few seconds Ebony was literally in a state of shock, completely unable to move or reply. When she was finally able to talk again, her voice came out in a hoarse whisper.

"I assume that I'm speaking with Lyn Dickerson."

"Your guess is one hundred percent accurate. Now, can you figure out where your two children are at this very moment?"

Ebony screamed into the receiver.

"Where are Paris and Derick? I swear, if you two butchering bastards have done anything to my children, as God as my witness I'll hunt down your asses and tear you both out a new..."

When Lyn Dickerson cut her off in mid-sentence and she heard the tirade that followed, Ebony knew for certain that she was dealing with a madwoman who could not be intimidated or reasoned with.

"And another thing, *don't you ever* speak to me like that again, you troublesome little wench," Ms. Dickerson warned in a tone of

379

voice indicating her absolute seriousness, "because I'll personally cut the balls off between your son's legs and stuff them inside his mouth until he chokes to death."

Ebony was unable to respond and, from that point forward, could only listen.

"I need your signature on some loan papers I have at my penthouse, so Conner will be giving you a ride to meet with me here. A limousine is waiting two blocks away that will come to pick you up. I want you to leave the house, walk down the street, and climb in the back seat. If you contact the police before you leave the house or if my driver is followed by anyone, your children will be dead before anybody has a chance to enter my building. Do I make myself perfectly clear?"

The line went dead before Ebony could respond.

Ebony rushed outside and headed straight for the taxi. She could tell the driver to call the police before Conner arrived to pick her up. The man appeared to be asleep as the cab's engine continued to run. Ebony tapped on the glass but he didn't respond. She went around to the driver's side and knocked upon the pane a second time, yanking open the door after she'd rapped. Now she could see that the shirt he wore was blood-soaked, that his head leaned unnaturally to one side. There was a fifteen-inch laceration starting from below his left ear, extending under and around his neck, and continuing across to the opposite ear.

Conner Davis pulled up beside them, rolled down the window of the limousine, and smiled at Ebony before he spoke.

"Because of all the running around and headaches you've caused me, I would have rather done that to you instead of him, but the boss doesn't want any witnesses left behind and still needs you alive. Well, at least for now she does."

Conner gave Ebony a look that was a mixture of extreme annoyance and contempt.

The very sight of him filled Ebony with utter sickness and absolute revulsion.

Their eyes bored deeply into one another, burning brightly with an unbridled passion that could only be described as profound hatred.

When Detective Williams and Nubian Prince landed at the Raleigh-Durham International Airport, the clock read exactly one a.m. During their flight from New York City to North Carolina, the Raleigh Police Department had gone through their case files, found a previous address for Ebony Hightower, and then secured a warrant to search through the premises currently owned by her mother. Waiting patiently inside a squad car parked next to the curb sat two officers who had come to pick them up from the airport. One officer handed Detective Williams some paperwork and warrant information, while the other started the engine and drove the quartet to Big Mama's house.

Conner led Ebony toward the penthouse suite, grasping her arm with a grip that reminded her of a wrestling hold. His other hand was holding a gun pressed firmly into her back. As they moved from the lobby area to where the elevators were located, Ebony could see the place was completely deserted...there was not a soul in sight. Considering the late hour of the night, anyone who might have helped Ebony would now be fast asleep. Once they rode upstairs and had reached the penthouse suite, Conner used the barrel of his gun to press the doorbell without releasing his hold on her. They watched as the entrance crept slowly open. Lyn Dickerson ushered them inside, but before closing the door, she looked out into the hallway and made certain that they hadn't been followed.

Suddenly Ebony realized something. Mitchell Dickerson was nowhere to be seen. Could it be that he and his son were not aware of what Lyn Dickerson was doing? Were they somewhere in the penthouse totally oblivious to what was transpiring, lying down sound asleep in one of the bedrooms upstairs?

Conner was leading the way as he dragged Ebony along with him. Every footstep she took was resistant and reluctant; however, each time Ebony lagged behind there came a violent shove to her back. As they moved through the foyer into the living room, Lyn Dickerson cattle prodded Ebony from behind until her spine became sore to the touch.

The lights were dimmed low in the room, which was comfortably furnished with a Moroccan sofa, two Queen Anne end tables, and an antique wingback chair. Atop each table were identical crystal vases.

When Lyn gave her a final shove into the room, it only took Ebony a split second to twirl around and slap the woman silly, even though Conner was still holding onto her left arm using the tightest of grips. Conner watched helplessly as the blow sent Lyn stumbling backwards where she landed squarely onto the chair's cushion.

"Stop pushing me around, you monster!" Ebony yelled at the top of her lungs, hoping desperately to awaken Mitchell or his son.

Just for added measure, Ebony kicked over an end table causing the vase atop it to come crashing down against the hardwood floors, shattering its glass into a thousand pieces.

When Ms. Dickerson climbed out of the wingback, she was boiling over in a blinding rage. Before Ebony knew what was happening, Lyn picked up an unbroken vase from the other end table and smashed it across her head. The strike made a hollow thud against Ebony's skull and within three seconds flat she collapsed to the floor, rolling and writhing around on the hardwoods in an incredible amount of pain. Conner picked up her semi-conscious body and propped Ebony sitting upright on the couch.

The entire room appeared to be spinning as Ebony drew in rapid, shallow breaths, gasping to take in air. While she remained slumped wryly on the sofa, there were two shapes looming above her, but Ebony could not focus well enough to distinguish which figure was the man and which was a woman.

The smaller of the two blurs rushed toward Ebony, but before it could reach or touch her, the larger shape pulled it back.

"No, Lyn, don't kill her yet. We need her to sign those papers and give your company an extension on the loan."

"I'm not signing anything for you people," Ebony protested.

An agonizing ache seemed to rip at the very fibers of her brain, but somehow, Ebony found the strength to continue. Realizing that Lyn and Conner were planning to kill them all, she needed to stall for time and decided to embellish the truth.

"I had an associate of mine contact the police department," Ebony explained. "They were on their way to my mother's house and have probably followed us here. If you do or have done anything to either of my children, both of you aristocratic hoodlums will surely pay for the crimes!"

The sound of laughter filled the room from its two other occupants.

"Do you want to tell her, Ms. Dickerson, or shall I?"

"This is just too sweet, Conner. Allow me to have the honor," Lyn lamented in mock sorrow then sat down on the couch next to Ebony. "Ebony Dear, how do you think Conner knew where to find you, by gazing into a crystal ball?"

"Brook Logan has been my girlfriend for the past six-and-a-half years," Conner confessed.

He too flopped down upon the sofa, sitting beside Ebony on the opposite side of Lyn.

"So you see," Conner continued. "I don't think the police will be looking for you or your soon-to-be deceased family members at your mother's house, much less searching for you over here."

His words cut into Ebony like a hot knife slicing through butter and, for the first time since this entire ordeal had begun, she could finally feel her spirit wane, feel herself starting to relinquish hold of all hope. Hard, body-racking sobs caused her head to scream with pain and her eyes to instantly swell shut, but as hard as Ebony tried to will the flow of water away, her deluge of teardrops would not stop falling.

"If you think that you're in great pain now, my dear," Lyn Dickerson said to Ebony, using the sweet and nurturing tone of a mother, then gently brushed back several of the flyaway hairs that were flowing freely across Ebony's face, "just wait until we take you over to that apartment complex you had built next door to mine. After you join your son and daughter in the basement for a brief family reunion, Conner and I are going to roast all of you alive. Burning flesh should be an agony beyond mortal belief. Considering all of the problems you and your family members have caused me these past few years, I want you all alive long enough to experience the sensation before your deaths."

"What about the loan papers?" Conner asked with gun in hand.

As they continued speaking, Ebony began to sob even louder.

"Don't forget, Ms. Dickerson, we still don't have them signed yet."

"I'll pay someone to forge her signatures," Lyn politely explained. "With Ebony out of the picture and a husband in mourning due to her recent demise, who in the world would question it?"

"You're a hundred percent correct, Ms. Dickerson. I don't know why I didn't think of doing that."

"My only desire now is to see them all die. Conner, take Ebony next door and tie her up with the others. I'm going to make myself a kettle of tea, then call my husband and son in Los Angeles."

"At this hour?" Conner exclaimed.

"California time is three hours earlier than it is here. So, for Mitchell and Tyree it won't be too late. Since my competitor's building is going to burn to the ground with all of them inside it, I'll need to have an airtight alibi. At the time the fire is burning, I'll be on a landline telephone with my son and husband, discussing how their business trip is going while also creating a phone record for myself."

"And what about *my* alibi?"

"In the same way that you arrived here, my pilot will fly you under the cover of darkness back to New York, without a record or paper trail of your ever having left the City. From the airport go directly to Brook's house and after you leave there in the morning, stop somewhere for gas and be certain to pay for it with your credit card. Your alibi will be that you were with Brook Logan all night long, making passionate love until the wee hours of the morning."

"Of course! This plan is absolutely brilliant!" Conner complimented as he and Lyn exchanged arrogant smiles with each other.

"Conner will take you to see your children now, Ebony. Paris and Derick want to see you very badly. Once they both awakened from the sedative I administered, I told them that you all are going to die very soon. You wouldn't believe how terrified each of them was at the prospect of not being reunited with their mother before your fatal accident occurs," Lyn Dickerson explained, before leaning forward to make eye contact with Conner as she continued. "Well, it's growing later with each passing minute, and I need to get this over with so I can go to bed and catch up on some beauty rest. Get rid of these people and do it quickly!"

"Yes, Ma'am."

Conner stood up, then yanked Ebony to her feet, forcing her at gunpoint to walk with him next door; ironically, over to the same warehouse that he'd assisted Ebony in converting into an apartment complex. Never could Ebony have guessed that, someday, the very same building that she had erected for the sole purpose of reaping vengeance for her only daughter, would soon become a graveyard for herself and her two children.

CHAPTER 22

Just as two paramedics closed the rear doors of the ambulance parked in front of Big Mama's house, a squad car came barreling into the driveway and screeched to an ear-piercing halt. Detective Williams and Nubian Prince bounded from its backseat and, before either of the paramedics knew what was going on, Nubian ran to the emergency vehicle and yanked open its doors. Both portals slapped against the sides of the vehicle with a thunderous crash from having been thrown open so violently, and as the doors made ominous squeaking sounds when they swung back and forth along their hinges, Nubian felt a surmounting, almost unbearable tension coursing through his veins.

Nubian leapt inside the rear of the ambulance and frantically began to search for Ebony. However, once he was interior the transport, instead of seeing the body of his wife inside, he saw a third paramedic administering cardiopulmonary resuscitation to an unfamiliar elderly woman hooked up to an IV bag.

For several moments Nubian just stood there completely still, stunned at the sight of a woman who was covered in blood and appeared to be dying. Detective Williams grabbed on to the jacket of Nubian's suit and pulled him back off the ambulance, allowing the paramedics to shut both doors and leave for Wake Medical Center.

"Where in the hell is my wife?" Nubian screamed out in anger.

Tears glazed over Nubian's sight, and its veneer was causing the vision in both his eyes to blur. He headed toward the house and, when Detective Williams attempted to stop him from entering the abode, Nubian broke free of the hold and ran inside anyway.

Scanning the interior from left to right with his every sense on alert, Nubian watched as several policemen and women moved from one room to the next, some taking photographs while others dusted the furnishings for fingerprints. He darted down a long hallway then began calling out for Ebony. When the corridor came to an end and he stood in the kitchen, Nubian saw that the contents of a silverware drawer had…either purposefully or accidentally…been tossed out or spilled onto the floor. From there he moved upstairs to search through each bedroom of the house, without discovering anything new inside any of them. Other than the authorities who were all milling about from place to place, the dwelling was completely empty of its original occupants, owners, or anyone else who might have been visiting.

"Where in the world is she?" Nubian asked himself aloud.

As Nubian retraced his footsteps and exited the house, heading back outside to where Detective Williams stood chatting with another officer, a surmounting sense of dread began to engulf his heart and mind. The two policemen turned around at the same time and, when they saw Nubian coming, each stepped forward to approach him.

"Mr. Prince, this is Officer Daly," Detective Williams cordially introduced. "He was the first patrolman to arrive on the premises after someone dialed 911 and reported to an emergency operator that there'd been a shooting."

Officer Daly reached out and shook Nubian's hand.

"Where's my wife, Officer Daly?" Nubian asked impatiently. "Have any of you found her yet?"

"At the moment we aren't certain of her whereabouts, Mr. Prince," Daly readily admitted.

His initial tone was saddled with gloom, but then Daly continued speaking with a modicum of optimism.

"However, earlier this morning one of the neighbors reported hearing a disturbance and, upon glancing out her bedroom window, she saw a black limousine leaving the area at that time. Given the hour of night and lack of light, she was unable to see the license plate or give us an accurate description of its driver. So, for the time being, we have no further leads."

"An officer is with the neighbor right now," Detective Williams chimed in, motioning with both hands in a gesture to express his own impatience and frustration. "We hope that, by continuing to speak with her tonight rather than our waiting until later in the morning or afternoon, we might uncover a forgotten piece of information that may lead us to identifying the driver and, in turn, to his ultimate destination. If we can track down that limo, I believe we stand a very good chance of locating the whereabouts of your wife."

For several moments Nubian paced back and forth in front of Detective Williams and Officer Daly in a state of deep concentration.

Then, in a sudden rush of excitement he stepped toward both men and yelled.

"God help me, I think I know where that limousine is going! I believe I know who owns it, and where we might be able to find my wife."

When Conner dragged Ebony into the basement of her own building, she began to shriek out in terror. But when he threatened to fire two bullets into the heads of her children rather then harming her, she abruptly stopped screaming and remained quiet, not knowing what else to do.

There was a single, forty-watt bulb hanging directly overhead and, when she and Conner entered the boiler room, Ebony could see that two people were sitting beside each other on the basement floor.

Derick and Paris sat tied together with their backs resting against the furnace. Both of their mouths were gagged and bound by handkerchiefs. Derick was the first one who looked up and saw them enter and, upon seeing his mother for the first time in over fifteen years, his face immediately brimmed with tears of happiness and joy…then, as suddenly as they had come, his joyous emotions were replaced by a frown of sorrow and regret.

Ebony could not get over how handsome her son was, or what a beautiful young woman Paris had become over the many years of her absence. When Derick began mumbling something that she could not understand, Ebony broke free of the hold Conner had on her arm, ran over to them, and yanked both gags from their mouths.

"Mama?" Derick called out, looking at Ebony for conformation of something that he already knew to be true in his heart.

"Yes, baby, it's me. I'm your mother," Ebony answered, then knelt down beside her son and hugged him fiercely.

When Ebony attempted to untie his hands, Conner warned her to stop immediately.

"Ma, I know we don't have much time left together but I need to tell you something."

The realization of his words cut Ebony down to the very quick of her soul.

"What is it, baby?" Ebony asked as she fought away tears, trying hard to be strong for her children in the face of their deaths. "What do you need for me to know?"

"I remember what happened now," he explained above the racking sobs of his sister.

Before Derick continued, Ebony adjusted her position so that one arm was around him and her other around the shoulders of Paris.

"For a long time I blamed you for leaving Paris and me, literally hating the ground you walked upon. But I'd blocked out what really happened on the day that you left us seventeen years ago."

Paris stopped crying and became very quiet, listening in a state of total confusion while her brother continued speaking to their mother.

"Recently, from my having attended therapy for the last two-and-a-half years, I've come to terms with my emotions and I know what really occurred on the day that daddy was shot. He yelled that he was going to kill you, and then actually tried to murder you. And he would have done precisely that if I hadn't come into the room when I did. I told myself that if you were still among the living, and if God ever allowed me to find you again, I'd turn myself over to the police and give the authorities an accurate account of what really happed that day so as to set the record straight. I now remember and understand that you didn't desert us because you wanted to, you left because you were merely trying to protect me from being placed in a reform school or going to jail for the rest of my childhood."

Paris hadn't realized that her tears had been rekindled, nor did she take notice of the tremor in her extremities. The only thing she understood was that, for the first time in dear life, she finally knew why her mother had left them so many years ago and ran away. Paris glanced at Conner, then back again at Ebony before she spoke.

"Mother, no matter what happens to me here and now, seeing you again is the happiest moment of my entire life."

Ebony felt a sharp blow from behind before she fell into a state of complete unconsciousness, landing faced down on the floor between the legs of her two children.

With hurried steps, Conner again placed the gags back over the mouths of Derick and Paris, and then withdrew a match and a small metal container of lighter fluid from an inner pocket of his suit jacket. Ignoring their muffled cries of terror, he sprayed the entire room with fluid, drenching the interior walls with a circular fan of his arms like a cuckoo clock gone berserk. He ended his ritualistic motions by sprinkling their clothing, moving from the mother on to the siblings alike. Conner lit a match and threw it in the center of the floor.

With one last glance behind him to make certain that the entire room was becoming ablaze, Conner closed the door and placed a padlock on the outside, making sure the exit was securely locked before he departed up the flight of stairs.

Conner walked up to the limousine, unlocked the driver's side door and was about to climb inside when, seemingly from out of nowhere, several squad cars drove up and surrounded him at the curbside. Nubian Prince leapt from the backseat of one of them, accosted Conner, and punched him squarely in the jaw. The sudden blow knocked Conner to the ground and left him in a daze that caused stars to appear before his eyes. Once his vision came back into focus, Conner found himself being handcuffed by Detective Williams and questioned by Nubian Prince.

"Brook is already in jail. You yourself are on your way to one right now, and as we speak, two patrolmen are on their way upstairs to arrest Lyn Dickerson. So the only thing I need to know from you is where you're holding my wife and her two children?"

"It's too late!" Conner said with the irritation of being caught while, at the same time, experiencing great satisfaction by causing Nubian immense pain. "I'm afraid that your poor family has had an unfortunate accident and, by the time you find them all, there won't be much left for you to recognize or identify. So if I were you, buddy, I'd hold on to the memories of how your wife looked during life while I still had the chance, because very soon now there won't be much beauty left for you to remember her by."

A blinding rage filled Nubian, and he was about to demand that the cuffs be removed so he could rip Conner apart using his bare hands when, all of a sudden, he smelled and heard something odd. Emanating from a distance away, the wind carried with it an unusual crackling sound mixed with a charcoal scent.

A moment or two later, rising up into the sky and disappearing against a backdrop of darkness, Nubian and the officers could see a thick, billowing cloud of smoke began to ascend from the base of the building next door.

"That's the building my wife bought and had renovated," Nubian yelled before he took off running in its direction. "They're burning it down! I'll bet anything that Ebony and her family are all inside of it."

While Detective Williams shoved Conner into the backseat of a black-and-white, Officer Daly radioed police headquarters, asked the operator to contact the fire department and have a crew dispatched to their location, then looked at Detective Williams before he spoke.

"A couple of officers have been sent to arrest Lyn Dickerson, so we're freed up to help Prince next door. Perhaps his wife and the rest of her family are upstairs with the Dickerson woman but, if they're nowhere to be found inside that penthouse, then at least we'll have all of our bases covered. Besides, we need to start alerting the occupants of that burning building and have the place evacuated as soon as possible. Looks like smoke is coming from the lower levels, possibly the first floor or basement."

In an effort to prevent Nubian from entering the burning building, several police officers chased him from behind, each calling out for him to wait until firefighters arrived on the scene. None of the officers was fast enough to catch up to Nubian before he dashed inside the flaming complex.

The lobby area was filled with fumes and Nubian immediately began to cough. Seeing that a billowing smoke was streaming from one particular service entrance, Nubian took a handkerchief from an inner pocket of his suit, placed it over his mouth, and followed the stairwell down to the basement. As he descended step after step toward the searing heat, holding onto the banister while thick, acrid smoke and extreme temperatures scorched his throat, he yelled out Ebony's name.

At the bottom of the stairwell Nubian saw a door leading into an area that probably held the furnace or a boiler. He spotted a padlock on the portal, locking the room from the outside rather than inward. Again, Nubian called out for Ebony. But still, there was only silence.

Nubian was just about to turn around and leave when he heard a faint scratching sound coming from the opposite side of the door. With a kick rivaling that of the National Football League's best punter, Nubian hit the door with such force that several screws flew out and both hinges were left dangling by two Phillips. Pushing the door open from where the hinges once held it securely in place, he rushed inside and almost tripped over something sprawled out on the floor. He could vaguely make out the shape of a woman using her fingernails to scratch at thin air. Once he bent down to get a better view of the person, Nubian could see that it was Ebony lying prostrate on the cement. She was barely conscious, gasping desperately in an arduous attempt to draw in more air.

For a moment or two the joy that filled his heart was all encompassing and completely overwhelming but, as Nubian looked around at the flames that were engulfing the room at an alarming rate, a sense of danger seized hold of his senses like never before. Flames were crawling up all four walls, eating away at the support beams that held the ceiling and surrounding structure above the minuscule room.

Making use of the adrenaline that coursed through his veins, Nubian summoned every ounce of strength he had left to pick up his wife. With his every step now labored, Nubian began to carry her back toward the stairs but, before he could cross the threshold and step from the room, Ebony grabbed hold of the doorframe and managed to point back at the furnace before she completely blacked out.

Nubian turned to look back into the smoke filled room. A burst of flames illuminated its interior long enough for him to see that two others were still inside the basement. A striking young man and a beautiful woman who reminded Nubian of his wife, was tied up and sitting on the floor with their backs pressed against the furnace. Knowing that he could not carry more than one person at a time, Nubian quickly set his wife down, moved back into the room and untied the man, then watched as Derick hoisted the body of his unconscious sister up from the floor. Nubian went back to the exit and picked up Ebony again, waiting at the threshold until Derick placed Paris atop his own back in the selfsame manner.

A swirling cloud of black smoke blinded them as they began to move forward, causing Nubian and Derick to stagger as though drink. Half walking and sometimes half dragging, they trudged up the stairs with what felt like the weight of the world atop their shoulders. Dodging roaring flames that surrounded them in every direction, both men bravely pressed on, managing to carry the women upstairs despite the heat that licked at their ears and singed their hair. On their way through the lobby area, they passed a fire crew who had their hands full with dousing flames within the building.

Upon exiting the burning complex into an open, night sky, Nubian could see by the moonlight shining from overhead that an ambulance had arrived and was waiting curbside to treat the injured.

Paramedics helped Derick and both women into the emergency vehicle, where they received treatment for severe smoke inhalation.

From somewhere in the distance, Nubian could hear someone screaming foul obscenities. He climbed from the back of the ambulance and hopped onto the pavement. He could see police officers leading Lyn Dickerson from her apartment complex next door. She was handcuffed from behind and struggled violently with

405

the police, creating a major disturbance. Tenants of both buildings emerged from their units dressed in nightgowns or bathrobes, forced out by the fire or curious about all of the commotion so early in the morning.

"You nasty, snaggle-toothed jackasses will pay for doing this to me!" Lyn Dickerson warned as she kicked backward and struck an officer who was guiding her from rear, in the shin. "None of you understand that I was just protecting my family from that crude girl and her criminal family."

When Lyn glanced in his direction and saw Nubian through the congregation of onlookers, she began to speak directly to him.

"Did you know that your wife shot her boyfriend in cold blood, the very man who's the father of those two bastard children she bore? She shot him in the back and the injury left the man in a coma from which he'll never awaken. If she hasn't already burned to death, then the authorities will lock her ass up and throw away the key! You can best believe that I'll either be dancing atop her grave or laughing aloud while she rots away in prison alongside me. Getting rid of her daughter and losing my business and freedom are worth seeing that woman die or put behind bars for the rest of her natural life."

Two officers shoved Ms. Dickerson into the back seat of a squad car and were just about to close the door when Nubian walked over to them and asked if they would wait for just a moment.

"I heard what you had to say. So, now let me tell you something, bitch! My wife won't be going anywhere, but you sure as hell will. For your information, the paramedics believe that Ebony and her children will make a full recovery, no thanks to you and your hired henchman, Conner Davis. And, for two, from what Derick tells me about what really happened to his father, the man was shot in self-defense. Believe me when I tell you that I have an army of lawyers who'll keep my wife from ever serving a single day inside anybody's jail. But as for you, with all the stuff that you've done here tonight...from the kidnapping and attempted murder of three people, on to homicide if Ebony's mother dies later on...your ass is, without question, going to prison for a *very* long time! While you're trying to explain to your husband and son what happened here tonight, why don't you think about that?"

407

With those parting words said, Nubian slammed the door in her face and watched as Lyn Dickerson began to cry. While she sat sobbing in the back seat, an officer hopped inside the squad car, cranked its engine, and pulled away.

CHAPTER 23

Ebony Hightower Prince

Dear diary,

It has been over seventeen years since I've seen or written anything upon your pages. The last time I held you in my hands was a few months after Joseph had been shot, when I was hiding out from the police and made an unexpected trip back to North Carolina during the wintertime. Back then, Derick was ten years old and Paris was only seven. I'd gone to the hospital where Joseph was lying motionless and mentally inert inside a gurney. The Raleigh News and Observer had reported that he'd fallen into a coma due to

409

a bullet wound through his back. I had to see for myself that the monster who'd fathered my son and daughter, the same man who'd tried to kill me in a fit of violent rage, was actually now living in a catatonic state and could no longer harm me or my children anymore than he already had.

Upon leaving Wake Medical Hospital, I walked several blocks toward downtown Raleigh to catch a Greyhound bus back to Virginia where I'd been living inside an abandoned building. It was then that this very diary had fallen from my purse and landed face down in the snow. How could I have known that my son would find you and return you to me these many years later?

Today, I went to the same hospital that I visited so long ago. Big Mama was transferred from the Duke Medical Center Burn Unit and Plastic Surgery Facility to an extended stay medical suite at Wake Medical Center here in Raleigh. If you have the insurance coverage or can afford the additional rates to be housed in one of their suites instead of a regular room, the surroundings and treatment there are as plush as you can get. The suites are like studio apartments, sporting a real gas log fireplace and a kitchenette, with the option of having a chef come in to prepare three meals a day specific to your own particular diet. They have units with not merely one, but two, bedrooms, just in case family members might want to spend the night or stay with the patient for several days at a time.

After Conner Davis had taken a gun, placed it against her throat, and pulled the trigger, there were many days when Nubian, Derick, Paris and I thought that Big Mama was only a breath away from an eternal sleep. However, six months and seven grueling operations later, the teams of doctors and plastic surgeons who've been working on Big Mama have assured me that she's out of danger and will make a full recovery. Other than some permanent scar tissue around her neck and jaw lines that she'll have to conceal through the use of theatrical makeup for burn victims, Big Mama is pretty much back to her old, loudmouth self. 'Get me a coke, make me a sandwich, and since you're already in the kitchen standing near the fridge, why don't you go ahead and grab me a beer for an appetizer?' are just a few of the demands that Big Mama has been making lately, before continuing on with other comments like, 'Ebony, you're my only daughter and you know that I love you, but your ass is getting small enough to see through. You better feed those cheeks so that when your husband gets back into town from one of those modeling jobs of his, the man has something to hold onto other than your ribcage! And I'm not talking about the cheeks on your face, either. Only a dog likes to chew on a bone at night.'

I'd almost forgotten what it felt like to have, and be surrounded by, such a loving family.

Nubian sold our home in New York and we've bought a beautiful four-bedroom condo near where Paris is enrolled in school. Once Big Mama is released from the hospital, which should happen within the next couple of weeks, she'll come to live here with Nubian and me. Paris and Derick are still living in Big Mama's old house until we can sell it. Thereafter, they'll move into one of the properties that I bought and had renovated. Not a day goes by that I don't spend time with my husband, mother, and children, even if it's just speaking with them on the telephone. Nubian commutes back and forth between here and New York City to pursue his modeling career, and both of my children are constantly here at the condominium spending time with me, all of us trying desperately to make up for lost time and never once take the miracle of our reunion for granted.

Derick has started dating a young woman named Thelma, who saw his photograph and read our story in the local newspaper. Once she realized that I wasn't a murderess and felt safe enough to get to know him, she dialed Information and got his phone number at Big Mama's house. Since there was a lot of publicity and media coverage surrounding the arrest and conviction of the well-known socialite, Lyn Dickerson, we'd requested new, unlisted telephone numbers. However, Thelma works as an operator for Bell South and apparently didn't have any problem obtaining his digits. I have no idea what she said to him or how Derick responded to her advances, but I do know that somehow the two of them hooked up and have been dating exclusively ever since, at least for the last three-and-a-half months that I'm aware of. Thelma is a pretty girl who reminds me of the actress with the same name that played on the television show, *Good Times.* Whatever it is Derick likes about her is cool with me, just as long as she continues to treat my son right and makes him happy. I can't complain or ask for anything more from their relationship than that.

Last but not least, there's Lyn Dickerson to write about. A judge and jury gave her and her cohorts so many years behind bars that, after Lyn finishes serving her sentence less any time off for good behavior, the only thing she'll be able to catch with a man inside it is a taxi! And even then the driver will probably be dropping her ass off at some daycare center because she'll be old enough to be his great-great-grandmother. Realizing this to be the case, the Christian side of me asked that I forgive and show mercy despite everything the woman did, and tried to do, to my family and me. However, the businesswoman side of me grabbed that bitch by the neck, placed her in one of those chokeholds like the wrestlers do on television, and dragged her ass off to the butcher to be de-feathered, quartered, and cleaned like a spring chicken. I took over the Dickerson Corporation, and then seized control of all their holdings and assets. I fired each and every one of the corporate lawyers who were working on Lyn Dickerson's defense team, including the staff attorneys who had any past affiliation with the company before I took it over.

Despite my doing all of this, Tyree and Paris are spending more time together than ever. Unbeknownst to Ms. Dickerson, Tyree's father had set up a secret trust fund for him, leaving their son quite wealthy in the aftermath of my taking over their family business. Mr. Dickerson never informed his wife about the monies for fear she might have tried to gain control of the trust for her own personal use.

Both Tyree and his father are preparing to open a brand-new startup company, something to do with marketing and web hosting on the

Internet. Just as long as they stay out of my way business-wise and don't try to compete with any of my realty acquisitions, I wish them nothing but the best of luck in developing, running, and profiting from their new online ventures.

But, should they ever get in my way...well, let's just say that 'Hell hath no fury like this woman if scorned!'

THE END

ABOUT THE AUTHOR

Edward Nubian James presently resides in Raleigh, North Carolina, where he is currently working on his next novel of fiction entitled, *I'M THE ONE YOU WERE BORN TO SEEK*...Among his many writing endeavors, Mr. James is a part-time print model and has been photographed in advertisements appearing in *FORBES Magazine, BUSINESS WEEK* Magazine, and *PC Magazine*. Edward James may be contacted at: SweetEbonyBLUES@AOL.com

A WORD FROM THE AUTHOR:

First and foremost, I would like to thank God for blessing me with the ability to share through writing the many stories that my mind conjures up. The talent is all His, and for as long as I'm blessed to live here upon the Lord's green earth, I'm merely borrowing it to use and entertain others.

Secondly, I'd like to give thanks to my mother, Darlene James. Her love and sacrifice as a parent have known no bounds. Much love to my brother, Andre, and to his wife, Cathy, who were dying to read my book before it was ever completed.

Last, but certainly not least, I'd like to thank two wonderful and supportive friends, Lieutenant Colonel Eric Meiers and Jeanie Renee White. I love you guys much.

Printed in the United States
997800003B

9 780759 694019